SUNRISE IN

Sometimes the only way forward is to go back.

A childhood in care has left Cat Radcliffe craving connection and a place to call home. When she takes an assignment for a company in the Scottish seaside town of Thistle Bay, her focus is on doing the work well to get a good reference for her fledgling copywriting business.

Nick Bell has lived in Thistle Bay his entire life. His last girlfriend headed to London to escape small-town living and he vowed not to get involved with another city girl. When he meets Cat, he knows he should ignore his growing attraction for the girl who's lived in eight cities in as many years.

Just as Cat is beginning to make plans for the future, an explosive secret shatters her world and sends her running back to the city.

Sunrise in Thistle Bay is a story of family, forgiveness and self-discovery.

Fall in love with Thistle Bay.

SUNRISE IN THISTLE BAY

CLAIRE ANDERS

A CIP catalogue record for this book is available from the British Library.

Published by TLC Publications Ltd

Cover Design by MiblArt

ISBN 978-1-8381777-6-8

For Gavin, Stuart & Evie

1

CAT PUSHED HER TROLLEY OF SUITCASES THROUGH THE OPEN doors of Edinburgh Airport's arrivals hall and scanned the white cards held by people dressed in an array of wildly different styles. Her eyes fixed on her own name, Catherine Radcliffe. She had expected it to say Thistle Bay Chocolate Company. On the handful of occasions she had been collected at an airport for work purposes, the card had always had the company name written on it.

The man holding the card was one of the more smartly dressed individuals. He wore a black suit, white shirt and a dark green tie. He wouldn't have been out of place at a funeral.

'Hi,' said Cat, managing to sound brighter than she felt. 'That's me.'

'Miss Radcliffe. Welcome to Scotland.' The man stepped beside her and took over the handlebar of her trolley. 'Allow me. I'm Arthur.' He placed the name card on top of her cases and steered the trolley through the horde of people gathered by the doors. 'How was your flight?'

'It was good, thanks.' Cat played along with the usual

airport small talk as they exited the terminal and walked to the car – black, of course – which was parked in a bay on the ground floor of the multi-storey car park. Arthur stowed her suitcases in the large boot and opened the rear passenger door of the sleek Mercedes.

'I'll return your trolley,' he said. 'You get yourself settled.'

Cat stared into the back of the car. This was the last part of her journey. The immaculate leather seats and the freshly vacuumed carpet in the footwells should have been inviting after fifteen hours of travelling. Instead, the hair on the nape of her neck lifted and beads of sweat dampened her collar.

'Everything OK, Miss Radcliffe?' asked Arthur, arriving back at the car.

'Actually, would you mind if I sat in the front?'

Arthur closed the rear door and opened the front passenger one instead. 'If that's what you would prefer. You get travel sick, do you?'

'Something like that.'

People who knew her story always presumed Cat would want to sit in the back of a car. After all, it was being in the back that had likely saved her life in the head-on collision that had claimed the lives of her beloved adoptive parents when she was six. But she preferred to sit in the front. The higher chance of death didn't bother her. You're dead – you don't know about it, she had always thought. The problem is what you miss when you can't see in front of you.

It had happened two years after the accident. Cat still remembered the crunching of tyres on the gravel driveway, the car pulling up in front of a house as she looked out of the window to see where they were stopping. Hartsfield Children's Centre. She could still feel the chill that had spread through her eight-year-old body, the look on her foster mother's face that told Cat everything she needed to know as she'd opened the car door for her to get out of the back seat. Cat had said nothing as she was led inside the building, her foster father trailing behind with her rucksack and a cardboard box. They'd all sat in a room with orange fabric chairs and a chipped coffee table while a woman introduced herself only as Mo. And then came those words that had stung her so badly as a child: 'With our own baby on the way,' her foster mother had said with a hand on her swollen stomach, 'we don't think we can help you become the person you are capable of becoming. We thought it best to let it happen as quickly as possible for you.' Those words that, as an adult, she saw were just a cop out – the kind of thing that people said when trying to make themselves feel better for doing things they knew weren't right. There had been no discussion, no time to prepare.

But Cat couldn't be angry. Biology mattered. It's why the adoptive parents who had loved her so much had always made sure she knew she had another mother somewhere despite Cat being too young back then to really understand. It's why her best friend Rachel still took care of her own birth mother despite twenty years of drug addiction that had left Rachel to be raised in care alongside Cat. And it's why Cat continued to search for biological relatives despite so many years of goose chases and dead-ends. There were no official records. If her adoptive parents had known any details, the drunk driver who'd hit their car when Cat was still so young had made sure they weren't around to tell her. Cat had been alone in the world since then.

Cat sat in the front seat of Arthur's car, the cool leather a welcome sensation to counteract the heat that had risen in her while staring at the back seat.

'One of my boys used to get travel sick,' said Arthur, putting on his seatbelt. 'He was always better in the front.

You'll find some water in the side of the door there and you just let me know if you need fresh air or for me to pull over, Miss Radcliffe.'

Cat opened the bottle of water and took a sip. 'I'll be fine from here, honestly. And please call me Cat.'

'OK then, Cat. Let's get you to Thistle Bay.' Arthur fired up the engine and pulled away.

'Thanks, Arthur. Let's hope the traffic is light at this time of night so you can drop me off and get back here at a reasonable time.'

'I'm from Thistle Bay actually. When I get you there, I'm already home.'

Cat glanced over at Arthur in his smart suit and swanky car. 'I wouldn't have thought there'd be much call in Thistle Bay for a professional driver.'

'You'd be right about that. I work for Mr Knight and the family – driving, deliveries, and anything else they need me to do, which includes picking up VIPs like yourself from the airport, although I'm usually taking them to the Edinburgh facility. It's not often I drive them all the way to Thistle Bay.'

Cat had never been described as a VIP before and she suddenly worried that Alan Knight, the CEO of Thistle Bay Chocolate Company, had greater expectations than she did about what she could deliver for his business.

The Forth Road Bridge loomed up on their right but instead of veering towards it, the car kept going.

'Oh, I haven't been on the new bridge before,' said Cat.

'Aye. The Queensferry Crossing. The three bridges over the water is quite a sight.'

The new bridge hadn't existed when Cat had last lived in Edinburgh, and as a visitor in the years since, she hadn't strayed too far from the city centre. Given how many years it takes to construct a bridge, perhaps the passage of time had changed more than just the view across the Firth of Forth.

'I thought you'd be American, you know. But are you a local lass?'

'I moved to Edinburgh when I was eight and lived here until I left university at twenty-two.'

'You didn't pick up much of an American twang while you were there.'

Cat had always had an accent that people found hard to place. The thick London accent she'd spoken with since she was old enough to talk had quickly faded when she'd ended up back in foster care, in Edinburgh. But she hadn't taken on a completely Scottish accent. To the Scots she sounded English; to the English she sounded Scottish.

'I was only in the US for a year – although it's easy to find yourself copying the accent a bit when you're surrounded by it all day.'

'And are you heading back there after your time with us?'

'I haven't decided yet,' said Cat. She was planning to go and stay with Rachel for a while after this assignment was finished and, right now, her best friend's spare room in Edinburgh city centre was about as far in the future as she could see.

When she'd lost her job, she'd also lost her visa. Launching a copywriting business had been part of a failed attempt to transfer visa categories. But she'd attracted clients and hadn't been as fazed by the uncertainty of it as she had expected to be. Self-employment gave her the freedom to go wherever she wanted to go; she just had to maintain a steady stream of clients to keep her income up.

Heading to Thistle Bay didn't thrill her – it was too close to a past she'd tried to shut off – but the assignment itself

could be fantastic. Alan Knight had offered her two weeks'
work rewriting his company's entire website. It was a signifi-
cant project, and having a multimillion-pound corporation
on her portfolio would add credibility to both her and her
embryonic business. All she had to do was make sure she
had happy clients at the end of the job.

The takeaway coffee cup in Arthur's cup holder was
emblazoned with the words Mystic Coffee in dark blue
block lettering.

'I've never heard of Mystic Coffee,' said Cat. 'Are they an
Edinburgh chain?'

'No. Mystic's is in Thistle Bay, but her coffee could rival
any from those fancy Edinburgh places and is much better
than the stuff at the big coffee chains.'

'That's good to know. I need a good strong coffee to wake
me up in the mornings.'

It wasn't long before the Mercedes had left the busy dual
carriageway and was heading along deserted country roads
bordered by fields and the occasional farmhouse that cast a
shadow on the darkening sky.

There was a road sign just before the roundabout that
indicated 'Thistle Bay 1 mile'. Cat took a deep breath. She
couldn't wait to get into her room at the bed and breakfast
Alan Knight had booked for her. She needed a shower and
to go through the notes she'd made before her first meeting
with the company. Thanks to the business-class lounge
access that Alan had arranged for her, she'd already eaten
dinner, which saved her from having to hunt for somewhere
to find food. But the first thing she wanted to do was stretch
her legs and get some fresh air to ease her pounding head.

'Is it your first time in Thistle Bay?' Arthur asked.

'Yes.' Despite all of those years she'd lived in Edinburgh,
she had never visited any of the Fife seaside towns. The car

climbed a gentle hill and Cat leaned forward to get a better view of the town once they reached the top.

Their arrival in Thistle Bay was pretty underwhelming. Cat had expected to see the town stretched out in front of her with lights glowing in the windows of tiny cottages. Instead, she saw nothing but a row of plain-looking houses. One thing was clear – there weren't any buildings higher than two storeys.

Arthur manoeuvred the car along narrow roads and Cat smiled as, street by street, the town began to reveal its charm. The further into the centre Arthur drove, the more the scenery shifted to match the image she'd had in her mind. Pavements widened as residential areas gave way to the town's hub. Independent businesses lined the main road with their pastel-painted shopfronts. Hanging baskets of autumnal flowers still bursting with colour hung at intervals from the Victorian-style lampposts dotted along the kerb-side. It was the kind of location she could imagine a film crew pitching up at to shoot a cosy murder-mystery drama series with a middle-aged amateur sleuth solving grizzly crimes in between bake sales and summer fêtes.

The car crawled along a street that led down towards the sea. 'Here we are,' said Arthur.

'Wow, that sunset is something else,' said Cat. The orange glow of the sun sinking into the sea created a trail all the way across the water that was broken only by the silhouette of a single wind turbine.

'Aye, we do a lovely chocolate and a sunset like no other here in Thistle Bay.'

Arthur turned the car at the end of the street and stopped in front of the first building. The exterior of the bed and breakfast looked exactly as Cat had expected. The double-storey building was painted white with black trims and had the cosy glow in each of the windows that she had hoped the entire town would have had. From the outside, at least, it looked just as cute as the photos on the website.

The cool evening air hit Cat when she opened the car door, along with an intoxicating scent of sweet cinnamon and caramelised sugar that brought back memories of Edinburgh's Christmas markets. It was coming from a small market stall opposite the bed and breakfast – the only stall along the entire length of the promenade. It had no obvious signage but its red frame and warm light from a heat lamp above two metal trays called out to Cat.

'Arthur, oh my gosh. Is that guy selling real sugared almonds?'

'Smells like it,' said Arthur, sniffing the air.

'I need some. Can you give me a minute?'

'Sure. I'll unload your luggage.'

Cat crossed the empty road and the man mixing the almonds caught her eye. He was older – in his seventies at least, Cat estimated – with a good head of grey hair peeking out from beneath a white cap. He wore a short-sleeved white T-shirt with a burgundy-red apron that stretched over his bulging stomach.

'I see you're tempted by my almonds,' he said in a thick German accent as Cat approached.

'I am,' she said. 'I love real sugared almonds, but I haven't had them in so long.'

'Try one.' He held out a stainless-steel scoop with an almond balanced on the end.

Cat took the almond and crunched it in her mouth. It was still warm and tasted like Christmas with its sweet yet spicy flavour. Cat hadn't had a family Christmas since she was little girl but she still loved everything about the season, especially the food and drinks.

'Delicious. I'll take two bags, please.'

'You have good taste,' the man said. 'Have you just arrived?' He filled a pink-and-white-striped paper bag with almonds and nipped it closed at the top. Passing it to Cat, he moved on to the second bag.

'Yes. I'm doing some work here so I'll be in town for a couple of weeks.'

'Excellent. I'm Josef. You stop by here anytime.'

'I will. I'm Cat, and thank you for these – such an unexpected treat.' She handed Josef cash and headed back towards the bed and breakfast.

Arthur was waiting on the wide pavement beside his car as Cat returned with her bulging paper cones. She popped one in her handbag and passed the other to Arthur.

'Thank you for the ride, Arthur. This one is for you.' She rummaged in her handbag with her free hand. 'Now, let me get you a proper tip.'

'Oh, no, there's really no need. I can't accept that. But I won't say no to these.' He took the almonds, unfolded the top of the bag and peeked inside. 'Your luggage is in the lobby, and I'll see you in the morning. About eight thirty?'

'Perfect,' said Cat. She waved Arthur off and moved to go inside and check in.

The entrance to Thistle Bay Bed and Breakfast sat directly on the pavement, although it was evident someone had tried to establish a garden feel. Planters in front of each window bulged with bright purple and pale pink flowers that looked like giant daisies, there was a wooden bench pushed up against the building's façade and bright blue pots of shrubs were placed in a row to create a short path to the front door.

Cat didn't expect anyone minded the obstacles since the pavement was plenty wide enough.

Cat pushed open the door and a bell chimed above her head. She smiled at the quaint metal bell that rocked back and forth before she spotted a woman with glistening silver hair waiting beside her suitcases.

'Hi, you must be Mrs Murphy,' said Cat.

'Call me Gloria. Goodness, look at you.'

Cat tucked her shoulder-length brown hair behind her ears. She'd had her layers trimmed just before leaving Los Angeles but she could imagine her hair was now plastered to her head after the journey. She smoothed her hands down her crumpled dress. There wasn't a crease on Gloria's blue jumper and, noticing the woman's chunky fuchsia necklace and freshly applied pink lipstick, Cat felt dishevelled. 'I've just come off a long flight.'

'Oh, no – sorry, hen. You look lovely. It's just you look like someone I've met before.'

'Really? Well, it's my first time here so it can't have been me.'

Gloria shook her head. 'No, it wasn't.' Her voice seemed to crack slightly and she cleared her throat. 'Let's get you checked in. Catherine Radcliffe, right?'

'Yes, and you can call me Cat.'

'You're the last guest to check in tonight. Let me get your key and I'll show you around.'

After taking Gloria's lead and poking her head into the immaculate eight-table dining room and the snug guest lounge, Cat made her way up the narrow staircase. Following the directions Gloria had given her, she found her door and put her key in the lock. She couldn't remember the last time she'd stayed in a hotel that had an actual key rather than a key card. She pushed the door open and fumbled for a light switch.

Inside was a generous-sized room and a bay window with a view of the sea. It was more homely, and bigger, than some of the flats Cat had lived in. Paying back her student loans hadn't left much of her salary for rent during her first few jobs. She'd wanted to be tied to those loans for as short a period as possible so had always paid back more than the minimum instalment due and had cleared them completely within four years of graduating.

Cat wheeled two of her suitcases into the room and Gloria appeared behind her with the final one, her already rosy cheeks now a little rosier from the exertion of hauling the suitcase up the stairs.

'Probably not what you're used to, hen. I expect Los Angeles is much fancier than my wee B&B.'

Cat took in the crisp white bedding with a lilac throw and two cushions, each adorned with a thistle print, propped against the fluffy pillows. The cream carpet was springy beneath her feet and the walls were a combination of light wood panelling on the lower half and ivory wallpaper with an embossed floral pattern on the upper half.

'It's lovely,' said Cat. 'And the view is amazing – I can't wait to see it properly in the morning.'

'I'm glad you like it. The rooms are all similar, but I keep this window for guests of Mr Knight, if I can.'

Cat was going to ask how Gloria knew Alan, but in a town with 1,400 people – as her research had told her – of course she would know him.

Instead, it was Gloria who asked, 'Have you known Mr Knight long?'

Cat shook her head. 'I've only met him once, actually.

But that's why I'm here. To get to know the family and the business a bit more.'

Gloria stood staring, lips pursed, as if waiting for further explanation.

'I'm a copywriter, so I'm rewriting their website for them.' On paper, Alan was taking a risk giving such a big project to her new company, but during their meeting in Los Angeles he had seemed quite taken by her thorough research, and perhaps knowing that she'd grown up across the water from his business had given him an extra slice of reassurance. That proximity was the main reason Cat had been reluctant to take the job, but she'd been left with no choice and, now that she was here, she was completely focused on the job and determined to impress him.

'I'd better let you settle and get some sleep,' said Gloria, closing the door and leaving Cat alone.

Cat's eyes dropped to the luggage that literally contained everything she owned. Renting furnished flats meant Cat had never acquired much stuff, and she didn't have a child-hood bedroom or space in her parents' attic to store away memories. The only thing she had from her childhood was a photo album of the first six years of her life with Jessie and Joe, her adoptive parents. Cat had been taken into care with nothing but the clothes she was wearing at the time of the accident. She later presumed it was her mother's brother who had tied up her parents' estate after they died. The only thing that had made it back to her was the photo album – it was the one symbol of home she owned and it was the thing she turned to whenever she had a big decision to make.

Cat unzipped the shoulder bag she'd taken with her on the flight, tugged the album free and laid it on the rustic oak bedside table. It fell open at a photograph of Cat dressed as Sophie from Roald Dahl's *The BFG*. Cat had watched the

BFG movie over and over again as a small child. Her mother, Jessie, had worried that the scary giants might give her nightmares but Cat had never dwelt on them. For Halloween, Jessie had made her a yellow dress with huge stitches joining the seams and bought her an orange wig and round-framed glasses. Cat had insisted her father, Joe, pretend to be the Big Friendly Giant. But then the worst had happened. Jessie and Joe, the only real parents she could remember having, had been taken from her overnight and, like Sophie, Cat had ended up in a children's home. Only Cat knew no one would come for her. This was the reason she looked at the album so sparingly. Each photograph invoked fond memories, but the bitter ones crept in too.

She still remembered her first day in a courtroom. Her parents' funeral hadn't even taken place and here she was, six years old, sitting behind a shiny wooden desk that she could only just see over while lawyers and social workers decided her fate. 'And the child has no other relatives to take her in?' the Judge had boomed from his platform at the front of the room. He'd reminded Cat of the BFG with his big ears and bushy white eyebrows – only he wasn't friendly. He didn't speak to her. He didn't even glance in her direction. 'No relatives that are *able* to take her in,' had come the reply from a flame-haired woman who'd introduced herself to Cat only moments before the hearing. That first court appearance was over in minutes. Cat had said nothing. No one had asked her to speak. She'd felt as though no one even knew she was there.

Cat moved to five different foster homes before relocating from London to Edinburgh. When she found herself back in a children's care facility, she realised no one was ever going to ask for her views. To be heard, she would have to step up and use her voice, whether invited to or not. So she did. It didn't change her childhood, but she grew into a self-assured woman who was skilled in her job and undaunted by relocating to new cities – new countries, even – on her own.

Cat closed her photo album, her palm lingering for a few seconds on the bronze leather cover, before picking up her phone. She logged in to her Find My Family account to check her messages. It had been fifty-two days since she'd read the words that made her skin tingle with nervous anticipation: 'You have a DNA match.' She had reached out immediately to the blank avatar identified only as CocoB13 – the only person who might be able to tell Cat who she was and where she came from.

She had played out so many scenarios in her mind. CocoB13 was her mother who had spent thirty years regretting the decision to give her baby away on the night she was born. Or her father who hadn't known of her existence until she had swabbed her DNA and made it available online for anyone that paid the registration fee to compare their own DNA against. Or perhaps it was a half-sister or half-brother. Of course, it would probably turn out to be some cousin twice removed who knew nothing about her mum – but even that would be further than she'd ever managed to get on her own.

She knew most people just did DNA profiling for fun, but finding out she was seventy-six per cent European gave her nothing new. She needed her DNA match to make contact with her if she was ever going to learn more. If they'd bothered to go through all the hassle of registering their details, surely they would follow it up.

Cat refreshed her screen. Inbox empty. She had to ration the number of times a day she accessed the app – the disappointment was taking its toll and it was proving to be nothing but a distraction. She opened her phone's settings and turned on her email alerts. Find My Family would email her when she had a reply. She usually kept notifications turned off for email so they didn't interrupt her flow when she was working, but turning them on felt like the only way to stop torturing herself with the app.

She turned back to the view from the bay window. The sun was gone completely now but the dusky blue sky was just light enough for her to still see the beach. Her head was fuzzy from the flight. Or perhaps it was from a swell of emotion that had been building inside her since her stop-off in London. Either way, a walk on the beach could only help. And she wanted to find the chocolate shop so she knew where she was going in the morning.

Cat pulled on her coat, snatched the sugared almonds from inside her bag and left the bed and breakfast without running into Gloria or any other guests. The only sign of life outdoors was the glow from Josef's heat lamps lighting up his frame as he mixed a tray of almonds, probably hoping for a few more sales before he headed home.

Seconds later, Cat was on the beach. Slipping off her tan-brown shoes, she sunk her feet into the sand and took a deep breath. She hadn't been looking forward to coming back to Scotland but, now she was here, she'd make the best of it and focus on doing a good job. She'd figure out where to go next once the job was finished. She unzipped her coat. The early-evening temperature was milder than she expected and Cat inhaled a deep breath. There really was no air like Scottish air.

2

THE COOL SAND BETWEEN CAT'S TOES FELT MAGICAL AND, with the gentle lapping of the waves on the shoreline, was already helping to clear the fuzzy head that came with half a day of travelling. She popped an almond in her mouth and crunched, breaking through the gnarly, sugary coating.

Walking down to the water, she had to negotiate a wide strip of egg-sized stones and dried seaweed that separated the dry sand from the wet. She had slipped her shoes off too early. Cat braced herself, stepped onto the stones and scuttled over them as quickly as she could. The address for the chocolate shop was Main Street, the same as Gloria's address, so it had to be further along the promenade, she reasoned. She'd make her way there by following the shoreline as it ran parallel with the street.

She sauntered along the beach for a few minutes when a dog appeared out of the darkness in front of her and dropped a miniature orange rugby ball on a rope at Cat's feet.

'Oh, hi,' said Cat, crouching down to pet the dog. 'Where did you come from?'

The jet-black dog wagged its tail fervently. Cat ran her hand through the dog's damp hair and it nuzzled into her knee. She scanned the beach for an owner but it was too dark by now to see properly.

'Skye. Here, girl!' sounded a voice from further along the beach.

'Are you Skye?' Cat said, and the dog turned in a circle and pounced on its ball with its front paws.

'Skye,' came the voice again, a bit closer now.

'She's over here,' yelled Cat. She scratched the dog behind the ears, sand from its fur pressing beneath her fingernails. 'Are you in trouble?'

'I'm sorry. Is she bothering you? Skye, here!'

The light from the moon up above illuminated Skye's owner as it bounced off the royal-blue sports shorts and T-shirt he wore. Sweat had turned his thick, blond hair dark at the edges of his face, suggesting he'd been out for a run along the beach when Skye had abandoned him and sought Cat's company instead. He had a deep suntan, discernible even by moonlight, which hinted at a lot of time spent outdoors, and his blue eyes reflected the shimmer from the sea.

Skye picked up her ball and bounded over to him. He bent down, prised the ball from her mouth and threw it back along the beach. The dog gave chase and disappeared into the blackness.

'It's really dark along there. Aren't you worried you'll lose her again?' said Cat, straightening up.

The dog came thundering back seconds later and dropped the ball at Cat's feet again.

'She always finds me,' he said.

The panting dog gazed up at Cat, tongue hanging out and tail wagging.

'She wants you to throw her ball, but don't worry, I'll get it. I'm Nick, by the way. And you've met Skye.'

'I'm Cat.' Cat bent down to pick up Skye's ball.

'I wouldn't,' said Nick. 'It's soggy from slobbers and the sea.'

Cat picked the ball up by the rope. She could handle a slobbery ball. She whipped her arm back and round and released the rope. The ball shot off to her left towards the promenade pavement and Skye ran away into the darkness ahead of her.

'Oops,' said Cat, hoping the lack of light would hide the flush on her cheeks.

'I bet you couldn't do that again if you tried. I'll get it.'

Nick jogged off and found the ball in seconds. He squeaked it as he walked back to her and Skye came tearing back towards the sound. Nick threw the ball down into the sea. No doubt exactly where he had intended it to go.

'Are you just visiting?' he asked.

'Is it that obvious?'

'Yeah, but only because it's a tiny town and I know I've not seen you around before.'

'I'm doing some work for Thistle Bay Chocolate Company. I arrived about an hour ago so I was taking a quick walk to find out where the shop is for tomorrow.'

'Well, you're going in completely the wrong direction. A bit like that ball.'

Cat looked down at her hands and pretended to brush sand off them. Great. She couldn't throw a ball or navigate her way around this tiny town. 'I was taking the scenic route,' she said. 'I needed to stretch my legs after the flight.'

'Given it's dark, you'd be better taking the direct route,' said Nick, pointing behind her. 'Where have you arrived from?'

'Los Angeles.'

Nick whistled and the dog scampered towards them. 'That's a long way to come just to visit a chocolate shop.'

'I'm a copywriter. I'm doing some work on their website so I'll be here for two weeks.'

Skye seemed to have had enough of chasing her ball around and criss-crossed in front of them, the dripping rope hanging from her mouth, as they headed back along the beach.

Cat padded over the wet sand, the occasional icy wave covering her toes. Nick, a good six inches taller than Cat, walked alongside her.

'The beach is so peaceful . . .' She let out a loud yelp as something jagged caught the side of her foot, causing a searing pain, and she fell into Nick as she hopped about and grabbed her foot.

Nick gripped her arms to steady her. 'What was that?'

'I don't know,' she shrieked, rubbing her stinging foot. 'Something bit me.'

'OK, just breathe,' said Nick, still holding her up. 'I don't see anything on the sand.'

'It must have come from the water.'

'Probably a jellyfish.'

Cat gasped. 'Are they poisonous?'

'Not the ones round here,' he said. 'You need to rinse your foot in the sea.'

'I'm not sticking my foot in there,' said Cat, taking a painful step back. 'And before you say it, I'm not going to pee on myself either.'

Nick laughed. 'That's definitely not what I was going to say. But you *are* going to have to put your foot in the sea.'

Cat shook her head. 'What if it's still in there?'

Nick took his hands away from her arms just by an inch

to make sure she was stable. He bent over, untied the laces on his trainers and prised them off his feet. He then tugged his socks off and tucked them inside one of his shoes.

'What are you doing?' Cat asked.

'Showing you there's nothing to be scared of.' He stepped into the sea and swirled the water around with his foot. 'See, nothing there. Now, come over here.'

Cat reached for Nick's outstretched hand and limped into the water. She gave a sharp intake of breath. It was freezing cold. She wanted to jump back out again but Nick probably already thought she was a baby without her needing to prove it further.

Nick, still holding her hand, used his foot to flush water around hers. He bent down a little to see what he was doing and they came face to face, his warm breath on her skin. His grip on her hand was tight and comforting and it was easy to ignore the sting in her foot with so many other sensations stirring in her body.

'That should do it,' said Nick. 'Let's get you off the beach. Skye, come!'

Skye, having ignored the commotion and continued further along the beach, now sprinted back to Nick.

'Can you walk on your foot?'

She said she could and they both stepped out of the water and back onto the sand.

'You sure?' He waited for her nod before he released her hand.

Nick collected his trainers and they made their way off the sand and back onto the promenade path. He put his sandy feet directly into his shoes and stuffed his socks in his pocket.

Cat held the wall to steady herself as she brushed sand off her feet, one at a time, as best she could and put her shoes back on. Skye, looking for attention, nuzzled her wet nose against Cat's bare leg.

'Is she a springer spaniel? She's quite small.'

'A working cocker spaniel.'

'I see you.' Cat scratched the spaniel on the top of her head for a few seconds. 'You're a needy one, aren't you?'

'She's not needy, she's loving.' Nick sank down near the ground and called Skye over to him. The dog hid her head behind Cat's leg and didn't budge.

'She doesn't seem to be loving you right now.'

Nick shook his head at the dog. 'She's loving, but fickle. Come on, have a seat over there.'

Cat followed Nick to a bench on the promenade and sat down. He gestured for her to lift her foot.

'It's fine now, really,' she said.

'I just want to check there's no sting in it.'

Cat slipped her shoe off, held her floral-print dress on her knee and lifted her foot. Nick cupped her ankle and held on to her toes with his other hand. He twisted her foot around to pick up light from the nearby lamppost.

'I don't see anything. It's just a little swollen and red. Soak your foot in hot water tonight and you'll be fine.'

'Thank you, Doctor Nick.' She had meant it sincerely but the words somehow came out with a sarcastic edge. 'Really,' she added.

'Are you staying at Gloria's?' asked Nick.

'I take it you don't have many bed and breakfasts in town.'

'Just the one. I'll walk you over there.'

'No, honestly, it's fine. Besides, I still want to find the chocolate shop before I go back.'

'You should really soak that foot.'

'I will. It won't take me long to find the shop.'

Nick glanced around him. 'It's on my way so I'll walk you there.' He picked up Cat's shoe and put it back on her foot, then clipped Skye's lead on and pocketed her ball. 'When you come out of Gloria's, turn right and you're on Main Street. The chocolate shop is at the very top of the street.'

They meandered along the promenade and Cat couldn't help but think how romantic a walk this would be under different circumstances. The sea was calm, the waves giving only the occasional gurgle, and patches of light shone on the dark street under the ornate lampposts. If she ignored the throbbing on the side of her foot, the cool air was a welcome change from a scorching Los Angeles summer.

They reached Josef's stall and he appeared to be packing up for the night. The scent of hot sugared almonds still lingered in the air and Cat took a deep breath and smiled as she caught Josef's eye.

'Goodnight, Cat,' the old man said. 'I hope you enjoyed your almonds.'

Cat patted the paper bag tucked inside her coat pocket. 'They were wonderful, thank you, Josef.'

Josef beamed and nodded his head. He waved to Nick as they turned to cross the street before he disappeared beneath the counter to continue closing up his stall.

'You like your food, then,' said Nick, tugging on Skye's lead to keep her moving when she tried to stop and sniff the postbox.

'Excuse me?'

'You've been here an hour and you're already on first-name terms at the local food stall.'

Cat glanced at Nick, unsure if he was making a joke or having a dig at her. His neutral expression didn't help her decide which one it was.

They walked straight up Main Street and there it was –

the Thistle Bay Chocolate Company shop. The streetlights gave off enough light for her to see the signage. She peered in the windows but all she saw were shadows; she would have to wait until the morning to get a proper look. First impressions were good, though. The location was great. It wasn't right on the beachfront but in daylight it must have a view of the beach, and the sign looked big enough to be seen from the promenade.

'Is the factory nearby?' asked Cat.

Nick pointed to the left-hand side of the shop. 'It's behind that wall, there.'

But it was too dark to see anything more. She'd wanted to see where the shop was and she'd done that now, so time to go back and soak her foot – although the throbbing had dulled already.

'Do you think you'll remember the way tomorrow?' It was Nick's turn to sound sarcastic, only Cat was sure his tone was actually intended.

Cat smirked. 'I think so. I also remember the way back to Gloria's, so thank you.'

'Skye and I will make sure you get back to Gloria's safely. We're heading that way.'

'Don't you live up here somewhere? You said the shop was on your way.'

'Actually, we live on the promenade. Your internal compass seemed a tad out of order and I didn't want to spend the night worrying about whether or not you made it to the shop.'

Cat put her hand on her hip. 'There was no need. I would have found it on my own. And even if I had gone off in the wrong direction, doesn't it take, like, ten minutes to walk around the entire town?'

Nick laughed. 'Not quite, but you make a good point.'

They strolled back towards Gloria's and another sign caught Cat's eye with its familiar deep-blue block lettering. 'There's Mystic Coffee,' she said. 'I'll be stopping off there tomorrow morning.'

The coffee shop was in darkness too. She'd forgotten that things closed earlier in small towns. She was used to stepping outside and picking up a takeaway coffee at any time of day or night. Coffee was a lifesaver when she had a deadline looming and needed something to keep her awake until she had finished her project.

'It's the best coffee in town,' said Nick.

Skye stopped to sniff a lamppost. She seemed intent on inspecting them all. Cat didn't mind. The fresh air had lifted her headache and, despite her earlier embarrassment, she wasn't in a rush to end her walk with Nick. She was quite content listening to him giving her the rundown of Mystic Coffee's food menu. Apparently it was where most of Gloria's guests ate lunch and the occasional early dinner.

'If you want to eat later, there's the local pub, The Smugglers Inn. The owners are from Greece and the food is authentic Greek cuisine. They also do takeaway,' said Nick. 'Other than that, you'd need to get a taxi out of town. There's not a lot choice around here but the food is homemade and delicious.'

Main Street was annoyingly short and two minutes later they were already standing in front of Gloria's. Cat scuffed her shoes against the edge of the kerb, reluctant to turn her feet in the direction of the bed and breakfast. She bent down to give Skye one last pat. 'Goodnight, cutie,' she said. The little spaniel closed her black eyes and stood perfectly still, revelling in the attention.

When Cat stood up, Nick was smiling at her. For a second she imagined she was in Los Angeles and free to give in to her overwhelming desire to reach out and kiss him. You're working, she reminded herself. And he thinks you're a hapless idiot.

'There you are, hen,' said Gloria. 'I was just locking up. Evening, Nick.'

'Evening, Gloria.' His voice was cheery, no sign of disappointment that their moment had been interrupted.

'If you ever need another sat-nav,' he said to Cat, 'just let me know.' He put his hand on her shoulder as he stepped off the kerb and a heat spread through her body. She wanted to turn and watch him walk away, wanted to see if he glanced back at her like in the movies, but Gloria was looking at her, waiting for her to go in.

'Soak that foot,' Nick said from behind her, giving her the opportunity to turn. He was standing in the middle of the road, his eyes locked on her. She smiled and nodded, then forced herself to turn away and go into the bed and breakfast.

Cat climbed the stairs to her room, curled up on the bed and powered up her laptop. She had to forget about Nick. She may have made a fool of herself on day one in Thistle Bay, but tomorrow was the day that mattered. Just seeing the chocolate shop had sparked some ideas and she was keen to note them down. Her foot would have to wait. This was only the fifth client of her fledgling freelance career but her biggest one to date and if the commission went well she could use it to attract more business.

The chime of a video call coming through interrupted her furious typing and Rachel's number flashed on the screen. Cat clicked Answer to accept the call.

Rachel Barnes, Cat's best friend, waved into the camera from the living room of her tenement flat in Edinburgh.

'Urgh! I was hoping your LA glow would have faded on the flight. You make me embarrassed with my pasty skin.'

'Nonsense, you're gorgeous,' said Cat. 'Your pale skin helps the bright blue of your eyes to sparkle.'

Rachel's eyes were a piercing blue that stood out against her porcelain complexion and chocolate-brown hair. Cat had experimented with hair dye over the years to brighten up her hair. She had the classic shade of mousy brown that made her look washed out when she wasn't sporting a Los Angeles suntan. Whereas Cat had no idea if her hair colour came from her mother or her father, Rachel knew her colouring came from her dad. Although she couldn't remember him, she'd shown Cat a few pictures that her mum, Heather, had kept. Besides, Cat knew Heather had blonde hair and naturally golden skin, although her complexion had transformed into a grey pallor as a result of long-term substance abuse.

'I might still break out the fake tan before we meet for mojitos.' Rachel clasped her hands in a prayer position under her chin. 'Friday, isn't it?'

'Nice try.'

'Oh, come on. I can't wait a fortnight to see you.'

When Cat had arrived at Hartsfield Children's Centre in Edinburgh she was already considered too old to be adopted. Rachel was already there, having fallen into a pattern of rotating in and out of Hartsfield each time Heather cleaned herself up then relapsed again. The longest block of time Rachel ever spent with her mother was five months, which was also the longest she and Cat went without speaking to each other. On the day Rachel arrived back at Hartsfield after that absence, her cheeks stained with tears and disappointment, she'd said that she hadn't visited Cat for fear it would tempt fate and push Heather to once again choose drugs over her daughter. For years after that, Rachel lived in hope that Heather would one day sort herself out so they could become the proper family Rachel had always longed for. Cat, on the other hand, accepted that she wouldn't leave Hartsfield until she was old enough to live on her own.

Now her friend was only an hour away and Cat was dodging seeing her.

'This town is seriously tiny,' Cat said. 'I don't want the Knights to think they're paying me to socialise. I just need to get the work done and then I'll be free to have as many cocktails as you want.'

'I don't think they'll mind you having one drink with your oldest friend.'

'Probably not. But I just want the job to go perfectly.'

'Are you sure you're not just avoiding dealing with the fact that you're home?'

'I'm not home.'

'Look,' said Rachel. 'I know you have this need to travel the world and find yourself or whatever, but the location doesn't actually matter. You've been to eight cities in eight years and what's changed? Maybe it's time to stop searching for a place that feels like home and just set up a home for yourself.'

Cat sighed at the familiar speech. Rachel had been asking Cat to come home for at least the last three years. But Cat had never considered Edinburgh her home. It was just the city she had grown up in, and the place she left as soon as she could. Cat touched the dark mobile phone on the bed beside her to light up her screensaver. It was a picture of her and Rachel on a rare sunny day at the Edinburgh International Book Festival in Charlotte Square Gardens. As a copywriter and a high-school English teacher, Cat and

Rachel found that the book festival provided the perfect platform for an annual get-together. Edinburgh was a great place to be a tourist, but Cat didn't want to live there again.

Her first move had been to London because that was where she'd lived with her parents after being given up for adoption by her birth mother. She'd been so certain she would settle there, build a life and put down some roots. She found a job and a room for rent in a shared house but instead of the homecoming she'd expected, it was a reminder of everything she had lost – the opportunity to know her birth mother; the chance to be part of a family. Five months later and Cat was on the move again. She had been avoiding London and moving every year or two ever since.

Now, here she was. Thirty years old and about to end up right back where she started – homeless in Edinburgh.

Not wanting to succumb to her despair, Cat changed the subject. 'I just met a guy on the beach.'

Rachel squealed with delight as she probed for details. Thinking about Nick for another half an hour couldn't hurt.

3

SEAGULLS SCREECHING WOKE CAT EARLY THE FOLLOWING morning. She looked at the green digits on the clock beside her bed. Five thirty in the morning. She snuggled her face into the plump pillow and tucked the duvet under her chin.

When Cat was offered the chance to transfer to Los Angeles she'd had visions of a sprawling mansion with a swimming pool, an outdoor terrace and a celebrity neighbour. In reality, Cat's apartment was a studio above a bar that seemed to get their glass recycling collected daily. The exterior of the building was beautiful but her early-morning wake-up call for the last year had been the beep of a vehicle reversing into the alleyway alongside her apartment followed by the clanging of empty glass bottles as they tumbled into the truck. Seagulls were a far superior wake-up call.

She lay in the middle of the double bed and stretched her arms out to touch the edges of the mattress. Her sleep had been a solid block and she'd woken refreshed, which was a good start to the day. It had to go well. She hadn't made a great first impression on the residents of Thistle Bay so far – Arthur had thought she was going to throw up in his car, Gloria had more or less suggested Cat looked a mess before quickly backtracking and Nick, well, she was better off not thinking about Nick.

Cat threw back her duvet and checked her foot. The swelling had gone down and she was relieved to see that the only bruise was the one to her pride.

She showered and dressed, choosing a navy dress with printed red flowers and short sleeves in case Alan Knight expected her to get stuck in with the chocolate. He'd thought she'd be able to do a better job writing about his business if she spent time in it. She wasn't sure what that meant, though.

'We need to do a better job of showing our customers who we are,' Alan had said during their meeting in Los Angeles. 'But before you can do your job, I think you need to spend some time in our business, getting to know it better.'

'Oh, absolutely,' Cat had said, full of enthusiasm. 'I can set up calls with key members of your team and . . .'

'No, Cat. You misunderstand me,' he'd said, cutting her off. 'I don't want you to talk to our team. I want you to become part of our team.'

Cat had narrowed her eyes, not sure she was following what he was asking of her. 'You mean in Thistle Bay?' Surely not.

'Exactly. To really get to know us, you have to see us in action. I want you to come to Thistle Bay for two weeks. We'll show you every part of the process and you'll meet the rest of my family.'

And here she was. Preparing to get to know someone else's family while simultaneously being rejected by her own. She refreshed her Find My Family inbox on her laptop, which still lay open from the night before. No messages. She groaned, logged out and headed downstairs for breakfast.

Gloria greeted Cat with a cheery smile and led her to a table by the window in the bustling breakfast room. She served her silky scrambled eggs, which Cat devoured with a slice of toast and a glass of apple juice before ducking out for a quick visit to Mystic Coffee ahead of Arthur's arrival.

Closing the door to the bed and breakfast behind her, she spotted Josef waving at her from his food stall. She waved back and crossed over the street to him.

'Good morning to you, Cat,' he said as she approached. 'Did you finish the almonds?'

'I did. They really were delicious. They took me back to a winter I spent in Munich eating sausages, mashed potato, sauerkraut and more than my fair share of sugared almonds.'

Josef nodded his head and closed his eyes briefly as though imagining he was in Munich. 'It's pretzels today.'

'I do love a pretzel. I'll take one, please.'

'You're a girl with good tastes.' Josef bagged a pretzel and handed it to her.

The heat from inside the paper bag transferred to Cat's hand and she smiled. 'It's still warm.' She opened the bag and couldn't resist biting off a piece of pretzel despite having just polished off a substantial breakfast. It had the perfect chewy crust with a soft, fluffy interior and was amply loaded with chunks of salt. 'It's so good. If you can make bratwurst for tomorrow, you'll make my day.'

'Tomorrow is pain au chocolat.'

Cat scrunched her eyebrows. 'That's not German.'

'My mother was French. Shall I keep you one?'

'Only a little one. Chocolate and pastry is not my favourite combination.' She loved chocolate but it had to be eaten on its own or drunk hot in a mug – she didn't even like chocolate cake or chocolate puddings. One of the boys in Hartsfield had once appeared with a giant jar of chocolate spread. His dad had brought it for him during a supervised visit having forgotten, or perhaps never known, that his son was allergic to dairy. Cat had followed Rachel's lead and taken two slices of toast and smoothed a thick layer of chocolate spread onto each slice. She realised her mistake as soon as the first bite made her gag. There was no way she'd be allowed to waste such a coveted luxury so she had shovelled it down as quickly as she could and left the rest of the jar for Rachel and the others.

Josef nodded, seemingly taking no offence that Cat didn't sound keen on his pain au chocolat. 'A Josef surprise for you tomorrow, then,' he said. 'OK?'

Cat grinned. 'I can't wait.'

'How long are you in town for?'

'Two weeks. I'm doing some work for Thistle Bay Chocolate Company.'

'Ah. Are you a chocolatier?'

Cat laughed. 'No. I wouldn't know where to start. I'm a copywriter. I'm helping them with their website.'

She put the rest of the pretzel into her bag for later and said goodbye to Josef. For now, she needed coffee. She could see the sign for Mystic Coffee and headed straight there.

There were two men in chunky high-vis coats in front of Cat in the coffee shop. They ordered a tea, a black coffee and two bacon rolls to go. The woman behind the counter scribbled their order on a notepad and took their payment, giving Cat time to browse the shop's homemade cakes.

There were fruit, plain and cheese scones as well as a selection of biscuits and two huge coffee-and-walnut cakes, yet to be sliced. Now, coffee and cake was a combination Cat *could* appreciate.

The tables in the coffee shop were busy already. Everyone seemed to be with someone, which was quite the contrast to Karen's Koffee, her local in LA, where the majority of early-morning sit-ins were people on their own with laptops. As a writer, Cat had really struggled with the K in Koffee but she'd felt a sense of loyalty to the café she'd gone to five mornings a week since the day she arrived in Los Angeles, when the place had simply been called The Coffee Shop. Her shiny new website even featured a few hard-at-work poses taken in Karen's Koffee, along with a profile photo of Cat looking intellectual yet approachable. The owners of Karen's Koffee had allowed Cat to take her photos inside the premises and she'd instructed the photographer to avoid capturing any of the café's bountiful branding in the final shots. The hiring of a professional photographer had felt like a necessary expense to Cat. Her business may have been cobbled together with haste but she wanted to make a go of it and so had invested the cash in building a sleek website.

The men in front of her moved to the end of the counter and Cat stepped into their place, a warmth from the roaring fire opposite the serving area skimming her back.

'Sorry to keep you waiting there,' said the woman behind the counter. 'I'm Mystic. What can I get you?'

Cat stared across the counter at the woman. She hadn't realised Mystic was an actual person. Cat estimated Mystic was, perhaps, fifty years old and looking great on it with her brown curly hair tied in a loose ponytail. Her magnetic green eyes were almost the same shade as the diamond-shaped emerald earrings she wore.

'I'll take a double-shot latte to go, please,' said Cat, glancing at her watch to check she wasn't going to be late for Arthur.

'Coming up.' Mystic wrestled a paper cup loose from the top of a stack and wrote her order on the side. 'And your name?'

'Cat. Do you by any chance know Arthur, the driver for Thistle Bay Chocolate Company?'

'Yes, sure, I know Arthur,' said Mystic.

'Do you know what he drinks?'

'He's a double-shot-latte man too.'

Cat smiled. She knew she liked Arthur. 'Then I'll take two, please.'

Mystic scribbled on another cup and rang Cat's order through the till. 'You can pick up your drinks from Susie at the end there,' she said once Cat had tapped her credit card to the card reader.

As Cat collected her coffees, her shoulders sagged at the familiar voice ordering a latte. She stooped forwards to glance around the side of the coffee machine and crept back out of view again. It was definitely him. Black shorts and a lime-green top that made him impossible to miss had replaced his blue running gear from the night before.

'Oh no,' she mumbled under her breath. She could do without bumping into Nick. She didn't need a reminder of the previous evening's fiasco – she needed to be on her A-game for her meeting.

Cat made for the exit, keeping her coffees raised and her head down in the hope of gliding past him and out of the door before he spotted her.

'How's your foot?'

Damn it!

'Oh, hi,' she said, turning to face him. 'It's fine, thank you.'

'Were you hiding from me?' Nick asked.

'What? No,' she said, flustered now. What was with this guy? Every time she saw him she managed to make a fool of herself. Granted, she had only seen him twice in twelve hours, and she could blame last night's mishaps on a day of travelling, but she had no excuse for this morning. Why hadn't she just said hello and kept walking?

'I was just . . . focused,' she said.

'Ah, yes. The big meeting.' Nick yanked open the door to the coffee shop and Cat headed out. 'Good luck.'

'Thanks,' she said, strutting away and not turning back. Given her luck so far in this town, she would likely fall over someone in the street and end up wearing the coffees if she took her eyes off the path.

Arthur was waiting for her outside his car and he opened the front passenger door for her as she hurried towards him.

'I'm reliably informed you're a double-shot-latte man, Arthur.' She handed him one of the coffees. 'I know we don't have very far to drive, but I need a strong coffee in the morning. Especially now.'

Arthur shot her a quizzical look.

'Don't ask.' Cat got into the front seat and Arthur closed the door, sealing her inside.

She took a gulp of her coffee and relished the first hit of caffeine as it swam through her body, re-energising her as it went. It's only two weeks. This job would go well. It had to. All she had to do to make a good impression was keep her mind on the job and avoid the man who seemed to bring out the less-than-professional side of her.

4

NICK SMILED TO HIMSELF AS HE WATCHED CAT CROSS THE road and hand a coffee to Arthur. Her brown hair was loose and sat just past her shoulders, with a slight wave at the ends as it swung with her movements. Last night he had found her utterly enchanting. Their encounter and the jolt he'd felt when he enclosed her tiny hand in his and they had stood barefoot in the sea was so unexpected. And it was the first thing he had thought about when he woke up this morning.

He'd passed Gloria's on his run and had found himself staring up at the windows, hoping to catch a glimpse of Cat. But his attraction was clearly one-sided. When he had seen her hiding behind her coffees he'd briefly contemplated letting her slip out. He couldn't do it, though. He would've kicked himself all day for letting the opportunity to speak to her again pass him by.

He'd noticed her hazel eyes had dark circles beneath them but, apart from that, they'd been wide open and bright, not betraying a hint of the exhaustion she must have been feeling after her journey. She had a sprinkling of freckles across her nose that he had missed in the dark and, as he watched her get into Arthur's car, Nick found himself wondering if they were always there or if they had been brought out by the Los Angeles sunshine.

'Nick,' came Susie's voice from the other end of the counter. 'Your coffee is ready.'

He turned and, aware Mystic was staring at him, kept his gaze fixed on his coffee.

'Thanks, Susie,' he said, picking up his coffee. 'How are you settling in?'

'Really well. I'm enjoying it, anyway. And I think I've finally mastered the coffee machine.'

He took a sip of his coffee. 'Tastes great to me.'

Susie beamed at the praise as she pressed the button to make an espresso for the next customer.

'So, you've already met the new girl in town,' said Mystic, leaning forward on the counter. 'She's cute.'

'Stop it.'

Nick was used to Mystic hinting at potential romances with every girl his age. She'd taken on the role of surrogate mother and chief matchmaker since his own parents had retired to the South of France.

'What's her story?' Mystic asked.

Nick glanced out of the coffee shop windows hoping for another customer to arrive and distract Mystic but the street was disappointingly empty. 'She's working for the Knights. She flew in last night and I took her up to the chocolate shop so she'd know where to go this morning.'

'I sensed a bit of heat in that little encounter.'

'That's coming from Susie with the milk steamer.'

Mystic smiled and gave a little laugh. 'I'm just saying it wouldn't hurt you to spend a bit of time with a pretty girl.'

'I spent an hour with her last night. That's enough.'

Although it definitely wasn't. Last night had been one of the few occasions when he'd cursed the town's size. He would have happily walked for miles in Cat's company. It had been the first time in over a year that he'd wanted to ask a girl out. In fact, the words were on the tip of his tongue when Gloria had appeared and interrupted them. Probably just as well.

'It takes five minutes to walk to Elizabeth's shop,' said Mystic. 'What were you two kids up to for the other fifty-five minutes?'

'She was on the beach getting stung by a jellyfish. Anyway, it doesn't matter. She's only here for two weeks. I probably won't even see her again.'

Mystic reached out and put a hand on Nick's shoulder. 'Look at you talking like you haven't lived in this town your whole life. You'll see her again; the only question is when.'

Her words rang in his ears as he headed home. Except for his time at university and two long years in London, Nick had lived in Thistle Bay his entire life. He couldn't wait to get back here. But something had been off since he'd come back and he couldn't quite figure out what it was or how to fix it. It wasn't his breakup with Lisa. In truth, they had both known since their move to London that it wasn't going to work out between them but neither of them had had the courage to say it.

Nick stepped inside Thistle Bay Art Gallery, the business he'd launched over a year ago, and flipped the sign on the door to Open. This venture had been his dream for so long, after two short-lived and disastrous jobs straight out of university had confirmed that he was never meant to be an employee. He was definitely more suited to being his own boss. The freelancing thing had paid the bills over the years and still made up a decent chunk of his income, but he benefited from the structure of having somewhere to go every day and had always longed for a bricks-and-mortar business that would still give him the freedom to indulge his creative side.

Lisa had worked in a gallery in Edinburgh and commuted from Thistle Bay for the first year that they were together. Nick had spent that time dreading a suggestion from her that they move to the city since he could work from anywhere, but the conversation never came. In the same way that he knew she wanted to move, she knew that he didn't, and so they had skirted around the topic for another year. Lisa had then been offered a job at a gallery in London, which caused immediate tension between them because she hadn't told Nick she'd even applied – let alone been interviewed – for the job. She was going, whether or not Nick went with her. Their compromise was to move to London for a year to try it out. Not going wasn't an option for Nick. They shared a vision of starting their own gallery, but Lisa had other career goals she was chasing at that time and he wasn't going to be the one to stop her achieving them.

Two years later the antique shop on the promenade came up for sale and Nick bought it. He came back to Thistle Bay straight away while Lisa stayed in London. They spent their weekends travelling back and forth, with Nick handling the renovations and Lisa agreeing to procure the art once they'd got the place up and running.

The antique shop sprawled over two floors with narrow passageways leading from one gloomy nook to the next. Nick knew he wanted a bright, open space and as soon as the planning permission was signed off he knocked the downstairs rooms into one, keeping only the supporting wall at the back to shield the staircase from view, and converted the upstairs into a generous two-bedroom living space. The whole refurbishment took six months to complete and by the time Lisa came back to join him, the gallery was ready to receive the art. But a month later, they'd both admitted it was over. Despite being Thistle Bay born and raised, Lisa had always had itchy feet. She acted like a girl plucked from city life and deposited against her wishes in the countryside. London suited her and Nick knew it. Expecting her to give that up would have gnawed away at their relationship until it fractured beyond repair.

Lisa had returned to London and he had opened the gallery on his own. But somehow it wasn't working for him. He'd realised his dream and it had fallen flat within a month. He struggled to embrace it fully because something tethered him from behind and he couldn't see what it was.

Getting involved with a girl from Los Angeles, no matter how short a liaison, wouldn't help. Besides, given how swiftly Cat had shoved her coffees in front of her face when she'd seen him, he didn't have to worry about keeping his attraction to her in check.

5

CAT STEPPED OUT OF ARTHUR'S CAR AND STOOD ON THE pavement looking up at the white sign with classic black lettering enclosed by painted purple thistles. Sitting right at the top of what she now knew to be Main Street, the Thistle Bay chocolate shop looked even lovelier in the daylight. Its eye-catching window display had a Halloween theme with orange pumpkins, chocolate cats and leaves in a variety of autumnal colours that looked like they were also made from chocolate.

Despite the company's old-fashioned website design, the shop looked pristine, as though it had only recently been opened or had at least been recently refurbished. A tall concrete wall to the left of the shop was decorated with a strip of haphazardly arranged seashells to cleverly conceal the factory building that Nick assured her last night was there.

'Wish me luck, Arthur.'

Arthur had got out of the car too and now stood beside her. 'You won't need it,' he said. He stepped forward and pulled the shop door open for Cat. It chimed with the same sound as the one in Gloria's bed and breakfast.

'Well, good morning. You must be Cat. I've heard a lot about you.' The woman behind the counter rushed forward and shook Cat's hand. 'Good morning, Arthur.'

'Good morning, Elizabeth,' said Arthur. 'It smells like warm chocolate in here already.'

'I got started early today,' said Elizabeth.

Elizabeth wore dark jeans with a pale blue floral top. Her white Thistle Bay Chocolate Company apron was immaculate except for one tiny smear of chocolate down the front. Her light brown hair was styled in a messy bun on top of her head and enclosed in a transparent hairnet. Cat touched her own hair, suddenly feeling as though she should have tied it back given that she might be around chocolate all day.

Elizabeth pointed to the counter. 'That bag there is just for you, Arthur,' she said.

Arthur picked up a clear cellophane bag of truffles, peeled back the sticker holding it closed and dug his hand in. 'It's never too early for chocolate. This will go nicely with the coffee that Cat here just bought me. You girls are spoiling me today.'

He popped the truffle in his mouth and Elizabeth seemed to glow with pride as he made an array of noises to show his enjoyment. 'Are the deliveries ready?'

Elizabeth nodded. 'They are. All packed up and waiting for you.'

'Where are you delivering to?' Cat asked.

'The whole of Fife,' said Arthur, digging in for another truffle.

'We supply our handmade boxes to garden centres, gift shops and cafés across the region,' Elizabeth explained.

'Arthur makes personal deliveries all around Fife and we use a courier for the bulk orders across the rest of the UK.'

'Aye. The local vendors know when they see my van that I have something one-of-a-kind for them.'

Cat felt a twinge of guilt at having allowed Arthur to drive her on a journey she could have walked in mere minutes. 'I hope I didn't delay your deliveries, Arthur.'

'Not at all,' he said. 'It was my pleasure to drive you.' He raised his bag of truffles on his way out of the door. 'Best batch yet, Lizzie.'

Elizabeth put a plate of chocolates in front of Cat. 'Can I tempt you? I'm with Arthur – it's never too early for chocolate.'

Cat thanked her and took one, noticing the familiar winged pattern on top. 'Raspberry?' she asked before popping the truffle in her mouth. The creamy chocolate melted on her tongue and the sweet raspberry filling oozed out – a delicious contrast to the coffee she had doused her taste buds in only minutes before.

Elizabeth smiled and raised her eyebrows.

'Your dad brought a box of chocolates to our meeting in Los Angeles and I recognised the pattern on top,' said Cat. 'These were one of my favourites. They actually taste like real raspberries. I have to say thank you for preparing that box for me. They really were exceptional chocolates.'

'I'm glad you liked them. There are no synthetic flavourings in them, just the natural tang from the fruit.'

Cat got the impression Elizabeth was going to say something else so she waited. Elizabeth's lips moved as she tried to formulate whatever was in her mind but she couldn't seem to get it out. The silence stretched between them and it was Cat who broke it.

'Your chocolate shop is lovely. If someone asked me to

picture a chocolate shop, this is exactly what would come to mind.'

'You might like this, then.' Elizabeth walked over to the left of the shop and drew Cat's attention to a large painting on the wall.

It was a depiction of the chocolate shop on a summer's day. The artist had taken liberties by surrounding the shop with trees that weren't there in real life but, otherwise, had captured every feature right down to the seashells along the top of the wall and the thistles on the sign. Cat leaned in for a closer look. The window display on the painting had a seaside theme, with shells, fish, starfish and pebbles. The attention to detail was exquisite.

'This is incredible,' said Cat.

'Isn't it?' Elizabeth stood staring at the painting too, her expression one of somebody deep in happy memories.

'Who painted it?'

'My sister Megan.'

'Ah, yes. The only sister not working in the family business, right? But she's left her mark in another way.'

Elizabeth hesitated, nodded her head, then walked back behind the counter.

Cat peeked over the worktop and took in the clear tubs filled with a wonder of ingredients. There were dried fruits, nuts, spices, oils, and a few ingredients you wouldn't automatically associate with chocolate such as dried mushrooms and what looked like breadcrumbs.

'What's this?' Cat asked, changing the subject. She had a feeling she'd struck a nerve when she mentioned Megan not working in the business and was keen to get back to more neutral territory.

'That's our flavour board. Ben and I are experimenting

with some of these infusions. Ben is my co-chocolatier. You'll meet him later today.'

'Great. I've seen his photo on the website.' Ben's professional online bio said he was from Edinburgh but had studied the art of chocolate making in Belgium and Switzerland. 'All of the flavours I've tasted have been amazing.'

'They certainly don't all end up amazing.' She sliced a chocolate down the middle and handed half to Cat. 'Smell this. I don't recommend eating it.'

Cat sniffed the chocolate and recoiled with a grimace. 'It's like sour milk with a touch of spearmint.'

Elizabeth laughed, her cheery demeanour having returned. 'Sometimes it just doesn't work. It's tricky because we're looking for a good balance of flavours. We don't want to overpower the chocolate, but occasionally we get it really wrong. The flavours are created here and then we test the production process to ensure we can replicate the quality on an industrial scale before we officially start making it.'

'What are you working on today?' Cat asked.

'It'll be a busy one. The shop should be quiet as there aren't many tourists around just now but we're preparing for the Pumpkin Festival next week. That's the town's Halloween celebration.' Elizabeth pulled a tray off a trolley near her and placed it on the counter. 'I'm making these for the kids.'

'What are they?' Cat asked, seeing only the smooth white chocolate and the back of whatever the designs were.

Elizabeth popped one out of the mould and flipped it over.

'Aw, it's mini Caspers,' said Cat, staring at the little white chocolate ghost. 'They're so cute. Did you do the window display too?'

'I did. I love this time of year. After Easter the window

displays get a bit boring but by the autumn I can be more creative, with pumpkins and ghosts, then Santas and Christmas trees, and then back to Easter eggs, chicks and bunnies again.'

'Plus Valentine's Day. I expect there's lots you could do with chocolate around that theme.'

'Uh-huh.'

The suggestion seemed to unsettle Elizabeth, who kept her attention focused on taking the chocolate ghosts out of their moulds. Valentine's Day, and her sister Megan not working in the business. Cat made a mental note not to touch those nerves again.

'Rebecca will be along to collect you shortly,' said Elizabeth.

Cat knew from what Alan had told her that Rebecca, his eldest daughter, would take over the running of the business whenever he decided to retire. The website listed her as Chief Operating Officer and Cat suspected Rebecca was the person who would have the final say on whether or not Cat had done a good job when these two weeks were over. She took a deep breath and waited for her arrival.

6

Rebecca Knight came to collect Cat from the shop just half an hour after she had arrived. At a couple of inches taller than Cat anyway, she wore heels that gave her at least another three inches. Her sleek mocha-coloured hair was much darker than Elizabeth's and styled with a heavy fringe framing her dark brown eyes. She wore black trousers and a red shirt that matched the shade of her lipstick. The woman was intimidating, which Cat sensed was intentional.

When Elizabeth introduced her, Rebecca shook Cat's hand with a firm grip and turned to walk straight back out of the door through which she had just appeared. 'Come with me. We're meeting in the conference room,' she said over her shoulder. Cat only just had time to wave at Elizabeth before she sped to catch up with Rebecca, who escorted her out through the back of the shop. 'Ryan is going to take you on a tour of the Thistle Bay factory this morning then the Edinburgh facility later in the week, if that suits.'

'Yes, that would be great,' said Cat. 'I'm excited to see

where the magic happens. I've had a flavour of it already from Elizabeth.'

The door to the conference room was open and Rebecca walked in first. She busied herself flicking through papers with her back to Cat. Cat got the impression her being here was not Rebecca's idea. The two Knight siblings Cat had met so far shared the same DNA and had the same upbringing yet were as different as standoffish cats and cuddly puppies.

Cat glanced at her phone. No messages. It was possible that she had siblings in the world somewhere. One of her parents might have had more children. When her birth mother had walked out of the hospital without even giving her name, she had made sure that her baby couldn't track her down and reappear at some point to disrupt her life. After many years of dead-ends, Find My Family seemed like Cat's last chance. Sometimes she would indulge in a little daydream that her mother welcomed her with open arms and had been hoping for years that Cat would manage to trace her. Most of the time, Cat knew she had to prepare herself for disappointment. There was every chance her birth family didn't want to be found.

Through the open door Cat spotted Gloria in the corridor with Alan Knight. The last time Cat had seen Gloria, she was rushed off her feet serving bacon and eggs at the bed and breakfast. The woman scowled at Alan and looked much more serious than the jolly person Cat had seen before. She was saying something to Alan in a volume low enough not to travel into the office, and their conversation was clearly personal.

Gloria's expression softened the instant another man approached them. Cat recognised him from her online research as Ryan Knight, the youngest child and only son of Alan. With his thick mop of blond hair, his casual navy trousers and an untucked striped shirt, he appeared less intimidating than Rebecca.

Ryan enveloped Gloria in a hug. He was a good foot taller than she was but he crouched down so she didn't have to stretch up too much to reach him.

'Good to see you, son,' Gloria said to Ryan loud enough that Cat heard. Gloria caught sight of her watching them and her face turned serious again for just the slightest moment before she smiled at Cat.

Cat returned Gloria's smile and gave her a wave. She couldn't decide if Gloria liked her or not. Her initial warmth when they'd first met seemed to have cooled a bit this morning and she had served Cat her eggs with barely a word.

When Gloria walked off down the corridor past a group of employees wearing white lab coats and hairnets, Alan and Ryan headed straight for Cat.

'Hi, I'm Cat.' She extended her hand to Ryan.

Ryan immediately hooked his arms around her and held her to him. 'It's good to see you,' he said.

His grip on her was tight and Cat only managed to get one arm round his back to pat it a few times. She wasn't expecting that and she wasn't quite sure how to handle it. Being lost for words was never something she had struggled with, but her new client hugging her so tightly on their first meeting brought her pretty close to speechless.

Alan Knight cleared his throat and Ryan released Cat.

'Sorry,' said Ryan. 'We're just one big happy family here. Sometimes I forget—'

'I'm so glad you arrived safe and sound, Cat,' said Alan, cutting Ryan off. His silver hair glinted under the glare of the conference-room lighting and his tall, broad frame towered over Cat. 'You've met Rebecca. Elizabeth, too, I understand. And as you'll no doubt have gathered, this is my son, Ryan.'

'Yes. Good to meet you, Ryan. And thank you again for choosing me for the project, Mr Knight. I'm excited to get started.'

'Call me Alan, please. Shall we all have a seat?'

Cat took her place at the rectangular table and the three present members of the Knight family sat opposite her. She had been in less daunting job interviews. Rebecca was still giving off a frosty vibe. Alan was as polite and professional as he had been in Los Angeles. Ryan was the friendliest of the three.

'So, what is it you need from us to get started?' Rebecca asked as Cat was logging in to her laptop.

'I think I just need to immerse myself in what's going on around here for a few days to get a clearer picture of what your offer is. I know from the brief that you want to expand your direct-to-customer sales.' Cat looked to Alan for confirmation that she had understood this part of his remit. His gaze seemed to be on the back of her laptop and she wasn't sure he was even listening. 'Um, well, I had some initial thoughts on how your website can achieve that by giving your customers more help to choose what they need. Let me show you.'

Cat brought up a file on her laptop and projected it onto the white screen suspended from the wall. It was hard to tell how this was going.

'If you check your website data,' she said, 'you'll find that one of the most visited pages on your site is the About page. Repeat customers will go straight to the products they intend to order, but new customers want to find out more about the person behind the business. To capture their interest, you need to show them who you are. People are increasingly choosing to shop with people they can relate to – the know, like and trust factor.'

'A return to old-fashioned shopping values,' said Alan, his eyes still fixed on the back of her laptop.

'Exactly. But now you can know, like and trust someone you've never met, on the opposite side of the world, just by reading their About page. I want to understand the heart and soul of your company and build a business personality that I'll reflect in the final copy. When we met in Los Angeles, Alan, you mentioned that you started the business using your mother's chocolate recipes when you relocated back to Thistle Bay.'

Rebecca slammed her pen on the desk and Cat flinched, fearing she had strayed into territory Rebecca wasn't comfortable with. Alan had been candid about his wife's illness being the driving force behind his decision to move his family back to Scotland from the Philippines, but Cat understood the impact of traumatic childhood memories and their enduring legacy.

'I'm not saying we put your personal life on the website,' Cat clarified. 'But your company has two sides to it – the wholesale channel and the direct-to-customer route. The wholesalers want a good product at a good price and probably don't spend too much time scrutinising your website. But those direct customers do, and they want to understand who Thistle Bay Chocolate Company is before they hand over their cash.'

Cat talked through a few more of her initial thoughts, but the Knights were difficult to read. Ryan was the only one who gave her the occasional encouraging smile and the only one who looked at all engaged. Alan was still somewhere else entirely, and Rebecca's expression could only be described as a glare.

'I've created this page mock-up,' she said bringing a new page up on her screen. 'It's a menu of options that allows people to shop by occasion. We'll keep the existing menu of boxes, bags and bars, but we can add an Occasion tab, too. This way people tell you what they're shopping for and the site gives them some inspiration.' Cat clicked on the drop-down menu to reveal the headings beneath. 'We have the usual holidays – Christmas, Easter, Valentine's Day. We can also have Mother's Day, Father's Day, Birthdays, Thank-you gifts, and this one that I'm calling Cosy night in. It's easy to tweak the menu options so it's seasonal. Your customer gets some suggestions they may not have thought to look at and you get data on what your customers are shopping for.'

'You seem to understand a bit about my company already,' said Alan, finally filling one of the many gaps Cat had left open for feedback.

Cat brightened, taking Alan's words as a compliment. The hours she'd spent on research hadn't uncovered much about Thistle Bay Chocolate Company but she did under-stand consumer-goods companies well enough from previous assignments to know what might help Alan's business.

'I think our website is doing pretty well as it is,' said Rebecca.

'I agree,' Cat said, desperately trying to think of a way to not annoy Rebecca any further but still get her point across.

Alan cleared his throat and Cat paused to give him time to interject. He said nothing.

'But wouldn't it be great if you could use it to attract even more sales? I've suggested you add an upsell to your checkout page,' said Cat. 'We can change the labels, but I've provisionally used *Go on, add a little treat for yourself* with links to your chocolate-drop bags and smaller boxes. Of course, these are just structural things. We can build it however you like.'

No one spoke for an uncomfortable few seconds.

'We haven't put much focus on the website or our direct-to-customer sales before,' said Ryan, 'but this is all making sense. I'm actually excited to see what a difference it could make.'

'Me too,' said Cat. She looked to Alan and Rebecca but it was clear neither of them was going to share an opinion. 'I'm looking forward to getting stuck in with the new copy. Your direct customers are not just buying chocolate, they're searching for the perfect gift for someone. Good copywriting doesn't sell to your customers; it shows your customers that they're in the right place, that they've found what they're looking for. People are turning away from faceless corporations in favour of artisan businesses where they can meet the maker. But they still want quality and they still want a fair price. You've built a business here that can give them that quality, can give them a great price, but can also let them support a company with a family at its heart. I'm just suggesting we showcase that more.'

Alan pushed his seat back and stood up. 'Will you excuse me? I need to go and take care of something else.'

'Of course,' said Cat, dragging a hand through her hair.

Alan turned and left the room without looking at her. Rebecca and Ryan glanced at each other, then back at Cat. Damn it. Had she been too harsh?

She decided to face it head-on and wiped her clammy hands down her dress underneath the table. 'I hope I'm not coming across as too critical,' she said. 'You've got a great business here. I like to come up with lots of ideas. We'll talk through what you think could work for your business and we'll implement those ones only. I won't make any changes you or Mr Knight are not comfortable with.'

'Don't worry, Cat,' said Ryan. 'You're doing a great job. We're just having an odd time right now. In the business.'

'Oh. Anything I can help with while I'm here?'

Rebecca gave what seemed to be a deliberately audible sigh. 'I think you should just stick to your brief. We can handle the rest. I need to get going too.'

'Well, thank you for your time. I'll keep working on the areas we've discussed.'

Rebecca stalked out of the room, leaving behind Ryan and an uncomfortable silence. Cat desperately wanted to ask how she had messed up. As she searched for the right words, Ryan seemed to know just what she was thinking.

'It may not feel like it, but the work stuff went well,' he said. 'You've clearly done a lot of thinking in advance and your ideas are good. I'm looking forward to seeing some mock-ups from you.'

The work stuff. So, what else was going on?

'Thanks.'

'I have an office here that you can use to work in, if you like. I spend much of my time in Edinburgh or on the factory floor here so I barely use it. Come on, I'll show you. It'll probably be more comfortable for you than working from Gloria's.'

Just the mention of Gloria's name took Cat back an hour. There was clearly some tension between Alan and Gloria. Was it possible that's what had caused the atmosphere? She might have the opportunity to ask Gloria later, but she wouldn't want the Knights to think she was gossiping if her enquiries got back to them.

The door to Ryan's office was open already. He ushered her in for the grand tour, as he called it, although there wasn't much to see. There was a desk and chair, one set of low cupboards and a small round table with four extra chairs. The only art on the walls were product shots. They looked professionally taken, not the amateur shots that featured on the website.

'This will be perfect for me. Thanks. I didn't get a chance to say before, but I'd also like to suggest new photos for the website. I know you just hired me to look at your website copy, but the shopfront is so cute and cute sells. You do mention the shop, but you don't show it. I think putting photos of it on your website would help people connect to Thistle Bay as a brand. And maybe some behind-the-scenes shots in the factory, too.'

'Great idea. Do it.'

'Excellent. I'm going to write copy that stands out and gives the company an identity. The right image can only enhance that. Do you know of any local photographers?'

'Yes. Nicholas Bell Photography. You'll find him on the promenade right across the street from Gloria's. He owns Thistle Bay Art Gallery.'

'Sounds ideal. I'll get some quotes from others, too.'

'Don't bother. He's the only photographer in town so his rates will be fine. And I went to school with him, so tell him I said it's a mates' rates kind of situation.'

'Will do.'

'I'll save the tour of the rest of the premises for when you're both free so you can get some pictures at the same time. See when he's next available and I'll work around that. Have you had much chance to explore the town?'

'Not yet. I had a wander along the beach last night but that's it.'

'Well, don't forget to take some time to look around. To fully appreciate Thistle Bay Chocolate Company, you've got to get a feel for Thistle Bay. It's not just our name, it's a big part of our story.'

Cat nodded. 'Thank you, Ryan. I really appreciate your support.'

She was warming to Ryan. He seemed to be on her wavelength. Or perhaps it was just because he was the only one who had actually been listening to her in the meeting. As first meetings go, that really was pretty awful.

7

CAT FOUND THISTLE BAY ART GALLERY EASILY. IT WAS ON THE corner directly opposite Gloria's bed and breakfast. She stepped inside and was met with silence and only one other customer browsing. As well as pieces along the walls, there were four square exhibition stands in the centre of the room displaying multiple artworks on each face. The white metal of these structures and the gallery's original wooden flooring seemed to add to the echo as she and the other customer moved around. She was grateful she wasn't wearing heels.

Cat wandered over to the first stand. It held a combination of landscape paintings and photographs, all by different artists. The only commonality to her uneducated eye was the colours. The photographs had been taken at dusk and the cool blue tones in the paintings made her shiver.

As she moved closer to the back of the room she saw a wood-burning stove. The glass door on the front of the stove had been left slightly ajar and she edged closer to feel the warmth emanating from it. She loved the concentrated heat that came from a real fire, regardless of the weather outside.

Stepping past the long and wide table to get closer to it, she spotted a familiar little black dog lying contentedly in front of the fire.

'Hey, Skye,' she said. 'Is that you? What are you doing here?'

Cat crouched down and Skye rolled onto her back, legs splayed in expectation of a belly rub. Cat obliged as her eyes darted around the displays in search of Nick.

'So, you're not hiding from me this time, I see. That's progress.' Nick appeared from behind a heavy wooden sliding door at the back of the room.

Cat took a deep breath to compose herself. She was going to keep her cool and just say hello.

'Hello again,' she said, giving Skye a final tickle before standing up. Her stomach lurched as it dawned on her why he was here. This couldn't be happening.

'You're not Nicholas Bell Photography, are you?' she asked, unable to muster even a smidgen of hope in her voice. Nick stood there and just smiled and nodded. 'Of course you are.'

Wearing grey jeans and a simple faded blue T-shirt, Nick didn't have the dapper look she associated with art collectors and gallery owners. But then a small-town art gallery probably had a different clientele from the chic galleries she was used to visiting. 'Were you looking for some photos?' he asked.

'I had a little project in mind but it's last-minute and it wouldn't be fair to ask you to try to squeeze it in. I can see you're busy,' she said, not daring to look around, knowing the gallery was all but empty.

Cat turned and retreated to the front door, where she paused, her hand hovering above the handle. The Knights' website really needed work. It wasn't bad, it was just clearly homemade and she was confident she could make it so much better. But their images were awful. And their chocolate shop was so lovely. New photos would complement her written words and really make the website pop. 'You're a professional. You can do this,' Cat muttered under her breath, then turned back to Nick.

He hadn't moved. He just stood there watching her. Amused by her, it seemed.

'On second thoughts,' said Cat. 'Are you free at some point today, or tonight even?'

'Are you asking me out on a date?' Nick said, the corners of his mouth twitching.

Cat forced a laugh to cover her embarrassment. Get it together, Cat.

She walked towards him again. 'I'm looking to shoot some new photos for the Thistle Bay Chocolate Company website and I'm hoping that, as the only photographer in town, you might be able to help me. Sometime in the next few days would be ideal. And Ryan Knight says to tell you it's mates' rates.'

Nick laughed. 'I'll bet he did. Let me check.' He pulled his phone from his pocket and swiped through it a few times.

Cat's shoulders relaxed. Nick seemed to now be in business mode, and that she could handle.

'I've got time tonight to talk it through,' he said and looked up from his phone with a glint in his eye. Cat steeled herself. 'Shall we say seven o'clock over dinner?'

And we're back there, Cat thought. 'Seven o'clock over coffee. I'll meet you at Mystic's,' she said, turning on her heel and striding back towards the door.

8

Cat knew without looking at her phone that it was Rachel calling for the third time since school hours had finished. Alone in her room at Gloria's, she had no excuse not to pick up.

'Hey,' said Rachel when Cat answered. 'Have you been avoiding me?'

'Of course not,' Cat lied.

'What are you up to?'

'I was just heading over to Mystic's Coffee to have some dinner. You?'

'Just calling you to find out how your first day went. And to find out if you've bumped into the sweaty-but-sexy beach guy again today.'

And there it was – the reason Cat had been avoiding Rachel's calls. She sighed.

'Oh, come on,' said Rachel. 'You know I have no love life and live vicariously through you.'

'Well, there's nothing going on there. I'm working . . .' Cat paused, swithering between whether or not to tell Rachel about seeing Nick again.

'Oh my God, you've seen him again, haven't you? I can tell by your silence.'

'I have seen him. But it looks like I'll have to work with him, so even if I did like him—'

'You definitely like him,' said Rachel, cutting her off. 'You as good as said it last night. What if he's the one?'

'He's not. Even if I believed that *the one* existed.'

'He could be. True love exists. If you ever gave anyone longer than a month, you might have felt it for yourself by now.'

One month was a bit of an exaggeration but Cat didn't feel like getting into a debate over it. Relationships always ended, so the break was cleaner if both parties got out before feelings were strong enough to make it complicated and messy. Besides, Cat was always on the move so it didn't make sense to get involved too deeply. Right now, she needed to focus on building her business and finding somewhere to live. Then she could think about a relationship.

'Maybe I would have gone on a few dates with him in different circumstances, but he's not the one. I need a photographer and it turns out he's the only photographer in this tiny town.'

Rachel laughed. 'So, you'll have to work with him. That's going to be interesting.'

'No, it's not. I'm a professional.'

'Look, I know you weren't looking forward to coming back to Scotland. I just think it would be good for you to have a little fun.'

'Not while I'm working. This is my biggest client so far, and my only client in this country. Besides, based on how today's meeting went, it looks like these people will be tough clients to satisfy and I need to stay clear-headed.'

'The job's just two weeks, right?' asked Rachel, not

waiting for an answer. 'Who knows what will happen after that?'

'I know what will happen. I'll be coming to sleep in your spare room for a few weeks and I'll never see Nick again.'

'Or . . . you can work for two weeks, shack up with Nick for a week, *then* come and stay with me.'

Cat laughed. Despite Rachel's traumatic childhood, she had a way of simplifying life that Cat had always admired.

'I need to go. I'm meeting Nick to talk about the photos I need.'

'What?'

'Goodbye, Rachel.'

Cat hung up the phone, cutting off Rachel's plea for details. She glanced at her watch. At least the call had distracted her until it was time to meet Nick. The guy made her nervous and she wasn't used to that. She didn't need to spend time overanalysing how a meeting that hadn't yet happened was going to go.

She spritzed some perfume on her neck and dragged a brush through her hair. Pausing at the door, she reconsidered her appearance and went back to the mirror, dabbed on some blush-pink lip gloss, then headed downstairs.

Gloria was standing behind her check-in desk. 'How was your first day, hen?'

It was weird, but she couldn't say that. After a brief internal debate, she settled for 'I think it went OK.'

Gloria spent a while straightening the plant pot, penholder and fruit bowl that sat on top of her desk. The woman almost looked disappointed as she plucked a few browning leaves from the plant.

Cat didn't want the Knights to think she was gossiping about them, but she had to ask. 'I don't want to pry, but when I saw you there today you looked a little upset. Are you OK?'

'Oh, I'm fine, hen. The Knights are like family to me, but we don't always agree, that's all.'

'I guess everyone is like family when you live in a small town.'

'Well, yes, but I also used to work for the family.'

'Really? In the business?' Cat couldn't quite picture Gloria in a hairnet and white coat.

'*For* the family. I looked after the kids when they were growing up. Ryan was just a baby when I started working for Alan. I set up this place after he left for university.'

'Goodness, they really are like family to you, then.'

'They are. And I would hate to see someone come in and cause them pain.'

Cat was lost now. Gloria was staring intently at her, but surely she wasn't talking about Cat. She was just a copy-writer overhauling their website. What pain could she possibly inflict? She was itching to ask Gloria to elaborate, but nosing into their private affairs would involve going beyond the terms of her contract with Thistle Bay Chocolate Company and was definitely not the way to get a good testimonial from them for her business.

'Anyway, hen, I'm fine. Thanks for your concern. Would you like me to rustle you up something for your dinner?'

Cat shook her head. 'That's kind, but I'm meeting Nicholas Bell at Mystic's. I'll grab something to eat over there.' Cat zipped up her coat in preparation for the rush of cold air she expected to feel from the North Sea.

'Another meeting with Nick, eh?'

'I'm looking to get some new photos taken of the choco-late shop,' said Cat, ignoring the insinuation in Gloria's voice and the arched eyebrow.

'Well, he's the man for that. He did my website photos. Business is thriving since I got myself a website,' said Gloria, seemingly happy to drop the Nick chat. 'Have a lovely date, hen. Don't stay out too late.' Or perhaps not.

9

CAT RUBBED HER HANDS TOGETHER AND BLEW INTO THEM AS she crossed the street from Gloria's. The early-evening Scottish air had already formed a light frost, bathing Main Street in a silvery glow. Despite what Gloria thought, her meeting with Nick was definitely not a date. OK, if she hadn't been working and Nick had asked her out, she probably would have said yes. But she was working and, anyway, Nick wasn't interested. He seemed amused by her, if anything. She simply provided some entertainment for him in this quiet town rather than being someone he might want to date.

It wouldn't take them long to have a cup of coffee and go over her photography needs. She'd had coffee meetings with hundreds of clients over the years and knew how to handle them. This meeting would be easier because Cat was in charge. She was the client this time. She wasn't trying to win work from Nick, she was offering work to him. If anyone should be nervous, it was him.

Nick was already waiting when Cat arrived at Mystic's. He was chatting with the lady herself and their conversation seemed intense. He'd chosen to sit at the sofas in front of the fire and Mystic was leaning over him, one hand on her hip, looking like the one in charge of the conversation. Nick nodded along, his gaze flickering everywhere except on Mystic. Cat hoped Mystic wasn't an unhappy photography customer and kicked herself for not checking out his website. Ryan had said he was the only photographer in town – meaning he may very well be the one responsible for the current mediocre Thistle Bay Chocolate Company photos.

Cat sighed. She couldn't charge the client to replace one set of shoddy photos with another set. Walking towards Nick, she strained to hear the conversation but Mystic had stopped talking and seemed to be waiting for an answer that wasn't forthcoming.

Nick didn't see her until she was right beside his table. 'Hi,' he said, a warm smile spreading across his face.

Mystic turned to Cat. 'Double-shot latte?' she asked her.

'Please,' said Cat. 'Actually, better make it decaf since it's late in the day.'

Mystic nodded and walked off to get their drinks.

'Have you ordered?' Cat noticed Nick didn't yet have a drink in front of him.

He nodded and Cat perched on the edge of the sofa opposite him. She would have preferred to sit anywhere else in the coffee shop – the sofas only had a knee-height table between them and the taller tables would have provided a helpful barrier between client and customer. The warmth from the fire was welcome, though, and Cat watched the flames dancing around with tiny flecks of orange sparking towards her as she shrugged off her coat and placed it on the sofa beside her bag. The metal grate surrounding the fireplace would stop any sparks getting too close.

'Are you OK sitting here?' he asked.

'Sure.' She could hardly say no and make him move.

'So, you need a photographer.'

'Yes.' Getting down to business. Good. 'Do you have a portfolio I can look at?'

Nick smirked and shook his head. 'You'll just have to trust me.'

Cat pulled her notebook out of her bag, laid it on the low table and flicked to the page she'd scribbled in earlier that day. 'I've made some notes about what I'm looking for.' She was just about to run through her suggestions when Mystic appeared over Nick's shoulder.

'Coffee's on the counter, Nick. Would you mind?' said Mystic.

'Sure, I'll grab it.'

When Nick got up to collect their coffees, Mystic put a plate with two pumpkin-shaped gingerbread biscuits on the table in front of Cat. 'Thanks, honey,' she said to Nick as he walked away. Then she turned to Cat. 'You be careful with that boy's heart.'

'Excuse me?' Cat furrowed her brow, not sure what Mystic was getting at.

'I've not seen him on a date for a long time.'

'Oh, no, that's not what this is. We're just working together. I'm looking to hire him to take some new photos for Thistle Bay Chocolate Company, that's all.'

'If you say so,' said Mystic. She smiled at Nick when he returned, then made her way back behind the counter.

Cat didn't turn around but she could feel Mystic's eyes on her. That was one of the peculiarities of small towns – everyone shared their opinions freely. In cities, people were more reserved until they got to know you better. At least, that had been Cat's experience over the last eight years. She should have been relieved that Mystic wasn't an unhappy photography customer after all, but Cat's instincts told her the tense conversation she'd walked in on when she arrived had somehow revolved around her.

'What was that about?' asked Nick.

'She thought we were on a date.'

'Aren't we?'

Cat raised her eyebrows. First Gloria, then Mystic and now Nick. Did he really think this was a date?

'I'm kidding,' said Nick. 'Mystic is a close friend of my mum's so she takes it upon herself to keep an eye on me. You planning to rob a bank or something?'

Cat had been lost in her thoughts and had no clue what he was talking about. 'What?'

Nick touched her notepad with his finger and she saw the last item on the list she had composed earlier: *Near an airport for a quick getaway*. 'That's quite a list,' he said.

While taking a break from all things chocolate, her mind had wandered to where she might go after Thistle Bay. Rachel had said it was time Cat started putting down roots of her own. It wasn't a terrible suggestion.

Cat took a gulp of her coffee and allowed the steam to warm her face. 'It's just silly, I have to decide where I'm going to go after Thistle Bay so I was making a list of what kind of place I fancied.'

Nick leaned over to read her list again. 'A beach, a good coffee shop, Wi-Fi, and near an airport for a quick getaway. It's about an hour to the airport from here. Is that near enough?'

Cat forced a laugh. She flicked the page over on her notebook and moved the napkin holder to the corner of her book to keep the page in place. 'I think I told you that I'm rewriting the website for Thistle Bay Chocolate Company.'

Nick nodded, allowing her to move the subject back to work.

'I'd like some new images to go with my words. I definitely want a photo of the shop. It's just beautiful and I think it'll help people to see the small, family nature of the business. Have you ever looked at the website?' she asked.

'Is that you trying to figure out if I took their awful photos?'

'It was originally set up to appeal to their business customers,' she said, ignoring his question. She wouldn't answer it without knowing who did take the photos. If it wasn't Nick then it might have been one of the Knights and she didn't want word to get back to whichever family member had been the photographer that she was criticising their camera skills. 'A good portion of their revenue now comes direct from consumers, and I think we can improve on that revenue by showing customers who they are buying from.'

She took a breath to sip her coffee, aware she was rambling. This was supposed to be the bit she was good at.

Nick nibbled on one of the pumpkin biscuits and she got the feeling he was watching her rather than listening to her.

'Most of the product photography is good,' she went on.

'Agreed,' he said. Maybe he was listening. 'That's because of Elizabeth.'

'How you do mean?'

Cat gave him a minute to finish chewing his biscuit. He brushed his hands together and took a gulp of his coffee.

'Eat your biscuit. It's good,' he said. 'When Elizabeth joined the business full time, I gave her some photography lessons. Nothing fancy – just some simple lighting techniques and key camera settings for picking up detail and colour accurately.'

Cat bit into her pumpkin biscuit. It was delicious. The ginger flavour was strong but not overpowering and the texture was chewy rather than crunchy, which she preferred.

Nick continued. 'Where Elizabeth has had a hand in creating the products, you'll find she's taken the photos. Some of the poorer shots are older products.'

He said it, not her. The product photography was hit or miss. Most of the shots were good but there were some truly awful ones too. He clearly had looked at their website. Perhaps he was better prepared for this meeting than she was.

'That's good to know,' said Cat. She could ask Elizabeth to take new product shots where needed and save money by using up less of Nick's time. With the added bonus that Cat would have to spend less time with him. For some reason, he turned her into a wittering mess – and the less time she behaved like that, the better.

She got down to business. 'I want a few shots of inside the factory – I'll need to get Ryan involved in that so we're not photographing any company secrets – and a few of Elizabeth and Ben working on some of their handmade creations. I'd also like new headshots of the family, although I'm not sure they'll all be up for that.'

'Why not?' asked Nick.

Cat shrugged. Rebecca was giving off strong vibes that Cat wasn't welcome here, but she couldn't say that to Nick without it looking as though she were bad-mouthing a client. Something she would never do.

'How about I come to the shop tomorrow and take some shots?' he suggested.

Cat's phone buzzed with an email alert. 'I'm sorry, do

you mind if I check that? I'm waiting for some important news.'

'Go ahead.'

Cat opened her emails and scanned her unread messages. Her eye was immediately drawn to an email from Find My Family. Her breath caught in her throat. It was just their weekly newsletter. The weekly reminder, as if she could forget, that the person who was potentially her only blood relative couldn't care less about her. She sighed and slumped back on the sofa. Being rejected by someone she hadn't even met was a new level of rejection.

'You OK?' The concern on Nick's face told her how miserable her own expression must be.

'I'm fine.' She hadn't intended the frosty tone and feigned a smile.

'Not the news you were hoping for?'

'No. And sorry, tomorrow would be great. I know it's last minute, so, thanks.'

'Happy to help. Can we eat now? I'm starving.'

Cat sighed again and ran her finger around the rim of her coffee cup. 'Nope. We said coffee, not dinner.'

'You've got to eat, right?' He picked up the menu and started reading.

She *was* hungry and she *had* planned to eat here. She'd just thought Nick might leave after they had talked about work. But he was right, she did have to eat. She put her hand out and Nick passed her the menu.

They ordered and Cat made small talk with Nick about his photography until their food arrived. Nick had studied for a photography degree and his dad was a photographer too, so he'd grown up in a house with lots of cameras and its very own darkroom. This renewed her hope that the suggestion she'd made to get new photos was a good one and, along with her new copy, would help show the Knights that such a transformation to their website could equate directly to a surge in consumer sales.

'Dad refused to get into digital photography,' said Nick. 'I think he just loves spending hours on his own in the dark.'

'And you?' Cat asked. 'What are your thoughts on digital photography?'

'Love it. I like working in the light. What's your story?'

'The only photos I take are with my phone.'

Nick laughed. 'That's not what I meant. You're staying here for two weeks and then you're looking for somewhere with a . . . what was it? A beach, a coffee shop, an airport and . . . oh, Wi-Fi. You're not going back to Los Angeles, then?'

'No,' said Cat, choosing not to elaborate.

'Well?'

'Well, what?'

'There's a story there, isn't there?'

Cat took a bite of the Cheddar-and-onion toastie Mystic had placed in front of her. This was a conversation she'd had many times before. With every new city, the people she met always wanted to know more about her story. It was understandable that they would be interested in where she had moved from, but she found that the more information she gave, the more questions were asked. She would give Nick the short version, then change the subject. 'Not much of a story. I've been travelling about a bit over the last few years. But I'm done with that. I'd like to settle somewhere – for a while, at least. Have you always lived in Thistle Bay?'

Nick cleared his throat and shifted in his seat. That should have been an easy question. Perhaps Nick had a story of his own.

'Mostly. Do you have a shortlist of places you'd like to

move to?' He took a bite of his BLT, avoiding eye contact with her.

Yep. He definitely had a story of his own.

'Not yet. I'm going to Edinburgh first and then I'll decide from there.'

'Is that where your folks are?'

'Em, no. They died.'

Nick looked up and did that tilt-of-the-head thing people always do when they feel sorry for you. They were veering towards another conversation she had become accustomed to having. Whenever anyone found out her parents had died and she had no brothers or sisters, it inevitably led to enquiries about grandparents, then aunts and uncles, then finally what it's like to be completely alone in the world.

'I'm sorry,' said Nick. 'That must be tough.' His eyes were locked with hers and he leaned forward. If he felt awkward by her revelation, he wasn't showing it. And he wasn't asking the questions that usually followed. He wasn't asking any questions at all.

'It was a long time ago,' said Cat. 'I was six. I had no other family who could take me in so I went into foster care. I moved from London to Edinburgh when I was eight, with a foster family. They moved back to London not long after and left me up here.'

Well, that felt like unnecessary added detail. Where did that come from? It wasn't that Cat hid her background – it just didn't usually come spilling out of her the first time she met someone. Although, this was the second time meeting Nick, not counting the coffee-shop fiasco and the five morti-fying minutes in the gallery that afternoon. If she wasn't stepping on jellyfish, she was questioning his ability to do his job and blurting out her tragic life story. What must he think of her?

Nick's lips parted and, just as he was about to say something, Cat cut in. 'Tell me about your gallery, Nick.'

Not the subtlest of subject changes, but he went with it.

10

Cat dialled Rachel's number on the way down the stairs from her room. She had ignored the texts last night asking how things had gone with Nick but she knew her friend was persistent. If Cat didn't call her this morning, Rachel would call between her classes until she got to speak to her.

'Hey, what's up?' Rachel said, having answered on the first ring.

'Not that you were waiting by the phone or anything, Rach.'

'Of course not. So, how did it go with the sexy photographer?' asked Rachel, getting straight to the point as usual.

Cat chose to ignore the sexy reference. 'It was pretty awful. He's going to do the work for me but the entire meeting was so awkward. It turns out Mystic is his aunt, or his mum's best friend or something so she's like his aunt. Anyway, she warned me to be careful with him as soon as I stepped in the door.'

'Oh my God. He must be a bad one if his own aunt is warning you against him.'

'Not like that. She was being protective of him. She thought we were on a date.'

'Ah. And let me guess. You still find him tongue-tyingly good looking and he got you all hot and bothered again.'

'Pretty much. What the hell is wrong with me?' She could have hurried through dinner and scarpered back to Gloria's early, but she hadn't. After they'd finished eating they had talked for a good hour about photography, copy-writing, the pros and cons of self-employment. Despite being on edge for much of their conversation, she hadn't been able to bring herself to walk away until Mystic told them it was closing time and they had to get out.

'Or . . . what's right with him?'

'Oh, shut up. It would go nowhere. Just a holiday fling, and I'm not even on holiday. I'm working. I cannot get distracted and risk this job. It's currently the only one I have.'

'You're worrying about this too much. You are the master at compartmentalising your life – which is not a compli-ment, by the way. But on this occasion, it might help. Put this guy in a box and don't open it again until November.'

'You're right,' said Cat, reaching the front door of the bed and breakfast. 'If there's one thing I'm brilliant at, it's keeping my emotions in check. That's all I need to do.'

Cat crossed the road feeling better already. She was good at dealing with guys. She closed herself off to relationships all the time. As soon as she felt herself starting to care whether or not a guy answered her call, she knew it was time to end things. There had been enough disappointment in her life; she didn't need to set herself up for more of it. She just had to see Nick as another one of those guys she could do without in her life.

'So, what's on the agenda today?' asked Rachel.

'Nick's meeting me at the chocolate shop this morning to start taking the photos. Ryan's giving us a tour of the factory first and then I'll get some writing done this afternoon. Anyway, I need to go now. There's an apricot pastry with my name on it right in front of me.' Cat hung up the call and slid her phone back into her bag.

'Good morning, Josef. These look amazing. I only had fruit and yogurt this morning because I knew whatever you had baked, I wanted.'

Josef's laughter bounced off the walls of his stall as he bagged up a pastry for her. 'You would have liked my mother,' he said. 'She was a writer, like you.'

'Really? Well then, we'd have had a lot to talk about.'

'She wrote for newspapers, then, in later years, for magazines. She wrote a couple of books, too. What kind of writing do you do?'

'I'm a copywriter so I write marketing material for companies – websites, sales campaigns, flyers. That kind of thing.'

'Not books?'

She had always wanted to hold a book in her hands with her name on the front cover – but wasn't that every writer's dream? Creative writing wasn't for her. She didn't have the patience to work on the same project for months at a time so a novel was out of the question, and she didn't know where to start to generate non-fiction ideas. A few people over the years had suggested she write about her life so far. Having no knowledge of her birth parents and then her adoptive parents being tragically killed when she was only six years old seemed to fascinate people, but she had no desire to write what she thought of as a misery memoir.

Cat shook her head. 'I struggled to find my own voice, but I realised I was good at embodying other people's so copywriting for different companies works for me.'

Josef nodded. 'As long as you like it. Maybe you'll do a book one day. Make sure you come back here and let me know about it.'

'If it ever happens, I'll bring you a copy.'

'Signed.'

'Deal.'

Josef smiled at this. She looked forward to their daily chats. The man radiated happiness and she felt a little bit rub off on her each time they talked.

'Do you have family around here, Josef?'

'No, it's just me. I lost my beloved wife of fifty years earlier this year. I miss her every day, but I decided I could follow her sooner or later. I chose later. She loved every minute of life so I didn't think she would mind. I retired here from Germany.'

She loved Josef's spirit. She couldn't imagine spending fifty years with someone and then them just being gone. Were those kinds of relationships now a thing of the past?

'You don't look retired, if you don't mind me saying,' said Cat, making a show of looking around his food stall.

Josef chuckled. 'Well, half-retired. I believe people that fully retire die soon afterwards. My father saw his hundredth birthday. I plan to see mine, too.'

The obvious next question was whether or not he had children, but Cat always avoided asking that question. She rubbed at the backs of her arms to dull the sensation of the hairs prickling on her skin.

'I have two girls and two boys. I can see you wondering.'

Cat laughed. 'Am I that transparent?'

'They have families of their own now and they live all

over the world, none of them here. Only my eldest daughter, Nadja, lived near me in Berlin.'

'That must be difficult for you.'

'No, I like to see them happy. It's good to know that they have the freedom to live their lives however they choose. It wasn't like that for every generation. In life, you should only do what makes you happy. And everyone else should do what makes them happy, too, and you cherish the times when your paths meet.'

'Nadja must miss you.'

'She does. But everybody misses someone.' He was right, of course. Separation was a fact of life, whether driven by geography, death or abandonment. Cat had experience of all three. She couldn't imagine Josef's daughter being happy about his decision to retire to Scotland – the death of her mother must have made her want to cling on tighter to her father. 'My daughter worries about me. They all do, probably. But my Eva was one of those happy people that irritate unhappy people. She was the manager of a department store for more than twenty years and had Christmas cheer for twelve months of the year. Whenever I, or any of our children, pondered trying something new, her response was always the same: do it. I reminded my daughter of this when I told her I was staying in Thistle Bay. She knew her mother would have wanted me to be here.'

'Why here?' Cat asked. 'Of all the places you could have gone, why did you choose here?'

'I was born not far from here and I lived in these parts until I was ten years old. My father was German and we moved back to what was his home. But Thistle Bay has a way of seeping into your soul and never letting you go completely.'

The only time Cat had felt that pull was when she

moved to London. But that tug had vanished within weeks and she'd never experienced it since. Her subsequent moves had all been practical and driven by where she had been able to find a job and somewhere to live. Perhaps that's why she was now struggling with her next move. She no longer needed a job to guide her. It was all on her.

Josef shrugged. 'I could have chosen to move closer to any of my children, but where's the adventure in that? I don't want to live a small life with whatever time I have left.'

Cat gazed at the town behind her before turning back to Josef. 'But isn't life in Thistle Bay kind of small?'

Josef leaned towards her. 'It's a small town. That's different from a small life. Life isn't about where you're living – it's about what you're doing, or what you're choosing not do to, with the time you have.'

Cat thought about that for a moment. Travel was supposed to broaden your horizons. So why did she suddenly feel as though she had used her travelling to keep her life small? 'You're very wise, Josef. I could do with some of your way of seeing the world.'

'It took me seventy-two years to see the world this way; don't be so hard on yourself.'

Cat nibbled on her apricot pastry on the way over to the chocolate shop. Those hairs on the backs of her arms prickled whenever anyone mentioned their family. It was a near-daily sensation that she'd never got used to. When you didn't have a family, your senses became heightened to any talk of other people's – and she had found that people talked about their families more often than they probably realised.

She swallowed the last morsel of her pastry and caught Nick's eye. He was waiting by the shop already and waved when he saw her approaching. Now, the hairs on the backs of her arms were prickling for another reason entirely.

11

CAT WATCHED NICK SETTING UP HIS CAMERA TO PHOTOGRAPH the outside of the chocolate shop. She didn't know much about photography but she imagined the light at this hour would help to create the perfect shot. The morning sun was still low in the sky and the shop looked bright, with no dark patches or shadows from neighbouring buildings to dull its appearance.

'Are these thistles real?' asked Cat.

'No one knows,' said Elizabeth. 'They're Arthur's domain. He grows them in pots then puts them out in front of the shop or gives them as gifts when they're big enough. But he also has top-quality artificial ones for between growing seasons.'

Cat touched one of the thistles poking out of the charcoal planters in front of the shop windows and yelped as its spike pierced her skin.

'Given you're bleeding, those will be the real ones,' Elizabeth concluded, making Cat laugh as she sucked the pinprick of blood from the tip of her finger.

'Can you guys move behind me?' asked Nick.

'Oh, can you hold on?' said Cat. 'Don't start yet.' She disappeared into the shop, had a scout around for a bucket and filled it with hot soapy water. Grabbing a handful of paper towels, she returned to the front of the shop. 'Seagulls,' she said to Nick and Elizabeth, who stood with quizzical looks on their faces, before she washed a mess away from the edge of the front window and dried it off with another paper towel. She grinned. 'I think it's better I use words rather than images to convey the beautiful seaside location of the chocolate shop, don't you?'

Nick laughed and started snapping his photos once Cat had moved herself and her bucket of water out of shot.

Elizabeth stood staring at Cat with a warm smile on her face.

'What?' asked Cat, folding her arms.

'Good spot, that's all,' said Elizabeth.

Cat peered around Nick to check out Elizabeth's window display. 'I love the leaves. Are they all made from chocolate?'

'Yes. It's very fiddly work.'

'Do you sell these designs?'

Elizabeth shook her head. 'Not the leaves, anyway. They're so delicate. I had to make double the quantity just to get those ones. We sell some of the seasonal designs, but I think you lose flavour when you make the more elaborate pieces so I just do them for window displays or local events. I've got another batch of these Halloween designs that I'll use to decorate our stall at the pumpkin festival. You need to come – it's such good fun.'

'Thanks. I'll be there.'

'The shots are looking good,' said Nick. 'Shall we do some inside?'

Cat poured her bucket of water down the drain on the side of the road and followed Elizabeth and Nick in through the door. 'Can you get some shots of the chocolate fountain?' she asked Nick, who glanced around the shop. 'It's in the back room – I spotted it when I went to find the bucket.'

Elizabeth led them through to her party room. 'You being here today is great timing, actually,' she said. 'We don't often have a chocolate fountain going but we're having a kids' party today and they requested one.'

Cat looked at the warm, glossy chocolate flowing down the three-tiered fountain. On the table around it were arranged platters of washed and chopped fruit – whole strawberries, mango chunks, juicy dates and slices of kiwi. There were also bowls containing marshmallows and cubes of fudge but Cat thought the fruit alone would produce a better photo so asked Elizabeth if she could keep the sweets hidden for now, to be brought out later for the party.

Nick was peering into his camera with his face scrunched up. 'The light is not great,' he said. The room had a long window at the far end and spotlights in the ceiling that were currently switched off.

'Should I put the lights on?' Cat asked.

Nick shook his head. He picked up a circular nylon bag from the kit he'd brought with him, unzipped it and allowed a bright white screen to pop out. 'Can you hold this up for me?'

Cat took the screen and butterflies took flight inside her as he held her shoulders and manoeuvred her into place beside the table. If he felt it too, he was giving nothing away. His focus was on the table.

'Can you move the fountain forward a bit?' he directed. 'I want more chocolate and less table.'

Elizabeth carefully moved the chocolate fountain forward and repositioned the fruit platters.

'Perfect,' said Nick.

He must have taken about forty photos from different angles by the time he was finished. It hadn't taken long but Cat's arms were aching from holding the screen up.

'I think we're done. Are you happy, Cat?' he asked.

'Yes, thank you,' she said, rolling her shoulders back and forth and stretching her arms out. 'When can I see the images?'

Nick packed away his camera and took the screen from her. 'Can you come by the gallery tonight? I'll upload them to my computer for you to look at.'

'Great,' said Cat, feeling the heat rise to her cheeks at the thought of seeing him alone.

Nick expertly twisted the screen, folding it into a circle small enough to fit back into the bag, and Cat stepped back to give him space.

'Oh God,' she yelled out. She could feel the warm chocolate on the back of her dress and knew instantly she had walked straight into the chocolate fountain. 'Is it still standing?'

'Yes,' said Elizabeth, turning Cat around. 'But I can cover a dozen marshmallows with the amount of chocolate dripping off you.'

'I'm so sorry,' said Cat. She peered over her shoulder and a feeling of relief when she saw she hadn't made too much mess on the table was followed by toe-curling embarrassment.

Elizabeth took off her apron and held it in place over the chocolate to stop it dripping onto the floor. 'It's fine. Your dress got the brunt of it. You'll have to go and change – there's too much chocolate for it to just wipe off.'

Nick had finished packing away his equipment and Cat was sure she detected a smirk on his face. 'I'll give you a minute to get cleaned up,' he said, heading back through to the main shop area.

'I blame him for this,' said Cat. 'Every time I see him, I end up making a complete fool of myself.'

Elizabeth laughed as she wiped the back of Cat's dress as best she could.

'I met him on my first night in Thistle Bay. He was running on the beach with his dog and he saw me getting stung by a jellyfish.'

Elizabeth laughed harder, then quickly apologised.

'It's OK. I know I'll see the funny side of it in a couple of weeks when I'm no longer here. For now, it's just mortifying.'

Elizabeth's face suddenly became more serious. 'He's a nice guy, you know.'

'Oh, it's not like that,' said Cat. 'Don't worry, my mind is completely on this job. When I'm not dripping in chocolate and ruining your event, that is.'

'Honestly. It's all fine. Nothing is ruined. Go and change,' said Elizabeth. 'And it looks like Nick is waiting to walk with you,' she added as they went through to the shopfront and saw him standing by the door.

'Hey,' said Nick. He held out his phone. 'That was Ryan. He's running an hour late. I'm thinking that's good for you, though, because you probably want to head back to Gloria's and change.'

'It is good. And I do want to change. Well, I need to,' said Cat looking down at her dress.

'I'll walk with you and then I thought we could grab a coffee at Mystic's and talk about what shots we need in the factory,' said Nick.

'Go. Enjoy yourself,' Elizabeth whispered into Cat's ear. Then she walked away, squeezing Nick's shoulder on her way past him.

12

Nick hadn't been inside the Thistle Bay factory since he was a student and he'd had a summer job packing boxes of chocolates. It was literally twice the size now. Alan had extended it as far as he could over the years, which no one in the town had objected to since he'd never proposed building upwards.

Once Cat had changed her dress they'd gone to Mystic's for a coffee before meeting Ryan for their factory photo shoot. He had purposely kept their conversation strictly business. Cat seemed more comfortable when they were talking about work and he didn't want to risk unsettling her when she was in professional mode. The Knights were good people but they were Cat's new clients and he understood her wanting to make a good impression.

Now, with their hairnets, white coats and freshly scrubbed hands, they followed as Ryan escorted them into the factory.

'Cat, just give me the nod if there's anything in particular you want me to photograph,' said Nick.

'Will do. And, Ryan, just you give me the nod if there's

anything in particular we're not allowed to photograph,' she said.

'It'll be fine. We don't have too many secrets. Not when it comes to chocolate, anyway,' said Ryan as he led them over to one of the production lines.

Nick glanced at Cat, who looked just as intrigued as he was. Ryan was what Nick's mum called an open book. It wasn't like him to make that kind of a comment and not expand on it.

'After you,' said Nick, allowing Cat to walk ahead of him.

'There's a lot going on in here,' said Cat, stopping to stand at the end of one of the production lines.

Nick followed her gaze up a line that had ten people working on each side of it. The chocolates made their way slowly along the conveyor belt and each person seemed to have a particular job. Some workers were icing, some were creating patterns in the still-warm chocolate and others were putting almonds on top of individual chocolates. There was even a person plucking out imperfect chocolates before the belt turned and headed towards another group of people, who were hand-packing the chocolates.

Cat caught his eye. 'I'll probably only need one or two shots from in here but I won't know what I plan to use until I write the material. Can you take a shot up this line here? I only want to see the chocolate and their hands, though.'

Nick switched on his camera and adjusted his settings to handle the movement in the shot.

'Is it working?' Cat asked as he clicked away, taking several shots, all from slightly different angles.

'Yeah, it looks good.' Nick checked the images on screen and could feel Cat's hairnet brush his neck as she peered over his shoulder for a glimpse of the photos.

'It does,' said Cat. 'I like that you can see the chocolates are handmade, but you can also see the number of hands making them. It says: we're a company with wholesome values but enough people to make sure we can reliably stock your favourites.'

Cat continued to give Nick his orders on what to shoot as it became her leading Nick and Ryan around the factory.

'She certainly knows what she wants,' Nick said to Ryan as Cat was off chatting to someone on one of the production lines.

'She's actually got some great ideas. I think she can really help us,' said Ryan.

Nick furrowed his brow. 'You sound surprised. That is why you hired her, isn't it?'

'Of course,' said Ryan. 'It's just that Dad had the contact with her. I didn't know what she would be like until she was here.'

Cat interrupted with a request for Nick to take a close-up. 'I want to get this lady's hand in the shot, with the chocolate and the icing,' she instructed.

'I see what you're looking for.' Nick took a single shot and tilted his screen towards Cat. 'Something like this?'

Cat cupped her hand around Nick's camera to remove the glare from the factory's overhead lights. If she felt the same tingle that he did when their fingers brushed together, she didn't react. 'Exactly,' she said.

Her twinkling hazel eyes were sharp as she scanned the factory as if searching for images he hadn't yet captured. Nick took another few shots then stepped back just as someone handed Cat a piping bag full of icing.

'Oh no,' said Cat. 'Now it's my turn.' She clenched her teeth theatrically and hovered the piping back above a fresh tray of chocolates. 'Here goes.' Nick couldn't help but laugh as the icing spurted out a lot faster than Cat had intended and made a splodge on the chocolate rather than the three neat lines she should have made.

He smiled as he watched her laughing and joking with the team on the production line as they all chipped in with their advice about a steady hand, taking a deep breath and just going for it. He liked seeing her relaxed, not jumping up and down with a sore foot or hiding from him in the coffee shop. And he liked hearing her laugh. Something sparked inside him the night they met, and each time he saw her that spark only grew.

'I've not seen that look on your face for a while,' said Ryan.

Nick jumped, having forgotten his friend was there. 'What look? And what secrets do you have?'

'Stop trying to change the subject.'

'Right back at you.' It made Ryan laugh, but Nick had known him long enough to realise something was up. 'Fancy a beer at mine one night?' he asked. They really hadn't spent much time together recently. Ryan had been spending more and more time in Edinburgh and had even bought a flat there, which Nick had avoided mentioning. Nick had been invited over to see it twice in the last month but he hadn't gone yet. Ryan would want to talk business and that was a conversation Nick wasn't eager to have.

'I really do,' said Ryan. 'Can we make it next week? I've got a lot going on just now.'

'Sure. Everything OK?'

'Just some family stuff. Megan might be back this week.'

'For good?'

'Nah, just for a visit. She's not ready to give up her sunrise yoga on the beach and watermelon juice for breakfast just yet.'

'Is she still with that same guy?'

'Unfortunately.'

Nick knew that Ryan had no time for Megan's boyfriend. He was more overprotective than Alan was when it came to people looking to date his sisters. Nick had watched Ryan, the youngest in the family, being mothered by his sisters throughout his childhood. But that had all changed when Ryan came back from university. It was as if he had grown up and for some reason felt as though he had to start playing the father figure.

'I've missed us chatting like this,' said Nick. 'Beers at mine next week, then I'll go to you the following week and see your new place.'

'Deal. You got some good shots?' Ryan seemed brighter now, having moved on from thoughts of Megan's boyfriend.

'Just need one more,' said Nick. He inched forward, camera in hand, and captured an image of a carefree Cat trying to ice a tray of chocolates in front of her.

'You make this look so easy,' she was saying with a laugh to Jane, who Nick knew from when she was a dinner lady at his primary school.

Jane shook her head. 'You'll need to practise a bit more before I let you loose with a piping bag again. Here's your batch,' she said, handing the tray to Cat.

Cat cringed at her pathetic attempt at decoration. 'Sorry about that, but thanks for letting me have a go.'

She brought her tray of messy chocolates over and offered them to Nick and Ryan. 'I doubt I'd get a job in production any time soon,' she said, and as they each helped themselves to a chocolate, she asked Nick how the photos were looking.

Nick lifted his camera and flicked through a few of his shots. 'I think I have what you're looking for. I'll show you when you come to the gallery tonight.'

'Thanks, I look forward to it,' said Cat, before stuffing another chocolate in her mouth just as Rebecca appeared from behind her.

'How's it going?' Rebecca asked.

'Great,' said Nick to give Cat time to swallow her chocolate. 'I think we'll have plenty of good images to choose from.'

Cat wiped her lips with the back of her hand and nodded in agreement.

'Good. You're done then?' said Rebecca in a monotone. It sounded to Nick more like an order than a question.

They turned and followed Rebecca out of the factory, a heavy silence sagging between them all.

'I hear Megan is coming home soon,' Cat said as they removed their white coats and hairnets. 'Her painting in the shop is amazing. I love that everyone in the family has worked in the business at some point,' she said.

'About that,' said Ryan

Rebecca glared at him. 'Now isn't the time.' She turned to Cat. 'For a writer, you don't spend much time writing.'

Nick was taken aback by Rebecca's direct criticism of Cat. Cat's cheeks flushed and he instinctively took a step towards her.

'The hardest part is capturing the spirit of the brand,' Cat said as if looking to reassure Rebecca that she was absolutely focused on her job. 'Once I've done that, the words flow easily.'

'That sounds good,' Ryan said to Cat. 'Ignore her. She must be hungry.'

'I'm just making sure we're getting value from our contractors,' Rebecca snapped. 'Last time I checked, I was still in charge of the company.'

Nick winced at Rebecca's brutal tone.

'Actually,' said Ryan, 'last time I checked, Dad was still in charge of the company.'

Rebecca stormed ahead of them. Nick couldn't help thinking Rebecca had deserved that bit of a jab back from Ryan. He just hoped it was brother–sister banter and wouldn't have wider repercussions for Cat.

'Sorry about that, guys,' Ryan said casting a glance Nick's way. 'We just have a lot on our minds right now.'

'Of course, it's no problem,' Cat said, but Nick detected a slight quiver in her voice. 'I'm probably taking up a bit too much of your time. I think I have what I need now so I won't be bothering you from here on in.'

'It's no bother. It's been good.' Ryan looked as if he had more to say but after he peered down the corridor towards the retreating Rebecca, he seemed to think better of it. 'I'll leave you guys to finish up.'

Nick turned to Cat once they were clear of the factory floor and Ryan was out of earshot. 'You OK?'

Cat nodded. 'I'm sorry about that. I don't think I'm Rebecca's favourite person. I hope it wasn't too uncomfortable for you.'

'You've nothing to apologise for. I grew up with these folks so I've had my head bitten off by Rebecca before. That was nothing.'

Chewing on her lower lip, Cat didn't look convinced and Nick squeezed the top of her arm in an attempt to reassure her. He hated to see her doubting herself. Rebecca wasn't shy about voicing her opinions but she was usually more considered about the direction in which she spewed her wrath. Whatever was going on between Rebecca and Ryan, Cat seemed to have unwittingly stumbled into the middle of it.

13

Nick opened the gallery door as soon as he received Cat's text saying she was on her way. Skye sniffed around on the pavement out front as he leaned against the door frame keeping his eye on her to make sure she didn't stray too far.

Skye alerted him to Cat's arrival by yelping and turning in a circle with excitement at seeing her new friend. Cat leaned over and stroked Skye. One pat was enough for the little dog and she scampered back into the warmth of the gallery.

Nick took Cat's coat and went to hang it on the hooks in the back room. She was looking apprehensive when he came back through to the gallery. He couldn't tell if she was worried about the photos or being alone with him.

He moved back to his desk and pulled out the chair. He gestured for her to sit down but she was craning her head towards the back room, her eyes scanning the images he had pinned to the walls there. She then turned back to face his desk and stood gazing at something of interest, her brow furrowed.

She picked up a loose photo. 'I know that sunrise. Did you take this?'

Nick nodded. 'From the beach.'

Cat stared at the photo and he saw her shoulders drop as though whatever tension she'd been holding there had evaporated. 'Why don't you sell these in the gallery?'

It was the question he had been asking himself since he'd moved back to Thistle Bay for good. He didn't have an answer – at least, not an answer he was prepared to admit out loud. In between gallery customers, he spent his hours editing shots from the photo shoots he'd been hired to do and also the innumerable photographs he'd taken of Thistle Bay. He kept those photos just for himself, with the exception of a few prints he'd given to Mystic for the walls of the coffee shop.

Nick leaned over his desk and, bringing the sleeping screen of his computer back to life, entered his password. The photos he had taken for Cat were already there for her. 'Do you want to flick through these on screen?' he said. 'I've pulled out the best shots and I'll polish up the ones you like the most.'

He sat down on the spare wooden chair he had pulled across to his desk and motioned again for Cat to sit in his leather swivel chair in front of the computer. 'Just click on the corner of your preferred shots. Or I can edit them all if you're not sure what you'll need.'

'I have a fairly good idea,' she said. 'These look perfect. They're going to make such a difference.'

Nick watched her as she scrolled through the photos. A small crease formed on the skin between her eyes as she concentrated on her task. She was certainly decisive, looking at each shot for only a few seconds before clicking the corner or moving on. Her floral perfume and the sight of her bare arm made the hairs on his own arm stand on end. He knew he could never get involved with Cat but he had craved her company since that first night on the beach.

He sprung up from his chair and walked to the window at the front of the gallery, aware of Cat's eyes following him. It was darkening outside, with the last sliver of the setting sun about to slip away, and he regarded her reflection in the glass as she went back to examining his photos.

After a while she joined him at the window. 'That's a pretty big pile of admin on your desk. Business must be good,' she said. 'I wasn't snooping – I just almost knocked it off the edge.'

Nick smiled at her. The concentration on her face had gone and she returned his smile. She was relaxed in his company tonight. There was none of the unease he'd felt from her before. 'It wouldn't have mattered. It's in no particular order.'

'In that case, you need a better filing system.'

'It's requests from artists looking for gallery space to show their work.'

'Brilliant. The Thistle Bay art world must be thriving. When's the next event?'

The more appropriate question was when the *first* event would be. When he had formally opened the gallery he had invited all of the locals to his launch party. He'd supplied the champagne and Mystic had made up trays of canapés. It had been such a celebration. After planning to start his own business for so many years he had finally done it, and it felt amazing. Seeing his name on the deeds to the building had been the grounding he'd been looking for. He had thrown himself into renovating the building. He didn't have the business partner he was expecting to have but he had come to terms with it being a solo venture.

By opening night, it hadn't mattered that he was on his own.

Six weeks after opening he had received the first letter from a recently graduated art student looking for him to host their show. More letters had followed, as well as an avalanche of emails about exhibition space and art installations. None of which he had replied to.

'I don't really do shows,' he said.

'Why not?'

'I guess I just never envisaged it being that kind of gallery.' That had been Lisa's vision. She'd seen invitation-only events with black-tie dress codes, selective showcasing of up-and-coming artists, and huge commissions with price tags to match. Nick had honoured the few commission agreements that he and Lisa had already entered into together but, as the commissioned pieces sold, he'd replaced them with artworks that he had bought up front. The maintaining of relationships with artists and the marketing efforts he felt obliged to make just didn't feel authentic. *Authentic*. He hated that word. Its meaning had been hijacked in recent years, but he felt like such a phoney when having conversations with artists about representing their work in the gallery. He was much happier now that the burden of commissioned pieces was off his shoulders. But much happier didn't mean totally happy.

'What kind of gallery did you envisage?' Cat asked.

Nick folded his arms across his chest and gazed out of the window. If he knew the answer to that question he wouldn't be in this limbo.

'The sunrises here are like none I've seen before,' said Cat.

He was relieved at the change of conversation and

pointed at the view from the window. 'That's a sunset,' he said.

She pounded him on the arm and laughed. That laugh again. Despite everything she had been through in her life and the uncertainty about what she was going to do next, the girl's eyes sparkled when she was relaxed. He was drawn to her in a way he hadn't ever experienced. Far from fizzling out, the spark he'd felt for her was becoming a flare, but he wasn't about to rush down that route knowing she was leaving in two weeks.

'I know that's a sunset,' she said. 'I was thinking about your sunrise photograph. It's the same sun that I saw in Edinburgh, and Los Angeles, but it really does look different here. That sounds crazy, doesn't it?'

'Not at all.'

'Maybe it's the uninterrupted view. It's hard to find a spot like that in the city – there's always something in front of you.'

'Do you hike?'

'Uh, I've done a bit of hiking, why?' The corners of her lips turned upwards.

Nick smiled at the bewildered look on her face. 'If you like an uninterrupted view, I can show you one tomorrow morning. We'd have to leave here at six o'clock to catch the sunrise but I think you'll love it.'

What he didn't think she would love was the journey. She was a city girl, used to bright lights, early-morning coffees and concrete underfoot. Seeing her struggling in his world might be enough to get her out of his head. Even if she did also have feelings for him, they were two very different people who could not see the appeal of each other's reality. He'd already been down that path and it didn't work.

14

Cat crept out of Gloria's front door. She reached up to hold the metal bell above her head still and slipped her hand out at the last second. The door closed and the lock clicked into place. She paused and listened for a chime or any movement inside. All was quiet. Nick said he would pick her up but she was ready early and didn't want to hang around at Gloria's in case she disturbed any of the other guests. Or, more to the point, Gloria. She didn't need any raised eyebrows or knowing smiles to rattle her before she left.

The sky was still pitch black except for the crescent moon, its edges blurred by mist. It was too early even for Josef. His food stall was closed and the air smelled of the sea instead of the sweetness of baked goods that she'd become accustomed to inhaling from Gloria's doorstep.

Cat glanced up Main Street hoping to see Mystic's lights on for a caffeine fix but she, too, was in darkness. The street-light on the corner opposite her flickered to life as if it were on a motion sensor and she was grateful for its glow as she made her way across the road. She had been out late and up early many times in her life but the darkness in Thistle Bay was something she had never experienced before. City streetlights seemed brighter and there was always illumination from the takeaway restaurants feeding hungry party-goers on their way home or coffee shops helping to wake everyone up.

Cat only had to wait outside the gallery for a minute before Nick came out of his door with an excitable Skye on her lead. His blond hair was flattened on the back of his head as if he had just got out of bed. When she greeted him, he looked her up and down.

'Morning,' he said, his voice still husky from sleep. 'You look . . .' His eyes darted around as he searched for the right word. Or perhaps a word that she wouldn't take offence at. 'Appropriate,' he said finally.

Cat laughed. 'I've never had anyone tell me I look appropriate before. Is that supposed to be a compliment?'

He shrugged. 'Just a fact.'

Cat presumed he was talking about her clothing. He'd said it was a bit of a hike so she had worn black sports leggings, a deep-purple waterproof coat and walking boots. She carried a small backpack with a water bottle in the side pocket. Her boots were well worn and comfortable. She had bought both them and the backpack when she'd first arrived in Los Angeles – she hated the gym and wasn't much of a runner so, at the weekends, she'd headed up into the hills for her exercise.

Nick wore shorts, hiking boots and a navy waterproof coat. She didn't know where they were going but, judging by Nick's outfit, her choice of clothing was indeed appropriate.

'Are you not taking your photography equipment?' Cat asked, seeing Nick's almost-empty backpack.

'Not today. I have a small camera in my bag but that's just for shots for me. You ready to go?'

Cat gave him the thumbs-up and within minutes they had left the town behind and were walking in open country-side, the little dog alternating between dashing ahead and stopping to sniff at the same spot for a full minute at a time. The sky seemed to brighten with each step they took.

'So, you're a morning person?' Nick asked.

'It just depends. When I have somewhere to be in the morning that's different from my usual routine, I always wake up extra early. Do you get like that?'

'Sometimes. You mean like when you have a flight to catch and you wake up loads of times so you don't miss it?'

'Yeah. Although I actually slept well last night. I only woke when it was time to get up. The bed in Gloria's is so comfy.'

'A comfy bed. You need to add that to your list.'

Cat laughed, but made a mental note to add *comfy bed* to her list. She'd never owned a bed before; there was no need to buy one when you rented furnished flats. Contemplating buying her own bed was surely a sign that she was ready to find somewhere more permanent to live. An image sprang to her mind of lying on dozens of mattresses to find one as comfortable as Gloria's. It would be like in the movies – she would bounce from bed to bed until one made her close her eyes and curl up in comfort, if only for a few minutes. Or she could just pull back the sheets and check the manufac-turer of Gloria's mattress and buy one of those. 'Nah, shop-ping sounds more fun.'

'Excuse me?' Nick stretched his left arm above his head and scratched the back of his neck.

'Oh, sorry,' said Cat. 'Just thinking out loud.'

'What are you mentally shopping for?'

'A mattress,' she said without hesitation. She was fed up with worrying about embarrassing herself in front of Nick. So what if she liked him? Nothing was ever going to come of it so why should she care what he thought of her? From this trip on, she was going to be completely herself. Rachel was right. Cat was the master at compartmentalising her life. In Thistle Bay she was in work mode – and at-work-Cat was confident and comfortable around people.

She shushed the little voice in her head that told her she wasn't very confident and comfortable around Rebecca Knight. Cat hadn't seen Rebecca since their clash in the factory. Nick had shrugged it off as nothing, saying he'd seen worse from Rebecca. But it didn't feel like nothing to Cat. It was yet more open hostility and Cat couldn't figure out what was driving it or how to get on Rebecca's good side. Perhaps it didn't even matter. She was doing the work for Alan and – if he was still in charge, as Ryan had said – all she needed to do was make him happy. Albeit that may be a challenge given she hadn't seen him since her first day here.

After they'd walked along a country lane for a while, Nick stopped beside a long wooden gate and crouched down to clip Skye's lead on. 'Grab one of those sticks if you want it.'

She followed his eyes to three long sticks on the grass beside the hedgerow. 'What for?'

'The cows,' he said.

Cat looked behind him over the gate. There were about twenty brown cows lying down in the corner of the field. She didn't quite know what he was getting at.

'If the cows get cranky that we're in their space, you can use the stick to shoo them away from us.' Nick tilted his head and Cat got the impression this was some kind of test for her. She knew animals could attack when threatened and she was pretty sure waving a big stick at them wasn't a great idea. She couldn't figure out if Nick wanted her to pick up the stick or not, or what her choice would mean.

'They look pretty settled. I'm sure we'll be fine,' she said.

Nick's expression was neutral and she had no idea if she had passed his test. He opened the gate and stood aside to let her through. 'Just watch your feet,' was all he said. Now, that she would do.

They crossed the field without incident and headed up hill, Skye running free once again.

'What are you doing?' Nick asked when Cat stopped and pulled her phone from her coat pocket.

'Photographing this flower,' she said.

'That's not a flower. That's a weed.'

'It's a beautiful weed.'

'It's still a weed, though.'

Cat snapped a few pictures. 'What's that saying? One woman's trash is another woman's treasure.'

'I don't think that applies to weeds. The dislike for weeds is pretty universal.'

'Isn't the thistle a . . .' Cat stopped speaking abruptly when Nick cleared his throat. His eyebrows were raised and his eyes wide, challenging her to finish her sentence. '. . . beautiful flower,' she added, then walked past him smiling to herself.

Forty minutes later, they cleared a scattering of silver-barked birch trees and arrived at the top of Blakely Hill just as the sunrise appeared on the horizon to signal the new day. The fragment of moon was now transparent in the rosy sky as it bid its quiet farewell. Thistle Bay was laid out beneath them, with more of the beach on display than Cat had yet seen thanks to the receding tide. Even from this height, the rhythmic ripple of the waves invoked a sense of tranquillity as the water crept towards the shore and glided back again moments later. The serenity of the town had begun to soothe something deep inside Cat, and she welcomed it.

The striking sky, with its blush pink shades and silky bands of gold, looked like an oil painting and the vibrant oranges, reds and yellows in the gardens below seemed more intense from this level than they did on the ground. Neatly cordoned pastures and fields framed the town like a patchwork quilt of calming neutral colours interspersed with bright greens and splashes of orange from clusters of pumpkins gathered for Halloween.

'It's stunning,' said Cat, unzipping her waterproof jacket to let out some of the heat that had built up. 'It's the view that should be on Thistle Bay postcards.'

Nick pulled his camera from his backpack and dropped the bag to the ground. Skye stuck her head inside it and rooted around for a few seconds before reappearing, seemingly unsatisfied Perhaps she was used to finding treats or toys in there. 'I'm just taking a couple of shots. I have lots of photographs of this view – although the town changes quite a bit with the seasons, so they all look different.'

'I can imagine that,' said Cat. She drew a deep breath and closed her eyes to appreciate the earthy aroma of fresh air and damp grass, reopening them on the first click of Nick's camera. As she watched him capturing the sunrise over Thistle Bay, Cat thought about Josef and his decision to move from Germany to Scotland after his wife died. That decision didn't diminish his love for his wife. It didn't make him miss her any more or any less. Cat hadn't wanted to come back to Scotland at all. Edinburgh was her past, and she wanted to focus on the future. She hadn't done that up to now – her drive to find out where she came from had kept her stuck in the past. She'd flitted from place to place, forming no real relationships, never finding a place that felt like home, never unearthing any more details of her birth family. She looked down now on the town that was beginning to feel more like home than it should. Maybe it was possible to build a life for herself and still look for answers.

'Penny for your thoughts,' said Nick.

For the first time in a long while, Cat didn't have a hundred thoughts swirling through her mind. She was content just to be in the moment, without the need to analyse what was coming next. 'That sunrise is pretty magical,' she said.

'It is.' A silence settled between them as they stood next to each other taking in the scene.

'Are you never tempted to put these views in your gallery?' The last time she'd asked that question Nick hadn't answered. She hoped it wasn't going to ruin what had so far been a serene start to the day.

'That's a long story,' said Nick.

Cat didn't miss the fleeting smile on his face and took it as an invitation to probe further. 'Well, lucky for you we're up early this morning and have a bit of time on our hands.' She plonked herself down on the smoothest rock she could find, rummaged in her backpack and pulled out two paper bags. 'I thought we might need a snack by the time we got up here. Apple-and-cinnamon croissants – I snagged them from Josef as he was packing up last night but they should still be OK.' She handed Nick one of the bags when he came to sit beside her. Skye wiggled herself between the two of them and rested her head on Nick's knee as he took a bite of his croissant and chewed slowly, nodding in appreciation of the flavours. 'Good, isn't it?' Cat tore her croissant in half and took a bite from the middle, relishing the sweet filling. 'Josef is a handy person to know. But back to your gallery. What's the deal, Nicholas Bell?'

Nick laughed and took another bite of his croissant. 'You're not going to let that go, are you?'

Cat smiled and shook her head but he continued to devour his croissant without speaking. 'The fact you're reluctant to talk about it makes me think there's a girl involved,' she said, filling the silence.

'There might be a girl involved.' He stared out into the horizon. 'Lisa. She wanted to get out of Thistle Bay and do something. That was how she put it. We agreed to go to London for a year, which turned into two years. We talked about starting the gallery together and planned the type of art we would include. I came back to Thistle Bay first to set up and she was going to follow.'

'And she didn't?'

'She did, initially. But she decided a small town wasn't for her. I couldn't go back to London. I like a small town.'

'You grew up here, right?' Cat said.

'Yeah, and maybe that means I should want to get out, but I like it here. She thought I was settling, or taking the easy way out. I've never felt like that. Sure, Thistle Bay is comfortable. It's what I know. But it's also what I love. I realised when I came back from London that there's nothing wrong with that. You're allowed to live in the place you love.'

Cat nodded in agreement. She'd lived in many places during her adult life and nowhere had felt as good for the soul as Thistle Bay did. She understood exactly why Nick wanted to live here. Cat gazed down at the town once again. She'd not even been here a week but already she knew it was going to be hard to leave. 'It's a pretty special place.'

'It is. Staying here was definitely the right decision for me. A small town is suffocating for some – I understand that – but this town gave me freedom from a very early age. As kids, we would run through the fields, play in the woods, steal strawberries from the neighbouring farms in the summer months.' Cat arched an eyebrow and Nick laughed. 'The farmer knew. He got his own back when we were a bit older – most of us local kids were sent to work on the farm picking fruit during our school holidays.'

'It sounds idyllic.' Although most childhoods sounded idyllic when she compared them with her own.

Nick nodded, lost in his memories for a few seconds. He held out his hand to give Skye the last sliver of his croissant. 'I thought once I'd made the decision, everything would fall into place. I got Skye, redecorated the flat – both of which were good for me. But I haven't yet figured out what to do with the gallery.'

'Was the gallery your idea or Lisa's?'

'It really was both of ours. I've been into photography forever and she studied history of art. It just made sense.'

'Does it still make sense?'

'I struggle with the vision sometimes.'

'How do you mean?'

'I don't know. The art is beautiful, but . . .'

'It's not Thistle Bay.'

Nick stared out at the sunrise and Cat got the feeling she'd hit on the problem. She had been behind the scenes at the gallery when she'd gone to get her coat last night and had snuck a closer look at the most stunning images of

Thistle Bay filling the walls in his back room, as well as piles of similar photographs on his desk. As far as she could tell, the art in the public area of the gallery was just a random collection of works with no link to Thistle Bay. She didn't even know if the artists were local. The gallery might have been Nick's idea, but Cat sensed the type of art on the walls was Lisa's.

'I don't want to create some cheesy tourist destination where people come for postcards and fridge magnets.'

Cat couldn't help but laugh, then stopped abruptly when Nick glared at her. 'So, don't sell postcards and fridge magnets.'

Nick laughed too now. 'You make it sound so simple.'

'It can be. You get up at five something in the morning to take photos of the town you love. Allow people to pay you for something you love to do anyway. Why sell other people's art when you're so good at creating your own?'

'I don't know. How many photographs of the same thing can you sell?'

'How many photos are on the walls in your back room? There must be more than fifty. Each one is different and not one of them is cheesy. You just said it yourself – the seasons change and every photo is different.'

Nick shook his head and nudged her with his shoulder. 'Do you have to remember everything I say, then use it against me?'

'It's a skill.'

Nick looked at his watch and must have moved just enough for Skye to think it was time to go home. The little spaniel sprung up and sniffed the ground for any remaining croissant crumbs before giving up and fixing her black eyes on her master. 'We should be getting back,' he said.

Cat couldn't tell if their conversation had been helpful or

if Nick thought she was sticking her nose in somewhere it didn't belong. She hoped it wasn't the latter, because she had an idea that might just help him see the way forward. For it to work, she'd need to engineer another rendezvous behind the scenes at the gallery.

But first, she needed coffee.

15

A WHIFF OF SIZZLING BACON FILLED THE AIR AS CAT PUSHED open the door to Mystic Coffee. 'Morning,' she said to Mystic with a smile. 'I really need a caffeine fix.' Her mouth watered as she looked at the juicy bacon browning under the grill.

Mystic was alone in the shop and was busy slicing bread rolls. She glanced at Cat. 'It looks like it. Double-shot latte coming up. Where are you off to?'

'I'm just back. I went up Blakely Hill to watch the sunrise over the bay.'

Mystic dusted crumbs off her hands with a tea towel and pressed a couple of buttons on the coffee machine. 'Beautiful, isn't it?'

Cat leaned on the counter and breathed in the enticing scents of a cooked breakfast. The way Mystic knew her coffee order before she even had to ask gave Cat a feeling of belonging. It was silly because the barista in Los Angeles had known her order on sight too, but it felt different. There was something about Thistle Bay that kept giving her an unfamiliar urge to settle down and make a home for herself. 'It's honestly a sight I've never seen anything like before. And now, I need that coffee. I'm going to Edinburgh this morning with Ryan and I don't want to fall asleep in the car.'

Mystic laughed and poured milk into a jug for steaming. 'Yep, an early start and a one-hour hike will do that to you. At least you were well kitted out. I hope you don't have blisters from those shoes.'

Cat looked at her feet. 'No, these are well worn in from hiking in the LA hills.'

'Can I tempt you with a bacon roll to go with your coffee?'

'I'm tempted, but I'd better not. Gloria will have breakfast cooking – although I was thinking about your bacon rolls all the way down the hill. Nick said he'd be along shortly to get one.'

'You were hiking with Nick?'

'Uh-huh.' There was no point in hiding it. Nick would likely tell her himself. Besides, there was nothing to hide. It was just two people going for a walk.

Mystic passed Cat her coffee and she took a sip. The hot liquid was soothing the instant it hit the back of her throat. She paused to see if Mystic was going to give her another warning about Nick but she didn't, and Cat lifted the cup to her lips again. Her smile widened. Even the threat of Mystic's disapproval couldn't diminish the joy she felt. That sunrise had been magnificent and she'd finally managed to spend time with Nick without embarrassing herself.

Cat's phone buzzed with an email notification. She grabbed it from her pocket and checked to see if it was a reply from CocoB13. It wasn't. The disappointment came flooding back to her. 'I know what to do,' Cat mumbled. She opened her mailbox and set up an email rule to sound an alert only when an email from Find My Family was received. Having notifications on for all emails was distracting her at work, but it was also causing her blood pressure to soar then crash with every buzz. Restricting her email alerts to just the one gave her a tiny sense of control again, which made her feel marginally less helpless about the situation.

'Thanks for the coffee.' Cat opened the payment app on her phone and held it above the card machine to pay. 'I'll probably see you or Susie tonight for some dinner.' On her way out she glanced at the flickering flames as they scorched the fresh logs in the hearth. Mystic's was the perfect coffee shop. It had good coffee, high stools facing the window for when you weren't up for conversation, cosy tables for two and comfy sofas in front of a fire that seemed permanently lit.

Gloria was lingering in the hallway when Cat arrived back at the bed and breakfast. 'Morning, hen. That was an early start for you today. How about a nice bowl of porridge to warm you up?'

Cat twisted her face in a grimace. Porridge had been a staple breakfast in the children's home. The aptly named Mrs Cooke, who had already been there for seventeen years before Cat showed up, prepared the meals. A cooked breakfast to Mrs Cooke meant porridge, and when it wasn't the usual cereal or white toast then it was a wooden spoon full of Mrs Cooke's stodgy grey gloop.

'Thank you, but I think I'll pass. I ate too much porridge as a kid and I remember it sitting heavy in my stomach all morning.'

'Your mum wasn't great at making porridge, then?'

'Actually, I grew up in the care system so it was one big pot of porridge that fed a dozen of us.'

Gloria's hand flew to her chest and Cat saw a glisten in her eyes that she didn't think had been there seconds before. The older woman reached out and cupped Cat's cheek. 'I'll make you porridge the way it should be made. We need to replace that memory for you. Do you prefer sweet or salty?'

Cat smiled at Gloria. Every now and again she caught a glimpse of the way Gloria must have been when she raised the Knight kids. If you were unfortunate enough to have no mother, Gloria would make a pretty excellent addition to the family home. 'Sweet, please,' said Cat.

16

NICK WATCHED IN ANTICIPATION AS MYSTIC LOADED A TRAY with his latte and a bacon roll. The hike up the hill had given him an appetite. She added a saucer with an extra slice of bacon for Skye.

'You must be hungry after your early-morning hike,' said Mystic.

He looked up into her eyes but he didn't see the playful look he expected. Her expression was serious and he waited for the rest of whatever she was going to say to come out. Mystic clearly had her concerns, and she'd never before been afraid to voice them.

'I'm just saying be careful,' she said, pushing his tray towards him. 'You've been spending a lot of time with that girl. Maybe you should give her a bit of space to finish the job she came here to do.'

'Last week you told me to have a little fun.'

'Just make sure neither of you gets hurt when it's time for her to leave. That's all.'

Nick picked up his tray, smiled at Mystic and led an

impatient Skye to a table at the back of the shop. The coffee grinder roared in the background and he could sense Mystic's eyes still on him as he tore Skye's slice of bacon in two and put the saucer in front of her. 'There you go, girl.'

Nothing had yet happened with Cat but that morning on the hill, he knew he wanted something to. Like a child denied a treat, telling himself she was off limits only made him want her even more. He hadn't expected her to cope so well with the hike up the steep slope. He'd thought it would be a chance to show himself that they were from two different worlds and so stop him thinking about her all the time. But it had had the opposite effect. She'd loved it. The early morning, the hike, the view. She had taken the hike in her stride and had loved it all.

Part of him was disappointed the climb hadn't been more difficult for her, though he knew that was cruel. But the other part of him was desperate to reach out and kiss her – and that wouldn't be good for either of them. Yes, Cat could see the beauty of Thistle Bay, but so could most people who came to visit. A two-week stay was charming, relaxing even. It offered a glimpse of a different pace of living, which most people would say they wanted. The reality of months, of years, in a small town was very different, especially for people like Cat who had grown up with the conveniences of city living.

Her being here was temporary. If he gave in to his feelings, he'd want more than just another week with her. He had already opened up to her in a way he hadn't done with anyone else this past year – his doubts about the direction he was taking with the gallery were something he hadn't shared with anyone. As enchanted as he was with this girl, he couldn't get involved. He'd been there before and knew it wouldn't end well.

Nick leaned over and picked up Skye's saucer. 'We're in trouble, aren't we?' he said, rubbing her behind the ears.

17

Having earlier polished off Josef's croissant and her latte, Cat now sat in front of a bowl of piping-hot porridge. It was already better than Mrs Cooke's porridge, which had never had steam rising from it. The porridge she'd eaten as a child had somehow always been lukewarm, even when she'd watched Mrs Cooke take the stainless-steel pot off the cooker just before serving up.

Gloria hovered beside the table and it was obvious she wasn't going to leave until Cat had tasted her porridge, so she dug her spoon in and scooped up a mouthful. She closed her eyes as the sumptuous heat filled her mouth. It was creamy and sweet with a hint of cinnamon – all the traits of a food so comforting that it reached right out from the bowl and enveloped you in its cosy embrace.

A memory of Jessie flashed into Cat's mind. Her adoptive mother was smiling in the kitchen as she cut a slice of toast into soldiers for Cat to dip in her soft-boiled eggs. Jessie had placed two ceramic egg cups painted with smiley faces on the table in front of Cat and when she brought over the stack of neatly trimmed toast, she cupped Cat's face in her warm hands and kissed her on the tip of her nose. Cat only realised years later how fortunate she'd been to have had breakfast with Jessie every morning. Joe, her adoptive father, had left for work before Cat was awake on most weekdays, making breakfast a time for mother and daughter. Jessie had always cooked Cat's breakfast before positioning herself opposite her at the table with a coffee, no food – unless it was a weekend and Joe was there too. She didn't recall being served porridge, but she did remember the daily hot breakfasts – every kind of eggs, beans on toast, cheese-and-tomato toasties. Jessie had never given in to Cat's whining for the chocolate cereal her friends said they had. Their conversations had covered the mundane topics you would expect from a chat involving a six-year-old – school, play dates to organise, plans for the weekend ahead – but those five minutes every day before Jessie stood up again to wash the dishes or wipe down surfaces while Cat finished eating were some of the clearest memories Cat had of her childhood before care.

Thistle Bay dialled up emotions in Cat that she usually shoved away to be dealt with later. Although later often came and went with her emotions still lurking in the shadows. When had she decided those memories that loitered just beneath the surface were things to avoid rather than tender reminders of people she had loved to indulge in? 'You're right, Gloria. This is a bowl of porridge I won't forget in a hurry.'

A delighted Gloria headed back into the kitchen to continue her breakfast duties and Cat savoured every spoonful of the porridge. This town was certainly proving to be good for Cat's taste buds. Between sampling chocolates, treating herself to Josef's baking, supping Mystic's lattes and indulging in Gloria's hearty breakfasts, she had never enjoyed her food more. No longer did she just chew food and swallow; now, she found herself pausing to appreciate the flavours that blanketed her tongue – which wasn't ideal when she just wanted a bit of chocolate or some pastry as a quick fix to cheer herself up.

Cat finished off her porridge and spent the next hour in the guest lounge drafting a few pages of website copy before Arthur came to collect her for her trip to the Edinburgh factory.

'It seems no time at all since I picked you up at the airport,' said Arthur as they headed along the motorway.

'It's not been a full week yet but I actually feel as if I've been in Thistle Bay for much longer,' said Cat.

'Aye, it has that effect on people.'

The three towers of the Queensferry Crossing came into view and Cat touched her stomach. She'd had pangs of dread during her last journey to Edinburgh. As Arthur drove onto the bridge, it struck her that, beyond Mrs Cooke's unappetising breakfasts, she hadn't given her bleak past in the city any thought at all this morning. Until now.

When they arrived at the factory, Ryan gave her a quick tour of the small open-plan office building before they headed over to the production facility.

Before they entered, Cat twisted her long hair into a bun and tucked it under the blue hairnet Ryan had handed her. Slipping on her white coat, she followed Ryan into the facility. After they'd washed their hands in the industrial-sized sinks, Ryan held open the opaque plastic sheeting that covered the entryway.

Cat looked around. It wasn't often she got to go behind the scenes of the businesses she had written for but when she did, she loved it. Seeing the product being made brought it to life for her in a way that no manager's explanation could do. 'Wow,' she said, raising her voice to be heard above the constant machine noise. 'It's very different to Thistle Bay.' It was a sea of white and silver – much more industrial – with machines mixing, moulding, cooling and wrapping chocolate. This was a stark contrast from the facility in Thistle Bay, where people did the bulk of the work and used their creative flair to hand-decorate the chocolates.

'It is,' said Ryan. 'Here we make buttons, bars, barrels and bags. It keeps operations simple and gives us the quality and quantity we need.'

'What does a barrel of chocolate look like?' Cat asked. 'I hear barrel, I think beer.'

Ryan laughed. 'Not quite. Over here . . .'

They walked the length of one of the production lines, passing only one person. The production lines in Thistle Bay had people working down both sides; the more automation there was, the fewer people were needed.

'This is a barrel,' said Ryan as he collected a tub of hot chocolate from the end of the line.

'Ah, that makes more sense.'

Cat was relieved that her only role on this tour was to observe. No hand-decorating required. After a walk along each of the production lines, Ryan led her out of the facility.

Removing her white coat and hairnet, Cat ran her fingers through her hair. 'Do you do any corporate gifting? You know, when businesses want to hand out gifts for corporate events or small perks for client engagement?'

Ryan took her white coat from her and hung it beside his. 'No, but I'm loving that idea.'

Cat smiled and nodded her head. 'I think it could be a good fit. You certainly have the capacity. You'd have to design new labelling and be able to personalise it for each order, but that's doable. It gives an additional revenue stream that's not wholesale to stores or direct to consumers.'

Ryan stared at her. 'I'm curious, what made you think of that?'

Cat shrugged. 'I went to a conference in San Francisco last year that had smaller breakaway training seminars. Each seat in one of the sessions had a goody bag with a notebook, retractable pencil and a tub of branded jelly beans. People loved the jelly beans; the speaker not so much – he was all style and no substance. The concept might work for you.'

Ryan tapped his fingers on his chin then broke out into a grin. 'I'm definitely going to explore that idea. But for now, are you hungry? Lunch should be ready for us in the conference room.'

'I'm starving, actually,' said Cat. 'I've already eaten one of Josef's croissants and breakfast at Gloria's, but an early start and spending the morning looking at chocolate whizzing around the place really builds up an appetite.'

They headed along the corridor and sat at a large boardroom table, the only two people on a table that could hold fourteen. The room was craving decoration to break up the barren magnolia walls. It wouldn't take much – some product photography, a few Thistle Bay prints from Nick, the framed certificates of the industry awards Cat knew from her early research that the company had won. Given Rebecca's immaculate personal presentation, the lack of personality in their offices surprised Cat. She made a mental note to drop it into conversation with Elizabeth if she got the chance. Suggesting new photos for their website was one thing but telling them their office decor was dull was beyond her copywriter remit.

'Greek salad? Or . . .' Ryan examined the other boxed

salad he'd picked up, holding it above his head to peer at the label underneath before replacing it on the table and frowning.

Cat leaned forward to have a look. 'Falafel,' she said. 'You take the Greek salad – you don't look too impressed with the other one.'

'Have the Greek,' said Ryan. 'I'll eat anything.'

'You're fine. I like falafel.' She took the box out of his hand and he peeled the covering off a tray of sandwiches.

'Black coffee, right?' asked Cat. He nodded in agreement and she poured coffee for them both, before tucking into her salad.

Ryan slipped the sandwich platter across the smooth surface of the dark wood-veneer table. The conversation between them flowed easily as they ate and Cat was grateful that Rebecca wasn't there so she could just enjoy the day instead of being on edge about what Rebecca might be thinking.

'Do you like copywriting?' Ryan asked.

'I do. It sounds odd but I like completing things. Everything is a project, whether it's starting something from nothing or taking someone else's words and making them better, so I can work on something for a few days or a few weeks and then I'm done. It's all very tangible. It's easy to measure the impact of my work, too. Did I increase sales for the client? Did I drive more traffic? Or whatever the objective is.'

'Yeah, I get that.'

'How about you? Do you like what you do?'

Ryan took a bite of a coronation-chicken sandwich and nodded. 'Dad didn't have any expectation that we would all go into the business. That's probably why we all ended up working in it. We didn't feel any pressure so we naturally gravitated towards it. He was very supportive of whatever we wanted to do – hence he doesn't mind Megan traipsing around Majorca doodling.'

She didn't usually pry into her client's personal lives, but it was Ryan who had brought Megan into the conversation. 'I take it you mind?'

'What I mind is the one she's doodling with,' said Ryan.

'Ah.'

'She'll be back, though.'

'Is the guy from Thistle Bay too?'

'No, thankfully. It'll give her a clean break when she returns.'

'You sound certain they're going to break up.' Cat speared the last falafel with her fork and used it to soak up the remains of the salad's creamy dressing.

Ryan grabbed another sandwich. 'They will. She tolerates him. She doesn't love him. What about you? Is there someone special in your life?'

An image of Nick flashed into her mind. 'No. Just me.'

'Same here. That's an area where Dad is less supportive. He'd like to see us all married off with families of our own. Rebecca is the only one who has managed it so far, though. She has twin boys. They're only five, and such a handful. But good kids.'

Cat wanted to ask more about Rebecca but Ryan put his sandwich down and Cat sensed a shift in his demeanour. His pale blue eyes glazed over and he stared at the table for a few seconds before looking up quickly as if he had just remembered she was there.

'Sorry,' he said.

'Are you OK?'

'I was just thinking about Elizabeth. She was engaged to Steven. Did she tell you that?'

Cat shook her head. Elizabeth had been warm and friendly, but they hadn't discussed anything personal.

'He died suddenly from an undiagnosed heart condition.'

'Oh, how awful. No wonder she doesn't like Valentine's Day.'

Ryan tilted his head and leaned towards her.

'We were talking about window displays,' Cat explained. 'She was quite enthusiastic until I mentioned Valentine's Day.'

'Their wedding was due to be on Valentine's Day. She's a romantic. She used to be, anyway. He died the day before.'

Cat dropped her fork and put her hands to her mouth. 'Oh no. How do you ever get over something like that?'

'I don't know. It was three years ago and I think she's still not over it.'

Cat touched her chest as she ached inside for Elizabeth. The life she'd planned had been ripped away from her in the most tragic of ways. She understood what that felt like.

'I'm sorry,' Ryan said. 'I didn't mean to depress you.'

'No, I'm glad you told me.'

'On a lighter note . . . if you've finished your lunch, how about we go and taste some more chocolate before Arthur takes you home?'

'The perfect way to end the trip,' said Cat. Hearing Ryan referring to Thistle Bay as her home loosened something in her chest.

18

IT WAS STILL DARK WHEN CAT GOT UP TO START WORK THE following morning. A piece of paper with *The Heart of Thistle Bay Chocolate Company* written on it lay in the centre of her bed dotted with Post-it Notes of the types of images she was looking for to sit alongside her copy. The family's story and the origins of the business were absent from the current website and Cat had written a draft that she felt showed it as a family-run business without giving away anything personal about the individual family members. Until her conversation with Ryan the day before, all she had really known was that Megan didn't work in the business and that their mother had died when they were all young.

When Alan Knight had met with her in Los Angeles en route to supplier meetings in Central America, Cat had probed him about his business over lunch in an airport hotel. She thought back to their conversation now, replaying the whole encounter in her head to try to extract any clues it might hold about how this family had ended up running an international chocolate company from a small town in Scotland. They were sitting at the restaurant table, having just ordered their food.

'Where did it all begin?' Cat asked Alan, raising the question she hadn't found the answer to during her research.

Alan picked up the cloth napkin in front of him and placed it across his lap. 'My mother used to make her own chocolates by hand and send them to us every Christmas. She even managed to get them to us when we were in the Philippines,' he said. 'My children would get so excited to see the parcel arriving. They always called them the Thistle Bay chocolates because of the postmark. Then, almost thirty years ago, we turned it into a business.'

Alan hesitated for just a second and Cat feared she had traipsed into territory he wasn't comfortable with, but he continued.

'I have four children. My wife wasn't well after the birth of our fourth.' Alan gazed at his wine and traced the stem of the glass with his finger. 'If I'm truly honest with myself, she wasn't well after the birth of our third child . . .' He trailed off and Cat was tempted to fill the silence but Alan looked deep in thought and she decided to let him stay where he was. 'I travelled a lot, and we lived overseas. After our son was born, I knew something had to change. We went home to Thistle Bay because we had family and friends there and it felt like the right decision.'

'Was it?' Cat asked.

Alan looked up at her. The waiter arrived with their food and forced a break in Cat's questioning that she thought Alan might appreciate. Her stomach fluttered, but not from the smell of Alan's steak that sizzled on his plate. She had pushed him too far. She thanked the waiter for her salad and braced herself for being told to mind her own business.

'It was,' Alan said after the waiter had gone. 'The right decision, I mean. My wife passed away some years later, but Thistle Bay was the right place for her and it has been the best place for the children.'

'And you?' she asked. He hadn't mentioned how he'd felt about the relocation.

He smiled at her and Cat knew he wouldn't be answering that question. It seemed she'd found one of the lines she wasn't to cross if she got the job.

'I used my mother's recipes and designs,' said Alan. 'Then I employed a chocolatier and invested in machinery. Quality has always come first, though. I wanted to create something that mattered to us, something we could all be proud of. Machines deliver consistent products and high quantities. They were operating under capacity for a few years but I knew from the beginning that I wanted to scale the business. A boutique business wasn't for me; I wanted a business that could sustain my entire family. Something that could provide the safety and security I felt we needed at the time.'

Cat got the feeling that there was a deeper, emotional reason that compelled Alan to seek the safety and security he spoke of. She found both his ambition and his passion for the product admirable. Her best experiences were always with clients who cherished the goods they produced. Sometimes she found that emotional attachments could get in the way of what she considered to be constructive suggestions – but the end results were usually superior for her clients who had passion than for those who started businesses their hearts weren't really in.

'My children have continued my work and have grown the business even further than I'd ever envisaged,' Alan added. His eyes had glistened as he'd gone on to talk about his children, and it was that sense of family pride rather than the specific personal details that Cat now tried to capture in her words.

She rolled the tension out of her shoulders, closed her laptop and pulled back the curtains that surrounded the bay window in her room at the bed and breakfast. The beach was empty with both the sea and the sky still dark. She'd been wide awake for over an hour already and needed to get out of her room.

She crept downstairs. The building was silent apart from the ticking of a clock somewhere. She opened the front door and the bell chimed, rocking back and forth above her head. 'Damn it!' She double-checked her key was still stashed in the pocket of her zip-up top, closed the door and headed for the beach.

Cat removed her shoes and walked barefoot along the sand. There was another set of footprints heading in the same direction that she was going. She smiled at the little paw prints beside them and sped her pace up a little.

She didn't have to walk for long before she caught up with them. 'Hello,' she said to Nick, who was peering through the lens of his camera.

He spun around, startled.

'Sorry, I wasn't trying to sneak up on you.'

'Why are you here?' His abrupt manner took Cat by surprise.

She held her hands up. 'I come in peace,' she said, trying to diffuse the sudden tension.

'Sorry,' he said, straightening up and dragging his hand through his dishevelled hair. 'I just meant it's not even six o'clock in the morning. Most normal people are still asleep.'

Skye trotted over and sat in front of Cat, her tail wagging in the sand. Cat patted her damp head. 'Someone has been in the sea already, I see.' She looked up at Nick. 'Delayed jet lag. Although I've lost track of what the real time is for me – I don't know if I'm supposed to be getting up or going to bed.'

There was a faint orange glow on the horizon now and the beach had brightened up. The early-morning light flattered Nick with his thick mop of blond hair and his suntan. His blue eyes reflected the waves that were lapping at his feet.

'Aren't you worried about getting that wet?' Cat asked pointing to his tripod, its feet sinking deeper and deeper into the sand with each movement of the approaching tide.

'Nah, it dries.'

'Are you shooting the sunrise?'

He nodded and fiddled with the settings on his camera. 'I have the perfect vantage point here. It's just the sun and the sea, but the photograph changes every minute as the sun gets higher and the light gets brighter.' Nick looked down at her feet. 'I see the jellyfish incident hasn't put you off walking barefoot.'

Cat laughed. Nothing could put her off walking barefoot on the beach. She'd lived in big cities and small towns but she always settled better in places that had a beach nearby.

As Nick busied himself taking photographs and adjusting the settings on his camera, Cat moved a few feet away to the dry sand and sat cross-legged beside Skye. The little dog seemed weary from her early-morning swim and was quite happy to snuggle up beside her. Cat pulled her hair into a ponytail, tying it with the hairband she had around her wrist, and yawned as she stretched her arms out in front of her and rolled her shoulders back. Seagulls circled above her head, their dawn chatter a surprising comfort.

She watched Nick work for the next half an hour, an easy silence between them. There was something about Thistle Bay. She could see herself walking along the beach every morning and never tiring of the view across the water. Her stomach growled and her thoughts immediately turned to Josef and what delights he would be selling that morning.

'That's a big smile for such an early hour,' said Nick. His camera was hanging around his neck as he carried his tripod out of the shallow water.

'I was just thinking about how much I like it here.'

Nick snapped his tripod closed, causing Skye to jump. 'Really? I thought you were a city girl.' Why did that feel like a criticism? 'I've finished editing your photos. I can email them to you.'

'Actually,' she said, formulating a plan in her mind, 'can I come by the gallery and take a final look? Viewing them on your big screen is better than on my laptop.'

'Sure. Tonight?'

'Works for me.'

They ambled back along the beach together and Cat was a little disappointed not to see Josef at his stall. 'No Josef yet?'

'He's still asleep like most normal people,' said Nick looking at his watch. 'Actually, he's probably not asleep – he's most likely in his bakery getting his pastries ready for today. I'd usually be heading out for a run with Skye round about now and he's always there setting up by the time we run back.'

Cat watched Nick and Skye cross the street before she unlocked Gloria's front door. She liked that she was no longer making a fool of herself every time she saw Nick. What she didn't like was the ache she got in the pit of her stomach every time she thought about leaving Thistle Bay.

19

CAT HAD SPENT THE MORNING IN RYAN'S OFFICE DOING business admin. She'd checked her business bank account and sent off receipts to two clients confirming their payments had been received. She'd also emailed a contract to a new client for approval – a personal trainer looking for Cat to write two blog posts and an email campaign targeting those wanting to improve their health and fitness in the New Year. The personal trainer was hoping to sell her January boot camps without using the same old 'new year, new you' diatribe. Cat was grateful for the business and it meant consistent income until at least the end of the year.

It had never been Cat's intention to start her own business but she was enjoying being her own boss and having greater creative control. She didn't even mind the admin side of the business; there was something relaxing about the repetition of handling invoices, payments and contracts. She had set up the procedures for each of these parts of her business from her very first client so now it didn't take much brainpower to handle them. Her creative juices didn't need to be flowing, and she got a bigger thrill recording payments received than she'd ever got on pay day in her previous jobs.

She had then spent the afternoon working with Master Chocolatier Ben in the shop while Elizabeth ran a chocolate-making workshop for a book club. With the pumpkin festival only two days away, Elizabeth and Ben were working flat out to finish the chocolate they needed for their stall. Cat wasn't much help with the chocolate so she took care of the customers and restocked the shelves under Ben's supervision.

Elizabeth had initially refused Cat's offer of help, saying they couldn't impose on her that way. Cat assured her the copywriting was going well so far and that she liked to roll up her sleeves and lend a hand to get to know her clients' businesses better. That wasn't actually true. Cat had never before given up writing time to immerse herself in the day-to-day duties of her clients, but Elizabeth had been so welcoming and Cat could see how up against it she and Ben were. The back wall of the shop was cluttered with boxes waiting to be crammed with sweet treats that still weren't decorated or wrapped. Some hadn't even been made yet.

The pumpkin festival was happening whether the chocolate was ready or not and Cat felt compelled to help. Besides, working in the shop had its advantages. She'd caught a glimpse from the shop window of Nick walking Skye and the wave he gave her had caused a surge of chirpy energy that dulled the throbbing in her legs. She'd only helped out for a few hours but she wasn't used to spending that long on her feet and her calves were still aching by the time she headed over to the gallery to view the edited photos.

Cat couldn't hide her grin when Nick opened the door

for her. Avoiding him in the coffee shop after their initial meeting on the beach seemed such a long time ago.

'Can I get you something to drink?' Nick asked after he had set her up in front of his computer.

'Please. Just whatever you're having is fine.'

'Tea, or I have red wine if you want something a bit stronger.'

Cat smiled and nodded. 'Wine sounds good.'

'It's upstairs. I'll be back in a minute.'

Cat saw her chance. She opened up Nick's photo files and scanned her eyes over the thumbnail images as quickly as she could. Seeing what she was looking for, she selected Mail, typed in her own email address and hit Send just as Nick returned holding two glasses of wine. Cat opened one of her commissioned photos and coughed to cover the whoosh sound of the email sending. Now she just had to hope he didn't check his sent-mail folder before she'd done what she needed to do.

'You OK?' Nick asked.

Cat stood up and took one of the wine glasses. 'I am now.'

'Would you mind coming upstairs with me? I want to show you something.'

Cat hesitated.

'Nothing weird,' Nick hastily added.

'Gee, that makes me feel better,' she teased.

He laughed and shook his head. 'You know what I mean.'

'Not really.'

'Just come. It's worth it, I promise.'

The door to Nick's flat above the gallery was already ajar, presumably so Skye could come and go. Right now, the little bundle of black fur was curled up in a ball on her dog bed in the hall. She opened her eyes, a dopey expression on her face, and promptly went back to sleep. The novelty of Cat seemed to have worn off for her already.

Nick led Cat along the short hallway and into the living room, where a navy-blue leather sofa was positioned in front of an unlit fireplace. The mantelpiece held small tealight candles in glass holders, which she somehow couldn't imagine Nick ever lighting. The walls were decorated with framed black-and-white prints and Cat's eyes lingered on a striking image of two women laughing and seemingly unaware of the camera lens on them. One of the women was Mystic and she wondered if the other was Nick's mother.

Nick directed Cat towards a pair of glass doors at the front of the room. He unlocked the doors and pulled them open. A tiny terrace appeared beyond, enclosed by waist-high black metal railings. The space was just big enough for two chairs, a small table and Skye, who had sprung up and shoved her way in front of them as soon as she'd heard the key in the lock.

'Have a seat,' said Nick.

Cat stepped out onto the terrace and sat on one of the chairs. Nick joined her and gave Skye a pat on the head as she stood in front of him sniffing through the railings. The lampposts lining the promenade gave off a dull glow against the dark night and, with no overhead light from the moon, the sky was lit up with thousands of twinkling stars. The only sound out here was the gentle lapping of waves against the shore, and their breathing.

'This is incredible,' said Cat.

'I thought you'd like it. There's a garden out the back but it's really just for Skye and for summer barbecues. It doesn't have this view.'

'How did I not spot this balcony from the street?'

'It sits in the space where the bay window should be, directly above the bay window downstairs.'

It was years since she had seen stars. City living meant lots of lights and not a lot of dark skies. She had lived on the opposite side of the water for more than a decade and hadn't ever seen a sky with this many stars. Thistle Bay was catching her out at every turn. The anguish in her stomach brought on initially by the thought of coming here had morphed into misery she now only felt when she thought about leaving.

She turned to look at Nick. 'Thistle Bay is just full of surprises.'

He held his glass towards her and nodded. 'Cheers.'

'Cheers.' She tipped her head back to marvel at the blanket of stars and take in the extraordinary silence that came with evenings in a small town. It was spectacular and, right at that moment, there was nowhere else on earth she wanted to be.

20

On the night of the pumpkin festival, Arthur pulled up outside the bed and breakfast in a small white van. Cat was already waiting for him on the pavement. City lights flickered in the darkness on the other side of the water and reminded her that her days in Thistle Bay were ticking down. She shivered and zipped up the quilted jacket she was glad she'd opted to wear. Arthur unbuckled his seatbelt to get out but Cat raised her hand to stop him and opened the van door.

She climbed into the passenger seat. 'Not your usual wheels today, Arthur?'

'I hope you don't mind. The van is easier for transporting chocolate pumpkins. Elizabeth and Ben are meeting me up there to set up their stall.'

'It seems a pretty big deal in this town. It's all I've heard anyone talking about today.'

'Community is important in small towns so any event that includes everyone is generally a hit.'

They arrived at the festival in just a couple of minutes. Cat could have walked if she'd had any clue where it was.

She silently chided herself for not paying attention to the route Arthur had taken so she could make her escape and get herself back to Gloria's if she needed to. She had offered to help Elizabeth set up, but once that was done there was only so long you could roam about on your own before it just felt awkward.

Arthur stopped the van behind a stall and Cat waved to Ben, who was standing by. Ben opened the back of the van and began unloading before Cat was even out of her seat.

A ring of temporary stalls and fold-out tables had been set up in a field and twinkly lights dangled from every available surface. The field was full of chatter and laughter already as those providing the food, drinks and entertainment set up their stalls. Cat was thankful the dry weather made the grass beneath her feet hard, although she did notice a few patches of hay had been laid down on what she presumed were muddy dips that were best avoided.

'What can I do to help?' Cat asked when Elizabeth appeared.

'Oh, no, you're a guest here. Just enjoy the festival. It officially opens in half an hour but you could always stroll around and get a preview of the stalls before the crowds gather.'

'I know you won't risk me touching the chocolate, but I can do anything else – it looks as though you've got a lot to do in only half an hour.'

Elizabeth looked around. 'If you're sure you don't mind helping, you could unload those two boxes there. It's bags of chocolates. Just line them up in rows, starting at the far side of the table.'

'I can do that,' said Cat, springing into action.

Cat lugged one of the boxes onto the table, careful not to encroach on Elizabeth's space. Elizabeth used her artistic flair to assemble her chocolate creations into an edible art exhibit while Cat unpacked the first box of clear plastic bags with mixed truffles. She put the empty box in the back of Arthur's open van and set to work on the second box, which was overflowing with ghosts, pumpkins and cats in a mix of milk, white and dark chocolate.

By the time Cat had finished emptying her boxes, Elizabeth had set up her feast with pumpkins, squash, ears of corn, red and green apples, and autumn leaves strewn around, all made from chocolate. Cat looked in awe at the spread and moved in front of the stall to snap a picture on her phone before anyone interfered with it. Ben was already serving the first customers with cups of hot chocolate.

'The display is exceptional, Elizabeth,' said Nick as he appeared behind Cat with Ryan.

Elizabeth's hand hovered above the biggest pumpkin. 'Just don't look too carefully at this one. It has a big crack down the back.'

Ryan moved round to the other side of the stall and poked a finger at the back of the pumpkin. 'You weren't kidding. Look at that.' Elizabeth smacked his hand away and Ryan put his arm around her shoulders and squeezed. 'I'm kidding, Lizzie. It's superb. How are you, Cat?'

'Good. I'm staying on this side of the stall so I don't end up breaking the pumpkin or wearing the hot chocolate.'

'Ah, yes. I heard you were dripping in chocolate the other day.'

Cat glanced at Nick and her cheeks warmed at the memory.

'Don't worry,' said Ryan. 'We've all been there. Consider it your Thistle Bay Chocolate Company initiation.'

'We've got everything covered here,' said Elizabeth. 'Why don't you two take a walk around?'

'Gladly,' said Ryan.

Elizabeth grabbed the back of Ryan's jumper. 'I was talking to Cat and Nick. I have a job for you.'

Ryan shrugged at Cat. 'I'm always in demand.'

Cat pasted on a smile and strode away from the stall with Nick following her.

'You OK?' he asked, speeding up for a few paces to catch her.

'Family stuff is a little hard sometimes.' She slowed her pace. 'Do you miss your parents being around?'

Nick tilted his head and thought for a moment as though it was something he had never considered before. 'Sometimes. They fly back often enough that I probably see them more than some people who live in the same country as their parents do.' He stopped and pointed in front of them. 'There's Mystic. Shall we go over and say hi while she's free?'

Mystic was watching them as she perched on a small stool with all of the accessories needed to paint the kids' faces. Cat waved. 'You go ahead,' she said to Nick. 'I think I'm going to head back to Gloria's.'

'Already? You sure you're OK?'

'Yeah, just a bit tired.'

A frown spread across Nick's face. 'Let me walk you back.'

'Honestly, I'm fine. You stay and enjoy the festivities. Really. You'd better go and say hello before that group of kids beats you to it.'

Six small children were noisily making their way over to Mystic. There were three witches, two cats and a pirate, all grinning with the excitement of knowing their bare faces were about to be transformed to match their outfits.

'You're right. I'd better run. I don't want to get stuck at

the back of that queue.' Nick picked up her hand and gave it a light squeeze. 'Text me and let me know you got back OK. I still don't trust that internal compass of yours.'

Cat laughed and watched him sprint over to Mystic before she weaved her way through the mass of people towards Josef, who was busy serving another group of kids with paper trays of mini doughnuts. As she waited for him to be free, Cat lingered beside three trailers brimming with pumpkins for festival-goers to take home for carving – presumably the same pumpkins she had spotted from the top of Blakely Hill.

A padlocked green metal box with a slot on the top sat on a table in front of the trailers. A handmade sign saying *Pay What You Can* had been taped to the table edge, meaning everyone in town could go home with a pumpkin regardless of their financial circumstances. Cat expected that doorsteps and windows across Thistle Bay would soon be adorned with spooky orange faces in preparation for Halloween night.

A small boy stood marvelling at the pumpkins, his purple knitted hat pulled down over his ears. He bounced up and down on the spot as his mother handed him a coin, saying, 'Go and put your money in the slot.' The boy toddled over to the table and, on tiptoes, dropped his coin into the money box then clapped his chubby little hands together. His mother smiled and lifted him up to get a closer look at the pumpkins. His hand settled on one and he bounced up and down again in his mother's arms. 'Good choice,' the woman told him, lowering the boy to the ground.

Cat stepped forward and plucked out the chosen pumpkin. 'Let me help you with that,' she said.

'Thanks, Cat,' the woman said, taking the pumpkin. 'I'm

glad he went for this one and not one of the huge ones – it's me who has to carry it home.'

Cat smiled and watched the pair walk off, the little boy clearly delighted with his pumpkin. She didn't recognise the woman and wondered if she had been one of the factory workers and the lack of a hairnet had changed her appearance.

Two teenage girls approached, each dropping a five-pound note into the slot before comparing the pumpkins, and Cat looked back at Josef. He had finished serving the kids now and Cat went over to tell him she was leaving.

'No, don't go yet. Once the kids are sugared out, the fun begins. You have to stay or you're not really experiencing the pumpkin festival. Please,' he added when she hesitated.

Everyone she knew had a job to do. Those who weren't working were supervising groups of little goblins and ghouls or choosing their pumpkins. She seemed to be the only person with no role to play in the festival and she wasn't enjoying being a spare part.

'I'll stay if you let me help you,' she said.

Josef's face lit up and he handed her a set of metal tongs. 'You do doughnuts, I'll do sauce.'

When the fifth stranger thanked her by name, Cat turned to Josef. 'Was there a Thistle Bay memo announcing my arrival?'

One hour and what felt like hundreds of kids later, Josef and Cat's duties were done. 'Now it's playtime,' said Josef, pulling his apron over his head. 'I'm off to the – what is it you call it? That potato-and-meat mush . . .'

'Stovies?'

'The stovies stall, that's the one. And I might wash my stovies down with half a pint of beer. What can I get for you?'

'Nothing for me, thanks. I think I'll take a wander. But I'll be back to help you pack up.'

'You might want to take a wander to the chocolate stall,' said Josef, giving her a wink before he made his way through the revellers.

Cat's cheeks burned even though Josef hadn't hung around for her reaction. She didn't need to turn around to see who he was referring to. She had spotted him there already. Nick had been chatting to Ben for the last few minutes. Their trade seemed to have died down, too, and she had a clear view of him.

He hadn't seen her and she contemplated walking in the opposite direction since Josef had left her and wouldn't know any the better. But her legs seemed to have other ideas and she found herself walking straight towards him. She had enjoyed spending the last hour with Josef and wasn't ready for the night to be over.

As if sensing her gaze, Nick turned as she got closer and they locked eyes. Too late now.

'Did you save me any doughnuts?' asked Nick. 'When you didn't text me to say you'd arrived at Gloria's I went looking for you and saw you helping Josef.'

'Ah. He didn't really need my help, but it was fun.'

'I'm glad you stayed. I really need you.'

'Me?'

'You. Mystic has roped me into the pumpkin-carving competition.' Nick looked down at his watch. 'We have an hour to carve our scariest pumpkin. Mystic is one of the judges and she doesn't do nepotism. If we're going to win, our pumpkin has to be amazing.'

'Give it up, man,' said Ben from the side of the chocolate stall. He moved his hand back and forth between himself and Elizabeth. 'The dream team here – we're going to win.'

'See you in the ring,' said Nick. He took Cat's hand and led her away. 'We'd better get started.'

They arrived at a table full of pumpkins and Cat was very aware that Nick still had hold of her hand. She glanced around to see if anyone was watching them and spotted Rebecca approaching the table with two boy wizards in tow.

'Oh God,' she said and wriggled her hand free from Nick's.

Nick turned and, without looking at Cat, spoke to the boys. 'Well, look at you two. You make very fine wizards.' He raised both of his hands and each boy slapped one with a hand of his own in a high-five. 'I hope you're not planning on casting any spells to help you win the carving competition tonight.'

The boys giggled and one of them waved his wand towards the pumpkins. Cat couldn't remember a time she'd ever believed in magic. She must have done when she was tiny, but being thrust into a world of strangers deciding her fate at the age of six had forced her to grow up far too young.

Rebecca stooped towards her children. 'Boys, this is Cat. Mummy and Cat are working together on something very important that I'm going to tell you all about one day soon. Say hello.'

'Hello, Cat,' they said in unison.

Rebecca placed one hand on each boy's head. 'This is Liam and this is Oliver.'

'Are you picking a pumpkin too?' asked Liam.

'We are,' said Cat.

Cat was struck by how different Rebecca looked tonight. She had only seen her in the office so far. Now, the high heels were gone. She was still a little taller than Cat, but wearing jeans and a jumper, with her dark brown hair loose and wavy around her shoulders, made her far less intimidating than she'd seemed at work. The bright red lipstick was still in place but now it highlighted her smile as her boys spoke.

'I'm carving my pumpkin with Mummy,' said Liam.

'And I'm carving my pumpkin with Uncle Ryan,' said Oliver.

'Well, have fun,' Cat said as the boys turned away to look at the choice of pumpkins.

Rebecca chewed on her lower lip and smoothed her hair down with her hand. 'Megan is arriving on Thursday. We're all having dinner at Dad's house on the Friday night. It would be good if you could join us.'

'Sure,' Cat said. 'I'd like that.'

'Great. Well, we'd better get started,' said Rebecca as she too turned away to assess the pumpkins.

When Cat and Nick had chosen theirs, they picked up their carving kit and plastic tub for the insides and found a spot on the grass to sit down.

'Is their dad around?' Cat watched Oliver giggling as he chased Ryan around with his wand.

'Jeremy. He's in the marines so he comes and goes. It kills him every time he has to leave those boys.'

'Are he and Rebecca together?' She knew she shouldn't be asking about her client's personal life and expected Rebecca would be furious if she found out. It was one thing Ryan volunteering information; it was quite another for her to ask someone who wasn't even family – that could be construed as gossiping – but there was something about Nick that made her want to talk about the things in life that she had missed out on.

Nick shook his head. 'I have no idea why not. High-school sweethearts and meant to be together.'

'Do you believe that – that some people are meant to be together?'

Nick picked up the small carving knife and stuck it into the top of the pumpkin. 'I used to. I'm not sure anymore.'

'Can I tell you a secret?' Cat whispered.

Nick leaned in closer. 'Of course.'

'I've never carved a pumpkin before.'

Nick laughed. 'That's good for me, actually. Your expectations won't be too great. Ben and Elizabeth won last year and there's no way my pumpkin-carving skills could beat theirs.'

'What?' said Cat in mock shock. 'You sounded so confident. I thought I'd signed on to the winning team.'

'Nick lifted the top off the pumpkin and offered her the miniature orange shovel. 'You can scoop. I'll get the wine to numb the disappointment we're about to experience. Red?'

Cat nodded and laughed as she watched him stride towards the mobile bar.

When their pumpkin was finished and sitting on the judging table, Nick traded Cat's empty plastic wine glass for a full one.

'I was going to ask if we should bother waiting for the results, but our pumpkin doesn't look too bad up there,' said Cat.

'It's certainly not the worst,' agreed Nick. 'Have you seen the one on the far left?'

'Yeah. I feel like it's watching me.'

'I know. There's scary and there's just plain creepy. I don't even want to know who carved that one.' Nick held out his glass. 'Cheers.'

'Cheers,' she said just as someone bumped into her left side, causing her wine to swirl too close to the rim of her glass. She turned to look into the eyes of the stranger swaying beside her.

'Sorry, Cat,' he said. 'I'm blaming that dip in the grass there. Nothing at all to do with the pint in my hand.'

She laughed as he raised his plastic beer glass and stumbled off. She didn't recognise him but he was another person who obviously knew her. She guessed there weren't that many new faces in Thistle Bay after the summer season ended.

Cat stared into the crowd, at the people chatting and laughing all around her.

For the first time, she felt part of it.

Mystic was standing in front of the pumpkin table tapping the microphone. The rabble that had gathered immediately hushed. 'The winner of this year's pumpkin-carving competition is . . . Rebecca Knight and Liam Lewis.'

Cat smiled as she watched Rebecca and her twin boys celebrate their victory. Rather than looking disappointed, Oliver was sharing in his brother's win and accompanied Liam to collect the prize bag from Mystic.

'Rebecca looks so happy,' said Cat. She hadn't seen Rebecca looking this relaxed before. Her skin had a glow and the frown lines Cat had become accustomed to seeing across her forehead were gone.

'Yeah, well, the pumpkin prize will do that to you,' said Nick, forcing a huffy expression on his face and crossing his arms.

Cat prised his arms loose and laughed. 'We might have better luck next year.'

'We? Next year?' he said, drawing out the words.

'I really want that pumpkin prize. Those kids don't stand a chance next Halloween.'

'That's the spirit,' Nick said laughing.

Cat liked hearing him laugh and was glad that she was in on the joke this time. Since she had decided to just be herself, the clumsiness that she'd developed since arriving in Thistle Bay had vanished. Tonight she had been able to just enjoy Nick's company without worrying about showing herself up.

The whizzing of fireworks being set off nearby drifted towards her on the breeze and she shivered as she looked up. The first bang lit up the night sky in a silver, red and green pattern and was closely followed by the screech of a Catherine Wheel and multicoloured balls of light careering through the darkness.

Cat and Nick stood so close to each other that their fingers kept touching. She wanted him to take her hand again but she reminded herself the Knights were all around her. This was a family-fun festival for everyone else. For Cat, it was meant to be work. She was here to show the Knights that she understood their business and their town. Besides, she had less than a week left. She could not deny that she felt something for Nick, but acting on those feelings and then leaving at the end of the week could only lead to heartbreak for one or both of them. *Leaving*. Something hung heavy inside her, as though weights filled her body and plunged to the base of her spine just at the thought of it.

Cat took a deep breath, looped her arm through Nick's and watched the rest of the show.

'That was impressive,' she said. Puffs of smoke drifting across the sky were all that remained of the fireworks. The field once again became a hive of activity as people headed home and the market sellers packed up.

'Can I walk you back to Gloria's?' asked Nick.

'I want to check on Josef first. Are you in a hurry to go?'

'Nope. I'll go and check on Mystic, you check on Josef, and I'll meet you back here.'

'Sounds good.'

She headed over to Josef's stall and found him loading boxes into the boot of his tiny blue car. 'Let me help you with that,' she said.

'No need. I have a packing system.'

'I'm sure you do,' she said, picking up a box anyway. 'I'll bring you the boxes, you pack them into their allocated spaces.'

Josef didn't argue and they had filled the car in less than a minute.

'Thank you, Cat.'

'Can I help you unload at the other end?' she asked, suspecting he would refuse.

'No, it's no problem. I do it on my own every day.'

She briefly contemplated insisting, but she also really wanted to walk home with Nick. Josef had boxes on his passenger seat, anyway, so she couldn't travel with him – and the boxes were now empty so would be light enough for him to lift easily.

Cat smiled at Josef and gave him a hug. She pulled back quickly, hoping she hadn't made him feel uncomfortable, but he looked his usual jovial self. His expression was permanently warm and welcoming, with eyes that put you straight at ease. If he really was going to live to see his hundredth birthday as he was planning, he faced almost thirty more years alone. But, somehow, despite his wife being gone and his children living in different countries, the man was joyful. He saw the good in everyday experiences, and that was a trait to emulate.

'I had a lot of fun tonight,' she said. 'I'm glad you made me stay. What's on the menu for the morning?'

'Pretzels. A little salt after all the sweet things tonight.'

'Perfect.'

After watching Josef drive off, Cat headed back to the centre of the field and saw Nick waiting for her. The smile he gave her when he spotted her made her stop mid-stride as her breath caught in her throat. Her feelings for this man were refusing to stay packed away inside the compartment she had boxed them up in.

21

Cat and Nick sauntered out of the field after the pumpkin festival and onto a country lane lit up by strings of bright white lights that were attached to the trees lining the pathway. She couldn't help but think this was the most perfect autumn evening. The wine she'd drunk had taken the edge off the chilly night air, the trees were bursting with colour under the glow of the fairy lights, and fallen leaves crunched beneath her shoes.

'That was a lot of fun,' said Cat. 'I've never been to anything like it.'

'It's always a hit with the locals,' said Nick.

'I thought it might be like the Edinburgh Christmas markets without the ice-skating, but it was nothing like that.'

'How do you mean?'

'Food stalls and a bar were the only similarities. It just had a completely unique vibe. I don't know, it's hard to explain.' She had begun the night on the perimeter looking in, but both the people and the festival itself had embraced her and she had become a part of it all. There had even been a thaw in her relationship with Rebecca.

'I think it's because most of the town is involved in some way or another,' said Nick.

'Yeah. Everyone was happy tonight. It was great to see.' Cat rubbed her hand up the sleeve of her coat.

'Are you cold?' asked Nick.

She shook her head. 'I have two glasses of red wine circulating round my body. I'm toasty.' Cat stopped suddenly and turned to face Nick. 'Can I tell you something crazy?'

'I like a bit of crazy.'

'I have the draft website copy written. It could be finished off in just a few hours. I just haven't done it and given it to the Knights yet.'

'Why not?'

She hesitated. How could she possibly tell him what she was thinking? His eyes bored into hers and she looked away. 'Because I don't want to leave here.'

Not only was that the first time she had said it out loud, it was the first time she had admitted it to herself. It was crazy. She knew it was. Her time in Thistle Bay had made her realise she wanted to settle somewhere. She wanted to plant roots for herself. But just because this town had helped her see that, it didn't mean this was the place she should do it.

Cat closed her eyes and her body swayed a little from the wine. She lowered her head to steady herself and sucked in a breath as Nick took her hand. She clasped her fingers around his hand as he ran his thumb back and forth across the inside of her wrist.

When she opened her eyes, Nick was watching her. 'Finishing the job doesn't have to mean leaving,' he said.

'Doesn't it?' Cat wrinkled her nose. 'Is that not weird?

What if the Knights think I'm hankering after a permanent job with them?'

'Why would they think that?'

'Because they hired me for two weeks. I'm sure they didn't expect me to stick around for longer than that.'

'They might not have expected you to, but why would it be a problem for them if you did?'

Cat shrugged her shoulders. 'I think I need to see Alan Knight again. I don't know why, but I haven't made the best impression on him. Plus, I need to make sure they're happy with my work. I couldn't stay in a town where I would bump into disgruntled clients every day.'

'Are you really considering staying?'

'It ticks everything on my list.' That was the best answer she could give right now. The thought of leaving made her stomach churn, but was staying really a viable option?

Cat's phone vibrated in the side pocket of her coat.

'Do you need to check that?' asked Nick.

Cat glanced at the notification on the screen. She could see from the preview that she had an email reply waiting in her Find My Family account. Perhaps it was because she was still overflowing with community spirit after the evening's festivities, but whatever CocoB13 had to say had lost its importance. She'd been searching for a connection in this world. It was dawning on her that she didn't need a stranger that she just happened to share a bloodline with to give her that connection. She had to stop allowing the search for her biological family to dictate so much of her life and just trust herself to make the decisions that were right for her.

'I really don't,' she said and tucked her phone back in her pocket.

Nick's gaze roamed across her face and her breath

caught in her throat as she drowned in desire. He squeezed her hand and the little voice inside her screamed at her to kiss him. She concentrated hard on not looking at his lips and tried to ignore his eyes continually dropping to hers. He inched towards her and it was clear what his intentions were. This was what she had been trying to avoid. In that moment, she couldn't remember why. Their lips connected and a rush of exhilaration enveloped her body.

22

When Nick woke the next morning, sunlight was already streaming through his window. He looked to the corner of the room where Skye lay curled in a tight ball in her bed. She seemed to sense him rousing and opened her sleepy eyes for a quick peek before closing them again.

Nick pulled on his running gear and forced Skye to get out of her bed and ready to go. They dashed across the street and headed onto the sand. The sun was bright but the morning chill nipped Nick's face as he ran.

He couldn't push thoughts of Cat out of his mind. His entire body buzzed just being near her. Something had shifted in her since their hike up Blakely Hill. A sense of fun had overtaken the nerves he'd picked up from her during their first couple of meetings. But she hadn't yet relaxed in his company. She was still a woman with a lot of feelings locked up tight and he longed to get close enough to crack her open. She'd gone from being an itch he needed to scratch to a woman he wanted to know everything about.

Their kiss had been everything he'd hoped it would be. And now it seemed as though staying in Thistle Bay was a possibility for her. After his last relationship failed, he'd wondered if he would ever meet someone who appreciated the life Thistle Bay offered. He certainly hadn't thought that someone might be a girl who had lived in countless cities and even countries over her lifetime so far.

Skye seemed happy to avoid the sea and run alongside him this morning. The wet sand flicked up onto the backs of his legs with each stride as he allowed himself to relive the events of last night. He could still taste the red wine on her lips and smell the coconut shampoo she'd used in her hair.

She had kissed him back without hesitation and he had known then that his feelings for her were reciprocated. The fact she trusted him enough to tell him that she had all but finished her copywriting project but hadn't handed it over meant a lot to him. She knew he'd grown up with the Knight kids, yet still she had faith that he would be loyal to her.

He stopped running and Skye slumped on the sand at his feet. 'Are you not quite awake yet, girl?' he asked, bending over to tickle her ear.

When Cat did finally hand over her project, would the bonds she had made and the pace of life she seemed to be enjoying in Thistle Bay really be enough to make her stay put? Or perhaps the real question was would *he* be enough? Nick tried to push away the doubt he felt as he turned and headed home, with Skye picking up her pace once she realised where they were going and the prospect of food that this offered.

After breakfast for Skye and a quick shower for him, Nick headed to Mystic's.

The coffee shop was already busy and Nick waved over at the table of retired women who had arrived just before him for their weekly coffee, cake and chatter, as they called it. Once their coats had been removed and their bags stashed under the table, one of them, Mrs Purvis, headed towards him at the counter.

'I'll let you go first, son,' said Mrs Purvis. 'Our order takes quite a while.'

'That's kind of you but there's no need. You were here first.' Nick stepped back and indicated for Mrs Purvis to go ahead of him.

'Don't you have to get the gallery opened?' she asked him.

'I've got plenty of time today.' He was happy to linger in the queue. Cat's daily latte was a habit and he hoped he was in early enough to catch her.

Nick had known all of these women his whole life. Mrs Purvis lived two doors down from the house he'd grown up in and she had always been the one yelling to the kids in the street that ball games weren't allowed and to jolly well keep their bikes away from her flowerbeds. She'd mellowed with age but she looked exactly the same, with her long grey hair tied in a messy ponytail and wearing her everyday attire of a skirt paired with a heavy knitted cardigan.

Mrs Purvis stepped ahead of him as instructed and handed Mystic a slip of paper. The women ate the same thing every week but they always gave Mystic a note with their order. 'How are your parents getting on?' she asked Nick.

'They're doing well, thanks. I'll let them know you were asking after them.'

'Is the heat not getting too much for them?'

He shook his head. 'They seem to like it.'

'I couldn't be doing with heat like that.'

Mystic cut in. 'Susie has your order ready, Mrs Purvis. She'll bring it over to your table.'

'You take care, son.' She turned to Mystic. 'Make sure she doesn't spill it over us like she did last time.'

Nick stifled a laugh at her bluntness. The old Mrs Purvis he remembered was definitely still in there. He stood back to let her walk past him and gave Susie a sympathetic smile as she followed behind with a tray of teas and coffees.

'She's not been in yet,' said Mystic.

'Who?' asked Nick.

'Cat. That's who you're looking for, isn't it?'

Nick shook his head. 'I'm just looking for a coffee.' His words were drowned out by Mystic grinding up a fresh batch of coffee beans.'

23

GLORIA HAD MADE CAT A CHEESE, ONION AND MUSHROOM omelette that morning. Cat had opted to forgo the toast, knowing Josef would be keeping a pretzel for her. Her plan was to wolf down her breakfast and head straight over to Josef's, but she could see through the window that his stall was still empty. The stall had a good view of the gallery and Cat was hoping that when she went over there she'd catch a glimpse of Nick, or he'd catch a glimpse of her and come across.

Last night, Nick had walked her to Gloria's door and kissed her on the cheek, his lips lingering next to her skin as if he, too, didn't want the evening to end. The pumpkin festival had turned out to be very enjoyable indeed, for more reasons than one.

Cat handed her empty plate to Gloria. 'That was delicious,' she said. 'I'm going to miss your breakfasts.'

Gloria's naturally cheery face turned serious. 'So, you're really leaving in a few days?'

Cat's breakfast churned in her stomach. Her lips parted to speak but she didn't know what to say.

'How are things going with Mr Knight?' Gloria asked.

'All fine, I think. I don't see him that often.' She hadn't seen him at all since her first day, which she thought was a bit odd. But she was clinging to his invitation for her to join the family for dinner and meet Megan as a sign that he was happy with her work here so far.

Cat glanced out of Gloria's dining-room window again. Josef still wasn't at the stall. She presumed he was just running a bit late, but it was unusual for the stall still to be empty at this time.

'Do you know where Josef lives?' she asked.

Gloria looked out of the window and frowned. 'He lives in the house next door to Seashell Cottage.'

'Where's that?' asked Cat.

'Head left along the promenade. You'll know it when you see it.'

Cat left the bed and breakfast and crossed the street towards the beach. She strode along the promenade, keeping her eye out for Seashell Cottage. She hadn't been this far along in daylight – her walks so far had either been early morning or later in the day. In contrast to Main Street with its businesses painted in pastel shades, Nick's gallery, the bed and breakfast and the homes along the promenade were painted in varying shades of white. The style of the houses changed the further along she walked. They sat further back from the sea and each one had a modest, enclosed front garden.

As she came to the end of the row of whitewashed cottages, there it was. Seashell Cottage. It was unmistakable. The very last house, its small garden wall was lined with seashells embedded in the concrete just like the wall that hid the Thistle Bay chocolate factory from view. An archway created out of seashells surrounded its blue front door. The grass in the front garden was overgrown and scattered with orange leaves and bright red berries from a rowan tree. The flowerbeds were scruffy and unkempt and a tangle of ivy had grown up the wall and partially obscured one of the front windows. It only added to its charm.

Even from across the street, Cat could feel a kind of good energy coming from the house. It was a reaction she had never had before. Houses, for her, were simply places to keep her stuff and sleep at night. Good energy would have to go on her list of essentials for her next move – it was so enticing.

She turned her attention to the house next door and her reason for being here. Josef was sitting in the window watching her. She waved and crossed the street. He waved back as she walked up his path and gestured as if telling her to come in.

Cat knocked on the door lightly, then let herself in. The door was unlocked.

'Come straight in, Cat,' yelled Josef from his window seat in the lounge. 'Are you here for your pretzel?'

'Kind of,' said Cat.

Josef had one leg resting on a footstool and made no attempt to get up as she entered the room.

'Are you OK?' asked Cat.

'Oh, I'm fine. I twisted my ankle a bit last night unloading the boxes after the pumpkin festival and the doc thought I should rest it for a day or so.'

A flash of guilt shot through Cat. She should have insisted on helping him unload his car. 'That sounds sensible. I'm glad you called the doctor.' From the little Cat knew about Josef, she suspected he wasn't the type to call a doctor out unless he really needed to.

'I didn't call him. He saw me fall over and he just made a

fuss, that's all. He lives next door.'

'In Seashell Cottage?'

'No, the other next door.'

'Who owns Seashell Cottage? I just adore their house.'

'She's called Mrs Dean but – would you believe it? – I've never met her. We lived next door to each other for six months and I never saw her once. Usually, I see everyone coming and going. Anyway, she went into hospital and she hasn't come back yet. They moved her to one of those community hospitals. You know the type – that place where they turf people out to who are not yet well enough to come home but they need the bed for new arrivals.

'That's so sad. She must miss her house. Do you know its story? Who put all the shells there?'

'No idea. Her granddaughter comes by every second Sunday to check on the place. I'll ask her. Nice girl.'

'Let me make you a cup of coffee while I'm here,' said Cat, and when Josef didn't object, she headed to the kitchen and filled the kettle with water. She snooped in the fridge to see how well stocked up Josef was – milk, cheese and beer. Not the ideal diet for someone convalescing for a few days.

'Where's all your food?' she called out. She flicked the switch on the kettle and popped back to the living room while the water boiled.

'Don't you worry about me.' Josef patted his portly stomach. 'You can see I eat well.'

Cat folded her arms across her body. 'I'm going to worry about you if all you planned to eat for the next few days was cheese.'

'I do love cheese.'

Cat pulled her phone from her bag and opened her Notes app. 'Let's write a shopping list.'

'I'm playing with you. The garage in the back is my bakery. I have plenty to eat in there.'

'Forgive me if I don't trust you right now. I'm going to have to go and see it.'

'The keys are hanging by the back door. Help yourself to some pretzels,' Josef called as she made her way through the kitchen and into the back garden.

The garage, sitting behind the house, had a solid wooden door and a long narrow window on the garden side. Cat stood on her tiptoes and tried to peer through the frosted glass. Seeing nothing, she unlocked the door and stepped into what could only be described as an industrial kitchen. The white walls and stainless-steel surfaces were immaculate. The oven in the corner was as tall as she was.

A sadness rippled through her as she stared at the trays of pretzels. Josef must have baked them last night or that morning before deciding his leg couldn't handle a day on his stall. There were six loaves of unbaked bread abandoned on the worktop too.

Cat looked around and saw that the open shelves held bags of flour and sugar and trays of eggs. She opened the tall silver fridge and found it brimming with ingredients that Josef could no doubt whip up into lots of tasty dishes. But there were no actual meals. Everything required preparation.

She locked up and headed back into the house to make the coffee.

'I have an errand to run,' she said as she put Josef's mug of coffee on the table beside him. 'I'll be back in half an hour. Don't move while I'm gone.'

Josef shook his head and sighed. 'What are you coming back for? I'm fine. You're a busy girl. You must have lots of work to do.'

Cat ignored his protestations and gave him a smile and a wave through the window as she strode back onto the promenade.

Mystic was busy when Cat reached the coffee shop so she sat on a stool at the window and waited, hoping to catch a break in the mid-morning caffeine rush.

Cat pulled her phone from her bag and texted Elizabeth just in case she was looking for her. The door chimed and Cat glanced up to see who had come in. It was just another customer joining the back of the queue.

Her thoughts drifted back to the pumpkin festival the night before. More specifically, to her walk home afterwards with Nick. Something was different with Nick. He threw her off her stride. She was used to being the one in charge in relationships, the one who made the decisions about how far to take it and when it was time to end it. But why was she even thinking about relationships? She had no relationship with this man. She wasn't even looking for a relationship. It was just one kiss. Unless she stayed.

'You looking for me, hon?' asked Mystic, interrupting Cat's thoughts.

'I am. I need a favour.' Cat stood up and moved closer to Mystic, who leaned forward over the counter with questioning eyes. 'Josef had a fall after the pumpkin festival. He's OK,' Cat added, seeing the concern on Mystic's face. 'He just needs to rest for a few days – although I think I'll be doing well if I can get him to rest for one whole day. Anyway, I'm hoping you could make up a few meals I can pop in his fridge so he doesn't have to get up to cook.'

'I'll get right on it,' Mystic said without hesitation and stepped back.

'Thank you.'

Mystic leaned towards Cat again, elbows resting on the counter. 'How did you hear about his fall?'

'He told me. When I didn't see him this morning, I stopped by his house to make sure he was OK.'

Mystic nodded and got to work.

Cat pulled out her phone, dialled Rachel's number and headed for the window seat in the corner. 'Hey, Rach, how's it going?'

'Pretty good. I've finally cleared out my spare room so it's all ready to go for whenever you get here.'

'Great,' said Cat, slumping down on a chair. Her mouth was suddenly dry and she wished she'd ordered a coffee before asking Mystic to make the food for Josef.

'You could try to sound a little more enthusiastic. It took me hours. What's up?'

'Nothing. It is great, thank you.'

'You need to work on your tone when you're lying. Seriously, what's up?'

'It's just the thought of leaving here.'

'The thought of leaving Thistle Bay or the thought of coming back to Edinburgh?' Rachel asked, knowing that the city held so many bitter memories for Cat.

'Actually, the first one. I mean, I know I wasn't exactly thrilled about coming back to Edinburgh. But Edinburgh wasn't really the problem. It was the fact that I was wandering aimlessly trying to capture that feeling of being home and I was frustrated because I hadn't managed it. I felt like a failure. You were right, though. I need to put down some roots for myself.'

'Did you just say I was right?'

'Is that the only thing you're taking away from that? I just bared my soul to you.'

'All I heard was that I was right. Although, I think I'm also hearing that you want to stay in Thistle Bay. Did something happen with the hot beach guy?'

'He's not the . . .' She was about to repeat Rachel's words but then realised someone was bound to overhear their conversation and, in a town this small, repeat those same words to Nick within the hour. 'Do you know what? It doesn't matter. It's not about him. I like it here. I feel like I could live here and be happy.'

'That's great. But something happened with him, didn't it?'

'We may have shared a moment.'

'Shared a moment? Who are you and what have you done with my best friend? It's not like you to be coy with the details.'

'OK, fine.' She glanced to the table next to her and saw a teenager wearing a back-to-front baseball cap, his phone in one hand and an iced coffee in the other. She lowered her voice to almost a whisper. 'We kissed. But that's not what this is about. The kiss was just . . . the perfect end to what had already been a pretty wonderful day.'

'I need details about this kiss. But I'll circle back to that. For now, can you really see yourself settling down in such a tiny place? You've never been attracted to the small-town thing before.'

'Maybe that was my problem.'

'How do you mean?'

'I'm not sure I can even explain it. I just feel good here.'

'So, are you staying?'

'I don't know.'

'Here's a question for you. If CocoB13 replied tomorrow and said they were your father or your brother or your cousin or whatever and they lived in London, would you move to London?'

Cat sighed and thought about it. The email she had been obsessing over had finally arrived and she hadn't even opened it.

'Cat, are you still there?'

'They replied.'

'Catherine Radcliffe! We've been wittering on for ten minutes and you wait until now to tell me this. Who are they? What did they say?'

'I don't know. And I don't know.'

'What do you mean you don't know?'

'I haven't read it.'

'You've been waiting two months for this reply and you haven't read it. Why on earth not?'

'I don't want it to influence me.'

'OK, you've officially lost me.'

Cat put her head in her hand. 'Things are going well here. I don't want anything to screw it up.'

'You've been chasing this for years.'

Rachel was right. She had been waiting for the email for weeks, but she had been seeking the information for a lot longer than that. 'I know. And I will get to it.'

'You make it sound as though it's just another task on your to-do list,' said Rachel.

'I've been trying to find out about my family for forever because I thought it would give me a connection to someone and some place. But you were right, Rach. I need to decide what's right for me. To put roots down that are my own. And I want to do that without being influenced by whatever this stranger has to tell me. To answer your question . . . if they're from Bath, or Newcastle, or Inverness, then I probably would go there. But I know that none of those would be the place for me, so it wouldn't be the right decision. You must think I'm crazy.'

'Actually, no. That's twice in one conversation that you've said I've been right. I believe you're actually thinking clearer than you have done in years.' There was certainly one thing guaranteed with Rachel – she always made Cat laugh. 'Seriously, though,' she continued. 'You're not crazy. That town is having a good effect on you.'

Cat spotted a reflection waving in the window she was facing and turned around. Mystic stood behind the counter with boxes of food ready for Josef. 'I need to go. Thanks, Rachel.'

'Just one thing before you go. The kiss. How was it?'

'It was . . . dynamite.' With that Cat laughed and hung up the phone. She could picture Rachel squealing with frustration and knew she'd have to call her back later with the details. For now, she had a food delivery to make.

'This should keep him going for a few days,' said Mystic, placing the last of her takeaway boxes on the counter. She had prepared three boxed salads and two sandwiches. 'The sandwiches will be good for today and tomorrow, and I've separated the wet and dry salad ingredients so they don't go soggy. All he has to do is mix them and drizzle over a touch of oil.' She turned away from Cat and brought forward two more boxes. 'This is a lentil soup and today's special, shepherd's pie, so he's got something warm, too. Those look OK, hon?'

'It all looks perfect. Thank you.' Cat hoped that a few ready meals would keep Josef off his feet and give his ankle a chance at healing. She dug around in her bag and produced her purse. 'How much do I owe you?'

Mystic reached forward and covered Cat's hand with her own. 'On the house. It was good of you to check up on him.' She gestured at the food boxes. 'This is my way of helping him out.'

Cat shook her head and prised her hand out from under Mystic's. She took her credit card out of her purse. 'No, honestly, I didn't come expecting free food. I want to pay for it.'

'You can buy yourself a coffee while you're here, but I'm covering the cost of this.' Mystic placed the boxes in a brown paper bag and pushed it over to Cat. 'Double-shot latte, is it?'

Cat nodded. Something told her that Josef, who didn't like to make a fuss, wouldn't want Mystic giving him free food. He valued his independence and she'd seen at first hand over the last couple of days that he didn't readily accept help.

'Mystic, do you think your customers would buy pretzels?' Cat asked.

Mystic slid Cat's coffee towards her with a smile on her face.

Cat squinted against the glare of the mid-morning sun as she made her way back to Josef's cottage. The heavy coastal clouds that were hanging overhead earlier in the morning had now parted and, with no breeze, the air was already as warm as a Scottish summer's day. It had drawn locals to the beach – parents supped on Mystic's takeaway coffees on the sand and supervised toddlers with buckets and spades, a bunch of wild swimmers swam back and forth in the sea, half a dozen dogs zoomed around a harassed-looking dog walker.

Josef was still sitting just where she had left him and Cat waved as she passed the window. His gaze dipped to the brown paper bag she was carrying. She let herself in and breezed straight through the living room and into the kitchen. A documentary about Japanese street food boomed out of the TV, the sound abruptly muted when Cat opened the fridge.

'I've brought you lunch and dinner for a few days,' she called out as she emptied the contents of her bag into the fridge.

'I don't want . . .'

'Before you complain,' Cat said coming to the doorway and holding up her hand to silence him, 'Mystic is going to sell the pretzels you've got in your bakery out there. She'll take what she's owed for the food and give you the rest. It would be such a shame if they went to waste.'

The lines across Josef's forehead softened and he broke into a smile. 'Sounds like you have it all figured out,' he said.

'Almost. What can we do with the unbaked bread?'

Josef shook his head. 'Don't worry about that. I'll bake it later today.'

'No you won't. You're resting that ankle,' said Cat. 'I could bake it.'

'Can you bake?'

She raised her eyebrows and he laughed.

'I don't need to be able to bake. You've already done the hard bit, surely. I just need to put it in the oven. I think I can manage that.'

Josef sat up straighter in his chair. 'I'll come and show you how to work the oven. It's an industrial one. You need to get the heat just right and the colour of the bread needs to be—'

'Stop,' said Cat. 'You'll sit where you are.' She looked around the room. 'Where's your phone?'

'Here,' he said, pointing to the landline phone on the table beside him.

Cat shook her head. 'Do you have a mobile or a tablet?'

He rifled through a pile of newspapers and pulled out a tablet.

'Perfect,' she said. 'I can video call you from inside the bakery. You can tell me which buttons to press and you don't even need to leave your chair.'

'You're quite something, Cat. Thank you.'

Josef may not have wanted to make a fuss but Cat could tell he was enjoying her company. He clearly loved baking, but she suspected he loved the social side of his food stall just as much. The man lit up whenever he had someone to talk to.

She looked down at her phone and fiddled with her apps. She connected a video call and passed the tablet back to Josef. 'I promise to do exactly as I'm told. Mystic is going to send Nick up to collect the pretzels so I can get started on the bread, if you're ready.'

Just saying Nick's name made Cat feel giddy inside. In a town this small it wouldn't surprise her if their kiss last night was already public knowledge, but Mystic hadn't mentioned anything and Josef hadn't seen anyone so he couldn't know yet. It was bound to get around soon, though. She had been so determined to avoid getting involved despite her attraction to him. She had no doubt the Knights would find out – she only hoped they didn't think she was completely unprofessional. She would hand her new copy over in the next day or so. Then they would at least have her work to judge her by alongside her personal life. Their approval meant more to her than that of any other client to date – but it was no longer just about getting their logo in her portfolio. Their endorsement would symbolise her acceptance here in Thistle Bay.

24

N<small>ICK PUSHED OPEN THE DOOR TO</small> M<small>YSTIC'S COFFEE SHOP FOR</small> the second time that morning and scanned the tables. 'Hey, I got your message. What's up?' he asked Mystic when he reached the counter.

Mystic gave Nick a rundown of her conversation with Cat earlier.

'You're asking me to help Cat? You – the woman who effectively told me to stay away from her?'

'It's only carrying a few boxes.'

Nick waited. As much as he was eager to see Cat again, he knew Mystic, and he knew there was more going on in her mind than she was telling him.

'I noticed Josef wasn't there this morning,' Mystic said finally. 'Do you know what I did? Nothing. Cat noticed and what did she do? She found out where he lived and went to check on him.'

'So, you're sending me to help Cat to ease your guilt about not checking up on an old man?'

'Giving him free food is to ease my guilt. There's more to

Cat than we've chosen to see. That *I've* chosen to see, anyway. I can tell you like her.'

'She's just . . .' A friend, he was going to say. She wasn't, though. There was a connection there and he knew Cat also felt it.

'I know you don't want to repeat mistakes of the past. But sometimes you need to take a chance and see where it leads.'

'You've changed your tune.'

Mystic gave him that don't-argue-with-me look she'd been giving him since he was in primary school.

He blew out a breath. 'Fine. But I'm only doing this for a free pretzel.'

'Deal.'

Nick went home to get his car and drove down the lane to the back of Josef's house. He parked beside Josef's familiar blue car behind his bakery kitchen and switched off the ignition. This was ridiculous. Why was he so nervous about seeing Cat? If he ever doubted that she felt something for him then surely last night had abolished those doubts. He hadn't actually asked her on a date, but they had spent most of the festival with each other. Then with the walk home and the kiss, it had certainly felt like a date.

He replayed her words again as he had been doing for most of the morning: she had said she didn't want to leave here. He knew she was already looking for somewhere to move to – so why not Thistle Bay?

He snapped up his keys and opened the door. 'Because you're not that lucky, that's why.'

'Talking to yourself?' Cat was standing beside his car and leaned over now to peer inside. 'Or have you got someone with you?'

'Just me.' He cursed himself for not seeing her there.

'Mystic told me you'd be coming to help.'

She looked beautiful. Her hair was scraped back off her face and her floral dress brought out the green flecks in her hazel eyes so that he couldn't tear his gaze away from them. He was desperate to kiss her again but her stance stopped him short. Her arms were folded across her body and she was facing to the side.

'The pretzels are just inside.' She turned and walked into Josef's kitchen.

He frowned, following her inside.

His mouth watered at the aroma of freshly baked bread. There were three trays of pretzels and six multigrain loaves cooling on wire racks. 'Did you bake the bread?' he asked.

She uncrossed her arms and leaned on the side of the metal table. A wide grin spread across her face. 'Well, I'm not one for bragging, but yes. I actually did. Of course, I mean *baked* in the strictest sense of the word. I physically put them in the oven and took them out of the oven. Josef made them last night.'

Nick laughed. 'Still, I'm impressed.'

'Do you want a pretzel?'

'Sure. Just don't tell Mystic. She's promised me a free pretzel for picking them up.'

She looked down. 'So, you had to be bribed to come here.'

'Not exactly.' If she really was thinking about staying, he had to show her what she meant to him. He walked towards her, passing through a wall of heat from the oven, and interlinked his fingers with hers. 'Of all the times I've been to the pumpkin festival, last night was my favourite.'

She smiled and her eyes glistened. 'Mine too.'

'Although, it was your favourite one by virtue of it being your only one.'

She squeezed his hand. 'True. But it was pretty great all the same.'

He leaned forward and brushed her lips with his. 'Hi,' he said.

Cat wriggled her hand free and wrapped her arms around his neck. The warmth from her palms sunk into the back of his neck and spread through his body. 'Hi,' she said back before she kissed him.

Nick's eyes darted open at the sound of someone clearing their throat.

'Oh God,' said Cat, letting her head fall into his body.

'Good morning, Nick,' came a voice.

Cat lifted her head and pointed to her phone resting on a shelf. The flush on her cheeks made him smile.

'Hey, Josef,' said Nick. 'How's the ankle?'

'I'm so sorry, Josef. I forgot you were there,' said Cat.

Josef laughed hard. 'It's just good to see you kids getting along.'

'Is that what you call it these days?' Nick whispered in Cat's ear and she elbowed him in the ribs.

Cat picked up her phone and raised her hand to Josef. 'We'll just load the car before we come in.' She ended the call and turned to Nick, cheeks still red. 'I was video calling him so he could see if the bread was ready. I told him I'd be right back when I heard your car and then I completely forgot about him sitting on the shelf there.'

'Just as well it was only a kiss,' said Nick.

'Oh God. What if that's why he interrupted us? What if he thought we were going to do it in his bakery?'

'I've never done it in a bakery before.'

She picked up a tea towel and threw it at him. 'Let's get these pretzels in the car before we get into any more trouble. You start loading and I'll wrap the bread. You need to take half of these loaves to Mystic. Then there's one for you, one for Josef, and I'll take the other one to Gloria.'

'I was going to call you today, actually,' he said.

Cat kept her eyes down and her hands busy with the bread. 'You didn't have to.'

He stepped towards her and lifted her chin with his fingers. 'I wanted to.'

Her smile reached her eyes and he was sure she felt the same way as he did. 'Can I take you to dinner tonight?' he asked.

Uncertainty crept back in as her smile faltered and she looked down. Nick stepped back, fearing he'd misread what had happened between them, but Cat reached out and caught his hand. 'I would like to,' she said. 'But I need tonight to work. I'm presenting my final website design to the Knights tomorrow. It has to go well and it wouldn't feel right to be . . . *socialising* on company time.'

Nick nodded. 'You'll be dazzling. You're ready for it,' he said and held her gaze for a moment before turning to pick up the first tray of pretzels. As Cat wrapped a loaf of bread, he paused at the door and looked back at her. She was radiant. Maybe it was the jet lag finally clearing or the blood that had rushed to her face when she'd realised Josef had seen them kiss. Or maybe it was the town. It suited her. When her project was complete, though, where would that leave them?

Once Nick had finished loading his car with pretzels and recited to Cat's satisfaction the instructions she'd given him about the bread when she came outside with the wrapped loaves, they re-entered the bakery. He draped his arm around her shoulders and she leaned into him.

'Can I give you a hand with anything else?' he asked. Knowing he wasn't going to see her that evening, Nick was reluctant to leave. He would have been happy to wash down the salt- and seed-splattered counters if it meant spending an extra few minutes with her.

'Nope, I'm fine. But I've got something for you.' Cat walked to the chair in the corner of the bakery and delicately slid a white envelope out of her bag. She opened it and passed the flyer from inside to Nick.

His gallery logo jumped off the shiny paper and he bristled at the text staring back at him. *Nicholas Bell Photography Exhibition at Thistle Bay Art Gallery*. She'd even gone as far as putting the date in.

He gripped the flyer and raised his eyes to meet hers. 'I see this is happening next month.'

She nodded. 'I plan to come back for it.'

'Come back for it?'

'I know what you're thinking. It's a lot of work to pull together an exhibition, but the prints in your back room are a brilliant starting point and I'd love to help. You could remove some of the existing art – just temporarily until you decided what to do with it longer term – and you'd have so much space to show your work.' Her arms flailed as she talked him through how he could lay out his photographs. 'The frames in the middle of the floor can easily accommodate different-sized prints so you can offer a variety of options depending on the image and the space the customers have available.'

Her cheeks were rosy from either the heat in the bakery or the enthusiasm she had for her exhibition plans. Her plans for *his* photographs. For *his* business. He'd already built his business to incorporate one woman's vision and she had upped and left anyway.

'That wasn't what I was thinking,' he said.

'What are you thinking?'

If she had to come back for the exhibition she'd decided he should have, then she had also decided she was leaving. He slammed the flyer down on the stainless-steel counter top in front of him and ran his hand over his face. 'I'm thinking it looks like you're meddling in my business and I don't understand why it even matters to you.' The words came out sharper than he intended them to but he was somehow reluctant to take them back.

Cat opened her mouth as if to retaliate but seemingly thought better of it and chewed on the edge of her lower lip instead. The wounded look on her face drove a shard of guilt through his chest. One little apology would fix this. He could take her in his arms, turn the clock back just a few minutes and kiss her again.

Instead, he turned and slouched out of the bakery.

'Afternoon, Gloria,' Nick said as he joined the back of the queue at Mystic's Coffee. Skye dropped to the floor from the exhaustion of their run, her pink tongue lolling to one side as she panted to recover. 'How's the bed-and-breakfast business today?'

Gloria, standing one place in front of him, swivelled around and gave Nick a cheery smile. 'How are you, son?'

'Can't complain,' he said, although he'd been better. A run always cleared his head and helped him burn off any tension. Today, that tension came from Cat. Or, rather, from how he had treated her when she'd given him the flyer she'd mocked up. He unzipped his running top to cool down. Afternoon runs always left him sweltering and Mystic's roaring fire didn't help.

Gloria nodded towards the counter. 'I'm making a

dinner reservation for a couple of new arrivals who want a quick bite to eat once they've checked in tonight.'

'You seem to be pretty busy despite the season.' Nick knew from conversations with Cat that the breakfast room was crowded in the mornings.

'I'm usually at half occupancy at this time of year, but it's been a profitable couple of weeks. I've had fairly local couples for long weekend stays – just people looking to escape their real lives for a couple of days without having to travel too far. And I've had a group of Irish guests who were all attending the same wedding – they arrived before the wedding and they've stayed on for a few extra days afterwards. The happy couple even joined us for a night before they flew to . . . oh, goodness, I can't remember where they went . . . some place exotic.' She glanced behind her and shuffled a step backwards to keep her place as the queue moved on, and Nick used the inside of his foot to nudge his dozing dog along the wooden floor; Skye knew the queue offered nothing exciting for her so had already begun to sleep off her exertion.

'Speaking of young love,' Gloria went on, 'will you and Cat be eating here tonight? I thought Cat could show my new arrivals where to come.'

Nick shook his head and folded his arms across his body. Dinner with Cat had been on his agenda, but he didn't feature on hers. She'd turned him down, then he had chewed her head off for trying to help him. He chided himself for his churlish behaviour. 'Cat needs to do some work tonight.'

'Never mind, I'll point the way myself.' Gloria reached over and squeezed his forearm. 'She only has a couple of days left, I suppose, before she has to leave. I'm going to miss her when she goes. I certainly don't say that about everyone who stays with me.'

'You never know, she might stay around a little longer.'

'I had hoped so too, son, but it doesn't look like that's going to happen. My heart sank when she told me she was going to miss my breakfasts when she checks out. Unless you know something I don't?' He sensed hope in her voice and knew it had nothing to do with the extra business Cat staying might provide. Mystic and Gloria had been known to work together to manufacture reasons for Nick to meet the occasional solo traveller. Despite his insistence that he didn't need their help, the well-meaning women's interference in his love life was part of their charm, and he'd become accustomed to making polite conversation with unwitting customers ambushed by the duo.

'Looks like you're next,' he said.

Gloria turned to give Mystic a wave, then said to Nick, 'Make sure she knows how much you want her to stay, son,' before spinning back around to Mystic again, leaving Nick to ponder her advice.

Nick had transformed the old antique shop into his dream space but the pieces that hung on the walls were Lisa's grand plan. He didn't want to sell paintings and, deep down, he had long known that. The fact Cat had articulated it with her flyer before he'd even admitted it to himself was what had caused his sour reaction.

Selling strangers' art wasn't what got him going in the mornings. The satisfaction he got from capturing the soft golden-hour light to create his own art was why he leapt out of bed when most people were still sound asleep. The flyer didn't represent Cat's vision for his gallery. It represented his. Cat had just been able to see what he had resisted acknowledging.

He thought about the night Lisa had told him she was leaving. 'I miss London' was all she'd said. He had simply nodded and they'd both known it was over without either of them having had to say the actual words. Five years together had fostered that instinctive communication. He didn't yet have a relationship with Cat, so if he wanted her to know what he was thinking, he was going to have to tell her. She might still choose to leave – but he wouldn't allow it to be because he hadn't offered her one more reason to stay.

25

THE FOLLOWING MORNING CAT HAD EXPECTED TO SEE JOSEF opening up his stall, but it lay empty still and she was glad he was taking the advice to rest for a while. Cat had spent all of the previous evening rehearsing her presentation. She'd really wanted to accept Nick's dinner invitation but she'd known she had to ask him to hold off until she'd finished the project. Her stomach had wrenched at the disappointment on his face when she'd turned him down. Then she had insulted him with her idea for his gallery. The flyer hadn't fallen flat, it had pulverised the floor and plummeted towards the foundations of Josef's bakery.

He'd texted earlier to wish her luck with her presentation but she hadn't yet texted back. She just needed to get this project handed over then see where that left her. And where it left her relationship with Nick.

Cat had made a fleeting visit to Josef's house to check on him before heading to the Thistle Bay Chocolate Company offices. She now stood in the boardroom beside the whiteboard presenting her work to the Knights. The new images

Nick had taken were stuck on the board beside her text to provide a visual overview of what the company website could look like with just a few tweaks.

Elizabeth and Ryan nodded their heads and smiled throughout Cat's presentation. They made a few minor suggestions, which Cat made a note to update before she sent the final files over. Alan Knight hadn't been able to join them, again. Rebecca rounded the table, walked over to the board and sighed. Cat braced herself.

'I think the images are perfect,' Rebecca said. Her normal brusque tone was absent. 'And the copy is excellent. You've done a wonderful job.'

Cat stood there trying to think of how to respond. Rebecca had so far not had anything positive to say. Often she kept silent, but that felt worse somehow. She was one of those people who managed to project their mood onto everyone around them.

'Thank you,' she said, fearing anything else would get her on Rebecca's bad side again.

'This could be interesting,' said Ryan.

'Sorry?' asked Cat, not sure if he was talking to her.

At that moment the boardroom door burst open and a tiny figure with a deep tan and sun-kissed hair strutted in. She wore a sleeveless vest with yoga pants and pulled a small purple suitcase behind her.

'Hey, I'm Megan,' she said. She marched straight over and gave Cat a hug.

'Oh, great,' said Cat with a smile. She had been hoping to meet Megan before she finalised the files, so her timing was ideal.

When Megan released her, Cat touched the photo Nick had taken of Megan's painting. 'This is your work, right?' she asked. 'I wanted to use it on the new website shop page – as long as you don't mind.'

'Oh my God.' Megan put her hands on her hips and glowered at her siblings. 'You haven't told her yet.'

Cat was suddenly nervous. Ryan and Elizabeth glanced at each other while Rebecca's eyes blazed at Megan. The atmosphere that had accompanied Megan's arrival told Cat she wasn't about to hear good news. She tried to ignore the twinge in her stomach as Rebecca sat down and instructed her to do the same.

When she'd been told she was losing her job in Los Angeles, Cat had felt matter-of-fact about it. There was a corporate restructure and she was one of many casualties. It wasn't personal and she knew that. If she was about to lose this job, though, it suddenly felt very personal.

'We haven't been entirely honest with you,' said Rebecca. 'Our mother, Catherine Knight, was also your birth mother.'

Cat froze and for a second thought she must be hearing things. 'Sorry,' she said. 'Your mother is . . .'

Rebecca nodded. 'Our mother was also your mother.'

Cat clutched her stomach, aware of everyone staring at her. What response was she supposed to give them? How on earth could this be true?

'You must have a thousand questions,' said Rebecca. 'We didn't plan to keep it from you. We planned to tell you as soon as you arrived.' Rebecca looked down at her hands. 'You being here has been harder on Dad than we thought.'

Elizabeth got up and walked over to sit next to Cat. 'We're so sorry. I don't suppose there was a good way to tell you, but this definitely feels like the wrong way.'

Ryan was speaking but his words weren't registering

with Cat. Her body was heavy as she stood up and made for the door. Someone called her name but she didn't stop. She couldn't stop. When she reached the street outside the shop, she slumped back against the wall and gasped for breath.

26

NICK RESTED HIS ELBOWS ON THE TABLE TOP IN FRONT OF HIM and cradled his coffee. He'd texted Cat to wish her luck for her meeting with the Knights; his apology would have to wait until afterwards. He knew Cat was obsessing over her presentation and her need for it to go perfectly and he hadn't wanted to drop by and create a distraction for her.

The door chimed and he looked up as he now did every time he was in Mystic's coffee shop. He felt like Skye sniffing underneath the shed in the back garden every morning because she'd once found a cat under there. When he looked back to the window, there she was – his Cat. He could tell immediately that something was wrong. Abandoning his coffee, he headed out of the door and crossed the street.

'Hey,' he said when he reached her. 'Slow down. What's happened?'

Her face was ashen and tears hovered on her lower eyelashes as if waiting for permission to fall. 'I have to get out of here,' she said, barging past him.

He followed her, with long strides to match her pace. 'Come to the gallery. You look like you need to talk.'

She shook her head. 'I need to leave. I should never have come to Thistle Bay. It's all just a big lie. I need Arthur.' She fumbled in her bag and pulled out her phone, not slowing at all.

'Wait,' said Nick. He gripped her shoulders and forced her to stop. 'I can see that something's wrong. You might not want to talk to me, but you need to slow down. I can call Arthur for you. What should I tell him?'

'I need him to give me a ride back to Edinburgh.' Cat looked at Nick for the first time. She dropped her arms by her sides and he snatched her phone before she dropped it. She looked utterly defeated, but her broken demeanour suggested this was about more than work.

He reached out and pulled her towards him, squeezing his arms around her body. A heart-wrenching sob shuddered through her body and her tears soaked into his top. 'Cat, I don't know what's going on, but Ryan Knight is heading straight for us. Do you want to see him?'

'No. Get me out of here.' She buried her head further into his shoulder and her fist gripped his clothes.

Nick raised his hand and shook his head at Ryan. Ryan came to an abrupt halt and nodded. He clearly knew something was up with Cat. Whether or not he knew what had happened, Nick wasn't sure. With one arm wrapped tightly around Cat's shoulders, he steered her to the gallery, locked the door behind them and eased her onto one of the chairs beside the warm stove. 'I'll make tea,' he said.

He slid open the door to the back room and flicked the switch on the kettle, watching her out of the corner of his eye as he waited for the water to boil. He saw her put her phone on the table without having called Arthur and wipe her face with her hands. He made the tea and when he turned back to Cat again, she was slumped in the chair with a glazed expression on her face. Whatever had happened was major.

Nick joined her in front of the stove and handed her a cup. 'I put two sugars in it,' he said. 'I don't know why. People just do that, don't they?' She held the cup between her hands, sipped at the edge and winced. 'Hot?' he asked.

'Sweet.'

'Do you want to talk about it?'

She took a deep breath and forced the air from her body as she breathed out. 'I don't know if I can.'

'Just take your time.'

'I mean literally. They're my clients.' She stared down into her tea. 'Although I guess they're not my clients. They never were.'

Nick wasn't following but he didn't want to interrupt her. There was no way the Knights had fired her – they just weren't that type of family, and he knew Cat's work was brilliant. He'd seen some of it when they were pulling photos together for her presentation and it was so much better than what was on the current website.

'Do you know Megan is here?' she asked.

Nick shook his head. 'Ryan told me she was coming but I didn't know when. Have you met her yet?'

'That's right, you're friends with the Knights.' She shook her head and shifted her gaze to the ceiling. 'I probably shouldn't be here.'

'I'm also friends with you, Cat.'

She seemed to be examining him now. 'Is that what we are?'

'We might be more than that. If you want to be.'

There was more going on behind her eyes than she was

showing. He sensed a storm was brewing inside her and it was about to be unleashed. He had no idea what had happened or how it might affect whatever was going on between them – all he knew was that it was something serious enough to make her want to bolt straight back to the city. He'd been in this position before and didn't think he could face it again.

She said nothing so he moved on. 'Look, whatever's going on, I know you can figure it out,' he said, trying to be reassuring.

She rubbed at her eyes with the palm of her hand. 'I can't. Something has happened that's changed everything.'

'So, change with it. From what I've seen you're good at that. I mean, I've seen you get stung by a jellyfish then walk barefoot along the same beach only days later,' he said, trying to lighten her mood so she could think a bit more clearly.

She took another sip of her tea and shook her head.

'You're brave, Cat. You can do this.'

Fury flashed in her eyes and she moved to the edge of the chair. 'What would you know about being brave? You're too afraid to show your own work so you hide behind other people's art even though it makes you miserable and keeps you stuck in the past.'

It wasn't her words that stung. They were the truth, but he already knew that. It was the arctic chill that spread across her face and seeped towards him.

'Can you please call Arthur for me and ask him to pick me up at Gloria's in an hour?'

Nick picked up his phone. As he dialled Arthur's number, he watched Cat gather her things and march towards the door. He thought about offering to drive her himself but he couldn't sit with her in the car for an hour knowing it was just to say goodbye at the other end.

'He'll be there.' He took her hands in his. Steeling himself, he looked up to meet her eyes. Every muscle in his body tightened as his gut implored him to stop her from leaving. 'I'm sorry that this is where we are.'

He pulled her closer and pressed his lips to her forehead. He'd known this day would come. She'd told him the day they met that she was only here for two weeks. They had both felt the spark between them that first night on the beach. And they had both tried to ignore it. He thought that had changed. When he'd kissed her, she had kissed him back. She had said she wanted to stay. Over the last few days he had allowed himself to imagine that she would. But if she couldn't trust him enough to talk about whatever had happened, he'd been a fool to think that spark was strong enough to make her stay. He opened the gallery door and watched her walk away.

27

CAT LEFT THE GALLERY AND CHARGED TOWARDS JOSEF'S house. She couldn't bring herself to look back. She had been horrible to Nick and there was no excuse. When he'd wrapped his arms around her in the street his heartbeat had thudded in her ear and all she'd wanted to do was blurt everything out. How could she have, though? She didn't even know what was going on herself. Nick didn't deserve the venom she'd spat at him. If she was going to snap at anyone, it should have been one of the Knights.

But she couldn't face them.

Josef was sitting in his garden chatting to a young woman when Cat arrived.

'Cat, I wasn't expecting to see you twice in the same day,' he said cheerfully. He was perched on what looked like a bar stool with a short back support.

Cat was grateful for the presence of a second person. It would force her to keep her composure. She didn't need to crumble; she needed to put some distance between herself and Thistle Bay. 'That's an interesting contraption,' she said pointing at the stool. She turned to Josef's companion. 'Hello,' she said with a nod.

'Hi there,' said the woman. Her hair was a glossy black and the gardening gloves sitting beside her on the bench explained the bead of sweat across her forehead.

'Do you like it?' asked Josef. 'Nick dropped it off this morning. He thought it might be easier for me at the stall over the next couple of weeks – just until my ankle gets completely better.'

Cat rubbed at the tightness in her chest that had come with the mention of Nick's name. 'You could always not to go to work for the next couple of weeks. That would also help you to get better,' said Cat.

Josef laughed heartily. 'That's what Nick said, but can you see that happening?'

'No, I can't unfortunately. How did you get on with the doctor this morning?'

'Something came up so he can't see me until this afternoon. Allegedly. He thinks I don't know he's trying to keep me away from my stall.'

'Good.'

'Have you met Iris here? She's Mrs Dean's granddaughter.'

'We haven't met, no. It's good to meet you,' Cat said to Iris, trying to sound chirpier than she felt. 'How is your grandmother?'

'It's good to meet you, too. I've heard a lot about you this morning,' said Iris.

'That's her way of telling you I chat too much,' said Josef.

'Something I already know, of course,' said Cat.

'My grandma is fine,' said Iris. 'She keeps hoping that she'll get out by the end of the week, she says, but another week passes and she's still in there. Unfortunately I don't think the doctors are thinking in terms of weeks.'

'I'm sorry to hear that,' said Cat. 'Seashell Cottage is spectacular. Has your grandma lived in it long?'

'Thirty-five years. In fact, I placed some of the seashells into the wall there when I was young. We used to bring a handful back from the beach every trip and my granddad would help us to cement them on.'

'It really is extraordinary,' said Cat. 'I've never seen anything like it. I can understand why she's so keen to get back home. Where do you live?'

'Edinburgh, but I don't often go to the beach so it's quite nice to come across, check the house is OK, and spend a little time on the seafront.' Iris turned to Josef. 'Of course, I don't need to come too often because you're keeping an eye on the place for me, which is so helpful.'

'That's her polite way of telling you that she thinks I'm nosy,' said Josef.

Cat winked at Josef. 'Another fact I already know about you.' Josef laughed. Not even his injury or a few days away from the stall could dampen his spirit. It was one of the things she admired about him.

'Cat's going to be moving to Edinburgh,' said Josef. 'Why don't you swap phone numbers? Perhaps you kids can meet up for dinner or something.' Cat stared at him. 'Go on,' he said.

Cat took her phone from her bag. 'I suppose I should be grateful you're just trying to fix me up with a friend and not with a man.'

Josef raised his eyebrows. 'That's because I think you already have the man sorted for yourself.' Heat rose to Cat's cheeks as she thought of Josef witnessing her kiss with Nick. She desperately wanted to go back to the gallery but she had to put some space between herself and Thistle Bay. How could Catherine Knight have been her birth mother? Her mind drifted to the times she had spent with the Knights and she searched her recollection of things done or said for any signs. 'Cat?' Josef's voice cut into her thoughts.

Cat shook her head. 'Sorry,' she said. She handed her phone to Iris. 'Feel free to put a fake number in there if you want to.'

Iris laughed and typed her phone number into Cat's contacts.

Cat looked at Josef. 'My plans have changed. I have to head back to Edinburgh today so I just came to say goodbye.' Josef moved to push himself off his chair. 'You stay where you are,' said Cat.

He stood up anyway and she reached her hand out to grip his arm. He patted the top of her hand. 'I'll see you when you get back,' he said.

Her lips parted and she shook her head. She wanted to tell him she might not be back but the words stuck in her throat. He threw his arms around her and wrapped her in a hug. She waved at Iris and walked out of Josef's garden and back along the promenade. Her life had seemed complicated when she arrived two weeks ago. She'd had nowhere to live and no plan for where she was going to move to. Then the idea of staying in Thistle Bay had started to form, but that idea had been ripped out from under her an hour ago and she felt worse off now than she had when she'd just got here. Tears welled in her eyes as she walked and she kept her gaze focused on the waves crashing on the shore.

Arthur was waiting for Cat when she got back to the bed and breakfast.

Gloria was also there, obviously having figured out that something was up and that Cat was checking out early. 'Leaving so soon, hen? I thought you were staying until next week.'

'I'm sorry. My plans have changed quite suddenly.' Cat scraped her hair to one side to get some air on her neck. She swallowed hard.

Gloria reached out and ran her fingers down a lock of Cat's hair. 'You look just like her, you know.'

Cat stared at her and wondered how long she had known what was going on. Gloria didn't volunteer any other information and Cat couldn't think straight enough to decide which question she wanted to ask first. She said nothing and just headed upstairs to pack her suitcase.

Her nomadic existence meant Cat travelled light and was an expert packer. She knew how to fold her clothes for minimal creasing at the other end of her journey and had leak-proof bags for her toiletries. This time, however, Cat piled her clothes into her suitcase and tucked the stray fabric down the sides. She opened a carrier bag and tossed her toiletries from the bathroom inside, folded over the top of the carrier bag and stowed it on top of her clothes.

After only five minutes, Cat was back downstairs with her suitcases. Arthur loaded them into the car and Gloria watched as Cat climbed in and they drove away.

'Thank you for driving me on such short notice, Arthur.'

'It's a pleasure. Did you get your project finished early?'

'Something like that.'

Ever the professional, Arthur seemed to sense she wasn't up for chatting on this journey and stayed silent. Cat texted Rachel to say she was on her way and stared out of the window, not really taking the scenery in. She hadn't given Rebecca or the others a chance to explain. But what was there to explain? They had lied to her for two full weeks. She had spent every day with at least one of the Knights and no one had told her. No one had told her why they had really asked her to come to Thistle Bay. Her work was just a sham.

It wasn't until they reached the Queensferry Crossing that Cat realised she'd been lost in thought for almost the full journey. Their mother was her mother. For so long she had sought any tiny detail about her birth mother and now there were numerous people who had the answers. But after their betrayal, how could she trust anything they had to say?

'Did you ever meet Catherine Knight?' she asked Arthur.

'Mr Knight's wife? No, I didn't. Sadly she had passed before I started working with the family. Her illness must have been devastating for Mr Knight and the children.'

Cat's eyes clouded with tears as it dawned on her that, even without any other information from the Knights, she now knew her birth mother's name, where she was from and a little bit about how she'd lived her life.

'I hear she was a lovely woman, though,' Arthur added.

'She was.' She had to be. Alan Knight still spoke so lovingly of his wife and Cat had seen for herself that the family were part of the fabric of Thistle Bay.

'Ah, so you met her, then?' Arthur asked.

'Once. A really long time ago.'

Rachel was sitting on the concrete steps leading to her flat when Arthur pulled the car over. She was on her feet and embracing Cat as soon as she stepped onto the pavement.

'Welcome home,' said Rachel, squeezing Cat tight.

'Thanks,' said Cat. She certainly didn't feel as though she was home. It was as if she had gone backwards in time. Here she was, again, arriving in Edinburgh with her world shaken. The only difference was that now she was more than twenty years older.

'Can we offer you a coffee or something before you head back?' Cat asked Arthur with as much sincerity as she could muster. She was desperate to talk to Rachel alone but was also grateful to Arthur for helping her out so suddenly.

'I'm fine, but thank you. You have my number. When you come back to Thistle Bay, please call me. I'd love to drive you back.'

'Thank you, Arthur,' said Cat. She refused Arthur's offer to carry her bags inside. She and Rachel hauled them up the two flights of stairs together and dropped them in Rachel's narrow hallway. They squeezed themselves around the suitcases and made it into the living room. Cat scanned the familiar room. A year after graduating from teacher-training college, Rachel had saved enough for a deposit and had borrowed the maximum her salary would allow to buy this place. They had spent many evenings in this very room planning their futures in the seven years since.

Rachel put her hand on Cat's shoulder. 'Do we need tea or wine?' she asked.

Cat burst into tears, unable to hold them in any longer.

'Wine it is, then,' said Rachel, leaving Cat alone to sob.

28

NICK PULLED ON HIS RUNNING GEAR AND CLIPPED SKYE'S LEAD to her collar. He headed across the road and onto the beach, Skye trotting ahead when he freed her again. He'd always preferred running on the beach. The sand made it more challenging and gave him a tougher workout in a shorter burst of time. Pounding the pavements wasn't much fun – there were always pedestrians to avoid and Skye had to be tethered to him – but he could run for miles on the beach and not see another soul.

Once they reached the wet sand, Nick jogged at first then broke out into a sprint, his feet pummelling the sand as the waves crashed onto the shore. Seeing him run, Skye did her best to keep pace beside him, her little legs whirring, until she'd had enough and pottered down to the water's edge to cool off.

When he stopped running, his heart hammering in his chest, Nick stood on the shore staring out across the water to Edinburgh. Skye sniffed her way along the beach, leaving Nick to kick at the sand in frustration. He picked up a handful of pebbles and threw them one by one into the sea.

He shouldn't have let her go. He'd allowed painful past experiences to influence his actions. But what did he really fear – history repeating itself or Cat's feelings for him not being deep enough to make her stay?

'You look like a man who's missing a beautiful woman.'

Nick jumped at the voice behind him. 'Josef, hi.'

'You didn't want her to leave, then?' Nick shook his head. 'She didn't tell me why she was leaving early,' said Josef. 'The tension I saw on her face told me she had no choice. Or thought she had no choice.'

'I'm not sure what happened either,' said Nick. All he knew was that it had something to do with Ryan Knight. One call to his childhood friend could tell Nick what was going on, but he had yet to make the call. He wasn't sure he was ready to face what he might hear. Nick looked at his watch. She would be back in Edinburgh by now, literally on the opposite side of the water in front of him. He glanced over his shoulder at Josef. 'Should you be walking on that ankle?'

Josef gave his usual hearty laugh. 'The doc just gave me the all-clear. I'm officially back on duty tomorrow. Or maybe later today.'

'I'm glad, but make it tomorrow, just to be sure. I've become accustomed to the smell of pastry when I finish my run in the mornings.'

Josef placed a hand on Nick's shoulder. 'This place changed Cat, just as it did me. She'll be back.'

Nick ran a hand across his jaw as he watched Josef trudge off the beach with tentative steps and amble along the promenade back to his house. An unfamiliar feeling had stirred inside him the night he met Cat on this very beach and he hadn't been able to stop thinking about her since. There was something special about Cat Radcliffe and he would make sure she knew that. But first, he had some changes of his own to make. 'Here, girl,' he called and Skye came galloping back to him.

Nick stopped by the coffee shop to pick up a decaf coffee and a steak baguette, grateful that Mystic wasn't around so he didn't have to force a smile, then headed for the gallery, Skye rushing in ahead of him as he unlocked the door. He gulped his coffee down as he walked along the row of paintings on the front wall. He'd known for a long time what needed to be done. He just hadn't admitted it to himself. Cat had seen it straight away.

Pausing in front of his favourite painting, he admired the artist's skill. It was a field of poppies and the artist had somehow managed to paint the flowers in such a way that you felt movement just by looking at the scene. The painting had been one of his first acquisitions but it had yet to find a home. Lisa had never liked it and, even once they'd gone their separate ways, he had allowed Lisa's preferences to influence his choice of artwork. It wasn't just that the gallery didn't represent Thistle Bay – it reflected a past that he had emotionally moved on from. It didn't represent Nick, and that was what he had to change.

'We've got some work to do, Skye.' The little spaniel wagged her tail and gazed up at Nick with her dark eyes. 'Come on, let's get started.'

Nick gave Skye a chew stick to keep her busy and switched on his laptop. If Josef was right and Cat did come back, he wanted to show her a new gallery. A gallery he was proud of. A gallery that was truly his.

29

CAT APPRECIATED RACHEL GIVING HER THE SPACE TO CRY alone. They had been through a lot together and her friend knew that Cat needed to get all of the emotion out of her body before she could begin to talk about it. Rachel was the polar opposite. She needed to talk to figure out how she really felt about something – a personality trait that had got her into trouble on the odd occasion when her thinking out loud would have been better processed internally first.

They sat together now on Rachel's living-room floor nursing glasses of red wine. Rachel had students' essays spread out in front of her and was occupying herself with them until Cat was ready to talk.

Cat flicked through her family photo album. It was something she did whenever she felt lost. She could reach for that album and somehow the answers would always come to her. It was as though her parents were still looking after her, steering her in the directions she needed to go. There weren't many answers forthcoming tonight, however.

'I haven't looked at these photos in so long,' said Cat.

Rachel dropped the essay she had been reading and

curled her feet underneath her body. 'Your mum would be so happy you still have them,' she said. 'I know it didn't last long, but it looks as though you had such a happy childhood. Do you remember it?'

Cat nodded. 'I think so. Or I just remember the photos. Either way, it makes me feel good to think back to when I was little. This is my favourite photo.' Cat passed the album to Rachel.

'You were so cute. Who are you dressed as?'

'Sophie from *The BFG*.'

'Ah, that's right.' Rachel continued to flick through the pages. 'Why do you think the Knights have just made contact now? You don't think someone needs a kidney, do you?'

'Oh, come on.'

'Well, why now?'

Cat stared into her glass of wine before taking a gulp. 'I don't know. It's weird, though. I always thought I had no roots in this world because I didn't know my birth family. But then I went to Thistle Bay and made these amazing connections and, ironically, it's biology that risks screwing it up.'

Cat moved to the window and stared out at the street below. Both sides were lined with parked cars. Rachel had a view of the tenement flats opposite her building and the black-lidded communal bins below. The location suited her. Rachel liked to be within walking distance of the city centre so she could drink red wine and walk home and the only bus she had to rely on was the one she took to work every day. Her car barely moved from its permit-holders-only parking space from one week to the next.

The sun was slipping behind the tenements and Cat's thoughts drifted to the pumpkin festival – the night she had decided Thistle Bay was the place she wanted to live. She had returned to Gloria's that night feeling as though she'd finally found a place to call home. And Nick. The red wine, the fireworks, the walk home, the kiss – it was all so exhilarating.

Oh, how she missed Nick. In her attempt to be professional, she had pushed him away. But whatever was happening between her and the Knight family was far from professional. If it was true that Catherine Knight was her mother then this was about as personal as it got, and she was quite entitled to talk to her friends about her personal life. She took another swig of wine. He may be Ryan's friend, but Cat knew he wanted to be more than friends with her. If she hadn't ruined it.

The confusion she'd felt when she fled had lifted. She turned and looked at Rachel. 'I'm done looking for family,' she said. 'I'm just going to build my own community. Starting with Nick.'

Rachel furrowed her brow. 'And how does Nick feel?'

Cat smiled, walked over to grab Rachel's car keys from the table beside the door and jangled them in front of her best friend's face. 'Only one way to find out.'

'I can't drive,' said Rachel, holding up her wine glass.

'Damn it!'

'But don't you think you're rushing into this? It's OK to take some time to process everything.'

'I already know,' said Cat. 'That place suited me. I made more real attachments in that town in just two weeks than I ever made in places I've spent years living in. And I want to be with Nick, if I haven't screwed it up completely. Not only was I horrible to him, I basically slated his business and tried to get him to do something he clearly doesn't want to do.'

Rachel nodded and patted the space beside her. 'It sounds to me like it's just his ego that's bruised. He'll get over that. What about the Knights?'

Cat dropped to the floor again. 'At this point, I don't really care what they have to say. Regardless of what happens with them, I'm supposed to be there.'

'Shouldn't you talk to them before you decide anything?'

Cat shrugged her shoulders. They'd had two weeks to talk to her and hadn't done it. Alan Knight had disappeared on day one and the others had kept up the charade of Cat being nothing but their copywriter. She had kept Nick at arm's length to make sure she did a good job and didn't get distracted – but it hadn't really been a job at all. It had been a way for the Knights to suss her out before being honest with her. The entire trip was a farce. Alan Knight could have told Cat the truth during their meeting in Los Angeles. Instead, he'd dragged her to Thistle Bay and allowed her to be abandoned all over again.

Rachel flipped the pages of Cat's photo album. 'Is this your mum's brother?'

Cat glanced at the photo. 'I guess so. I never met him. Well, obviously I did, but I don't remember him. I would've been about five then.'

'Who's the girl?'

Cat took the album and studied the photo. Her eyes widened and she gave a sharp intake of breath. 'Oh my God.'

'What?'

'That man is Alan Knight.'

Rachel snatched the album back. 'It can't be. Oh my God. Could it be?'

'It was twenty-five years ago but it definitely is.' Cat pointed to the girl next to him. 'And I think that's Rebecca.'

Cat drained her wine glass, put it on the table beside the sofa and studied the images of Alan and Rebecca. Alan's complexion was smooth without the lines he now had. His dark hair was the same shade as Rebecca's. Rebecca looked like a teenager, which would fit the timeline. Their younger faces beamed towards the camera, with Joe and Jessie on their left and five-year-old Cat grinning in the middle.

Cat couldn't remember the day this photograph was taken but she'd seen it in the album over the years. It was near the back of the book. There were only four other photographs after it in the album and Cat's attention had always been drawn to her parents. Their time together was almost over at that point and none of them had known it.

This photograph was proof that the Knights had not only known about Cat, they'd known exactly where to find her. A tear slipped down her cheek and Rachel's question hung unanswered in her head. *Why now?*

'Maybe I do care a little bit about what they've got to say,' said Cat.

30

Nick logged out of his computer, flicked off the lights and lumbered upstairs to the flat. He had just reached the flat door when he heard a thumping on his front door downstairs. He glanced at his watch. He'd locked up the gallery an hour ago and wasn't expecting anyone. For a brief second he allowed himself to hope that Cat was standing on the other side of the door. She wasn't. He opened it to find Ryan there, pain etched all over his face.

'Got time for that beer?' Ryan asked.

'Come on in.'

Nick led Ryan upstairs to the flat and opened two bottles of beer while Ryan took a seat on the sofa in the living room. He handed Ryan one of the beers, sat at the opposite end of the sofa and listened as his friend blurted out everything that had happened over the last two months – locating Cat, Alan meeting her and asking her to come to Thistle Bay, Megan's arrival and, finally, Cat's reaction. Nick had seen that reaction. Her heartache must have been unbearable and he understood now why she had chosen to flee.

'And Cat just found out about all of this?' Nick realised

that in between the confusion of trying to work out how this was all possible, he was a little relieved – the thought had crossed his mind that something romantic might have blossomed then soured between Cat and Ryan when he'd seen it was Ryan she was running from the day she left.

'Yes,' said Ryan.

'What the hell were you thinking?' asked Nick.

'What were we supposed to do?'

'Oh, I don't know,' said Nick. 'Tell her the truth.'

Ryan gave a heavy sigh and clawed at the back of his neck. 'I know. That was our intention. We just didn't anticipate how hard it would hit Dad. He's had years of making decisions that he thought were right for everyone and then decades of feeling guilty about those decisions. Seeing her here just brought it all back to him.'

Nick nodded. It was never going to be an easy situation to deal with. He could see that. 'How's Alan doing?'

'We haven't told him she's gone yet. I was hoping I could get her back before he realises.' Ryan took another mouthful of his beer and then rubbed his eyes with his hand. 'Do you know where she is?'

'No. Well, I know she'll be at Rachel's but I don't know where that is. I don't even know Rachel's last name.'

Ryan swore under his breath. 'She's not answering her phone. Not that I can blame her.'

'Have you tried emailing her?'

'Rebecca has.'

'Did you know that she was thinking about staying in Thistle Bay?'

Ryan's mouth dropped open. 'No, I didn't,' he said, his voice flat.

'She was worried about what you guys would think.'

Ryan's eyes narrowed.

'She thought you might think it was odd. You'd hired her to do a job and wouldn't have expected her to hang around. She grew up in care and has been looking for somewhere to build a life of her own ever since.'

Ryan put his head in his hands. 'I hope we haven't ruined that for her.'

Nick hoped the same thing. This news was life-changing for Cat and he needed to give her space to talk to the Knights and figure out what kind of relationship she wanted with them – if only he could find her. Nick had never been clearer about the kind of relationship he wanted with Cat. But now wasn't the time to ask her if she wanted the same.

31

THE NEXT MORNING, CAT HAD A SUITCASE PACKED AND waiting by the door before Rachel was even awake. Only one night away from Thistle Bay and she found herself craving the tranquillity of the town. In her search for somewhere to call home, she'd always stuck to big cities; she could be anonymous and she found it easy to connect with other people who had relocated for a variety of reasons. In truth, those connections were superficial and had ended up being reduced to the liking of an occasional photo on social media without any of these people having a real idea of what was happening in each other's lives.

Rachel came out of her bedroom and squinted a sleepy look at Cat's suitcase. 'Have I got time for a coffee, at least, before we go?'

'I'll get the train. I'm sure Arthur wouldn't mind picking me up from the station.'

'Nonsense. I'm driving you. And before you protest, I've got two free periods this morning. So, do I have time for that coffee?'

Cat smiled at her friend and glanced down at the phone in her hand. 'Of course. It's still early.'

Rachel gestured at the phone. 'Did you call Nick?'

'No, that was Gloria. She's got a room for me so at least I'll have somewhere to stay until I get something else sorted.'

She followed Rachel to the kitchen and wiped down the surfaces as Rachel made them both coffees. Cat rinsed the sponge under the hot tap and sprayed a lavender-scented cleaning product into the sink.

'Are you really staying up there?' asked Rachel.

'If I stay here I'm just running from it, and that's not me.'

'So, you're going to talk to the Knights?'

Cat nodded and dried her hands. She took her coffee to the living room and perched on the sofa opposite the one Rachel had just sat down on. Her heart thumped against her chest at the magnitude of it all. 'I know it's not going to be a quick fix. There's thirty years of history and heartbreak on both sides. But I need to face it. I don't know what they want from me, but I certainly have questions for them. I think I must have been in shock yesterday.'

Cat picked up her photo album from the coffee table and slotted it into her handbag alongside her laptop. She pressed the button on her phone to check the time.

Rachel nodded at the memory stick sitting beside Cat's phone on the table. 'What's that?'

'The final copy and photos. It's done. They may as well have it, even if they don't plan to use it.'

Rachel took a gulp of her coffee and stood up. 'I can't stand it anymore. Let's pour these into takeaway cups and get going.'

'I have one more call to make, but I can do that from the car.'

Cat arrived at Gloria's bed and breakfast with one suitcase this time instead of three. She'd packed light, uncertain about the duration of her stay.

Rachel leaned forward to look up at the building from the driver's seat. 'It's so pretty. It's funny seeing all these places you've talked so much about. You sure you don't want me to stick around? I have no issues about phoning in sick to work.'

'Thanks, but no. I'll give you a call.'

Cat climbed out of the car and took her suitcase from the back seat. Gloria had already opened the front door and was waiting for her. She was immaculately turned out as usual. Her navy trousers had been paired with a lilac knitted top and a chunky navy-beaded necklace.

Cat turned back to Rachel. 'Thanks again.' She closed the car door, watched Rachel drive off along the promenade, and took a deep breath.

Gloria ushered Cat into the lobby. 'I was so happy when I got your call. I've kept the same room for you, hen. Come on inside.'

Before Gloria closed the door, Cat tried to give Josef a wave but he was busy with a line of customers. She did notice, though, that he was using the chair Nick gave him – that was about as much rest as they could force him to have, such was his independence and stubbornness.

She hadn't told Nick she was coming back to Thistle Bay. She was torn between her desire to rush to the gallery and kiss him and feeling desperately ashamed about what she had said to him the last time she saw him.

'Have you spoken with Alan yet?' asked Gloria.

Cat shook her head. 'They don't know that I'm here yet.'

'Goodness, why not? They'll be delighted to see you. I know Alan was devastated about how things turned out. They're a good family. None of them wanted to hurt you.'

'Does everyone in town know?'

'Goodness, no!'

'So, I'm a secret, am I?'

'Only if you want to be.'

'Alan wants me to be. I think that's why I've barely seen him. The sordid little secret of the Knight family.'

Gloria squeezed Cat's hands. 'Alan doesn't think that way. He values family above all else, and he's your father.'

'Is he?'

'Well, of course he is. That's what we're talking about, isn't it?' Gloria's voice had suddenly gone higher as though in fear that she had let something slip that she shouldn't have.

'Rebecca said Catherine Knight was my birth mother. I left before she could tell me any more.'

Gloria's shoulders slumped with visible relief. 'He's your father.'

'Then why did they give me up? Did they just not want a fifth child?'

Gloria paused and she squinted her eyes as if trying to work out what she should say and what she shouldn't. 'From the minute you walked in here, I knew who you were. Catherine, your mother, was my best friend. You look just like her when she was your age. The day after you arrived, I went to see Alan to find out what was going on.' Cat remembered. She had seen Gloria at the chocolate shop on her first day and Gloria hadn't seemed too happy about something. 'He said he brought you over here to tell you the truth, but he wanted to wait until all of the family were together.'

'Meaning Megan?'

Gloria nodded. 'Honestly, I think he got scared. You look so much like your mother. I think that brought back lots of painful memories for him, which upset him more than he realised it would.'

Cat was finding it hard to feel sorry for Alan because she still didn't understand what had happened to cause this situation. She'd heard how lovingly he spoke of his children and seen how much affection he had for them when they were together. She couldn't imagine what might have happened to make him want to give her away.

'My parents – my adoptive parents – told me that my birth mother was too ill to look after me.'

'Oh, she was. That's how I came to work for the family. When they moved back to Thistle Bay, I spent a lot of time with Catherine and the kids. Catherine was so distraught over losing you that she struggled to function. I helped out where I could and eventually Alan asked me to help on a full-time basis.'

'If she was so distraught, why did she give me up?'

'You need to talk to Alan about that. But she didn't give you up. She cried for you every day of the life she had left.'

Gloria pulled a tissue from her pocket and dabbed at her eyes. If Gloria and Catherine really had been best friends then Gloria must have known a lot more than she was telling – there wasn't much that Cat wouldn't discuss with Rachel, and vice versa. But Cat was grateful for the details that Gloria had felt able to share with her. Somehow, their chat had dampened her nerves and amplified her need to see Alan. She was ready to hear the full story and he was the only person who could give it to her.

32

THE SOLE CUSTOMER IN THE GALLERY WAS A MAN WHO LOOKED to be in his sixties. He had spent so long staring at the same painting that Nick wondered if he was one of those people who could sleep standing up. Even Skye had interrupted her snooze a few times to check if the man had moved. The gallery wasn't exactly known for its noise, but never had a customer stood for so long in the same spot without even the occasional shuffling of their shoes.

'It's a lovely piece, isn't it?' Nick said, unable to stand the strange silence any longer.

The man simply nodded, still transfixed by the field of poppies in front of him and obviously not up for any conversation.

'Just call me if there's anything I can help you with.'

'Actually,' the man said, finally breaking his gaze on the painting as he turned to face Nick, 'I'll take this one. Can you keep it for me and I'll be back to pick it up tomorrow?'

'Of course. Just let me take your details.'

Nick led the man to his desk and picked up his order

book. 'That painting is one of my favourites. It's actually the first piece I found when I was setting up the gallery.'

'There's something special about it. I can't put my finger on what exactly, but I know I have to buy it.'

Nick nodded. 'It had the same effect on me. Can I take your name, please?'

'Arthur Jenson.' He slid a credit card across the desk.

Nick processed the payment and took his contact details. 'I'll just pop a sold sign on the painting until I can package it up for you. Is it for you or is it a gift?'

Arthur Jenson shook his head. 'Honestly, I don't know yet. I just felt as though I had to have it.'

Nick placed a sold card on the wall just beneath the painting. These were the sales he liked – when the customer bought a piece just because it spoke to them. It was how he now chose all new art for the gallery; he selected only the pieces that his intuition told him to show. 'Well, you've picked a fine painting. I'll have it ready for you first thing tomorrow, Mr Jenson.'

As the man left, Nick looked down at his completed order form and the name he'd just taken down leapt out at him. He didn't know exactly where Cat had gone, but he knew a man who did.

'Skye, here girl.'

Skye stood up and groggily stretched out her back. Nick grabbed her lead from the back room and locked up the gallery as they left.

On the walk to Alan Knight's house, Nick contemplated speaking to Arthur directly and going after Cat himself. He so desperately wanted to see her and bring her back. What Ryan had told him was too huge, though. If the Knights were Cat's biological family, she needed the space to process that and consider the implications. She had to talk to them, regardless of whether or not she wanted a relationship with them. Nick tracking her down and telling her how he felt about her could only add to her stress.

Nick noticed Arthur's car in the driveway and an abandoned sponge on the car roof, but no Arthur. He headed around the outside of the house expecting to spot Alan and whoever else was there through the kitchen windows. The family always gathered in the spacious kitchen-diner at the back of the house and since he was a boy he'd used their back door when visiting. They were all in the garden, though – Alan, Rebecca and the boys, Elizabeth, Megan and Ryan. Ryan and Megan appeared to be keeping the kids occupied while the others sat huddled around Alan on the patio furniture. Nick had hoped to see Ryan there and was glad his hunch had been right. He wasn't sure if anyone else knew that Ryan had told him everything.

Alan jumped to his feet as soon as he saw Nick approaching. 'Have you heard from Cat?'

'No.'

Alan looked dejected and he looked older, as though he had aged considerably over the past few weeks. 'How was she when you last saw her?' he asked.

Nick glanced at Ryan but decided there had already been too many secrets. 'She wasn't good. She needs to hear how this happened and what you expect from her going forward.'

Alan ran his hands across his face. 'We expect nothing from her. I hope she'll want to get to know us and become part of our family – her family. It won't be that easy, I realise.'

Alan turned away, shuffled back over to one of the patio chairs and slumped down into it. Nick had never seen Alan like this. He was always so assured and in control. Ryan was watching his father, deep worry lines etched on his face. Nick couldn't help thinking that although it must be a shock for Ryan and the others to see their dad like this, they had only prolonged Alan's agony by not being upfront with Cat as soon as she had arrived.

'Grandpa, you look sad,' Nick heard Liam say.

'We're going to do a show to make you happy again,' said Oliver. 'Mummy, can you help us?'

Rebecca was receiving her orders from the boys as Megan and Elizabeth chose the chairs on either side of Alan.

Ryan sighed and scratched his head. 'It must have been pretty full on to go from having no family to having us lot. We've still not heard from her.'

'Arthur took Cat back to Edinburgh,' said Nick. 'He probably took her straight to Rachel's door.'

Ryan relaxed his shoulders at this news and he reached out and hugged Nick. 'I'm going. I need to speak to her. Her silence is just torture.'

Nick slapped his friend on the back a few times and pulled away. 'Just remember that she's been waiting thirty years to figure out where she came from. That must have been worse.'

'I know.'

'Uncle Ryan,' yelled Liam. 'We're about to start.'

'Shall we go and watch the show before I get Arthur and head off to find Cat? It looks like your hound has a starring role,' said Ryan nodding in the direction of an obedient Skye being led around the grass in a circle by Oliver, her tail wagging in excitement at all the attention.

33

ARTHUR WAS WASHING HIS CAR ON THE DRIVEWAY WHEN CAT arrived at Alan Knight's house. She had spent the afternoon in her room at Gloria's pretending she was finishing up some work when in reality she had been unsuccessfully scouring the Internet for details about the Knight family.

Now, she stared up at Alan's sprawling two-storey home and wondered what it would have been like to grow up here. The house sat on a sizeable plot with a roomy gravel driveway that led to a double garage. The crisp white exterior was capped with a slate roof that matched the charcoal-grey front door. Natural stone paving slabs formed a path to the front door then wrapped around the side of the house, out of sight.

There were pots of ornate shrubs on the path and an expanse of lush green grass to the left that Cat could imagine a young Elizabeth or Rebecca playing on. Neatly trimmed hedges provided privacy from the street but the double gates to the driveway were decorative wrought-iron railings with lots of gaps for anyone to peer through if the gates were closed.

The driveway had three cars parked on it, including Arthur's, and there was easily space for another three. It occurred to Cat that Alan probably wasn't alone. She had squandered almost the entire day and it was likely that some of the other Knights were there too.

Arthur, who must have known she was there by now, continued to sponge the windows on his car. Discreet as ever.

'Hi.' Cat forced a smile and tried to ignore the pounding in her head.

'It's good to see you back,' said Arthur. 'They're all in the garden. Just head round the side of the house.'

So, he wasn't alone. 'Thanks.'

Cat edged towards the back garden. The nerves in the pit of her stomach were once again strong but she kept her feet moving forwards. At least this time she didn't feel ambushed, as she had been in the office.

Children's voices carried towards her – Rebecca's boys, she presumed. She pushed open the blue iron gate and saw the boys whizzing around with Skye. Everyone had their backs towards Cat as they watched the children, but her eyes locked on Nick instantly. He was sitting with Ryan, and Rebecca was kneeling on the grass in front of them.

'Turn around,' she whispered, keeping her eyes trained on Nick. Her heart thudded in her chest. Seeing the entire family together was too daunting. Her shoes clung to the stone path and she couldn't move any closer.

One of the twins – she wasn't sure which – tumbled on the grass. Skye barked, thinking it was a game, and clambered on top of the boy. The laughter made Cat jump and she backed away from the garden.

'Did you find them?' Arthur asked when Cat returned to the driveway.

'I did, thank you.' Cat paused and reached into her bag. 'Can I ask you a favour, Arthur?'

'Of course. Do you need a ride?'

She shook her head. 'Not this time. Please would you give this memory stick to one of the Knights?'

'I can do that.'

Cat placed the memory stick on the wall near Arthur but safely away from the bucket of water he was using to clean the car. With shaky hands, she rooted around in her bag again and fished out the key for her room at Gloria's.

'I'll see you around, Arthur.'

'I'm glad.'

Cat stalked away from the house. Her nails dug into her sweaty palm as she gripped the key. Bile rose in her throat and she swallowed hard. She sucked in a deep breath and ignored the urge to sit down, forcing her legs to keep moving forwards.

34

Cat shivered even though Gloria's lounge was cosy from the late-afternoon sun streaming in the window. She cursed herself for not having had the courage to speak up at Alan's house. All she'd had to do was take another step into that garden and she would have the answers she sought. But she'd chosen to run away. Again. She wasn't even sure what she was afraid of. Thistle Bay was where she wanted to be for a number of reasons. What if the Knights didn't want her to stay? What if her horrible words had already broken what she and Nick had?

From her vantage point in the window, Cat had the perfect view of the sun sinking lower in the sky. She also saw Ryan racing straight for Gloria's front door. She wilted further back into the chair and looked away. Her breath caught in her throat when the door opened and the now familiar chime rang out.

'Hello, son,' she heard Gloria say.

From the silence, Cat knew Ryan was likely hugging Gloria. He was a hugger, she remembered from the first time she met him, and he seemed to hug Gloria every time they met. She knew now that Gloria had been the only mother figure he had really known since his own mother . . . their own mother . . . hadn't been around.

'I'm looking for Cat. Is she here?'

'No. She went to your dad's house about an hour ago.'

'I've just come from there. Arthur said she'd been there, but she left without seeing us.'

'Oh no, poor girl. This must be so hard for her.'

Cat contemplated staying quiet and sneaking back upstairs to her room. She shook her head. The gathering in the garden had unnerved her, but here was Ryan and he was on his own. She could at least get some of the answers without everyone sitting around watching for her reaction.

'Let me give her a call,' said Gloria.

Cat stood and moved to the door, the cool air from the hallway causing her to shiver again. Gloria saw her first and gave her a gentle smile. Ryan turned and let out a loud breath when he saw her. He walked towards her and scooped her up in his arms for a hug. His grip was tight and he held her for a long time. Tears threatened to flow and she closed her eyes, gripping Ryan back.

The door chimed again and Ryan released her.

'You two kids need to talk,' said Gloria. She put a hand on Cat's shoulder and nudged her back into the lounge. 'You can talk in here.'

Gloria watched them until they were seated in the window. Cat chose the same comfy armchair she'd just vacated and Ryan sat on the sofa opposite her.

'Your mother would be so happy to see you kids together.' Gloria's cheeks were rosy and her eyes glistened as she pulled the door closed to leave them alone.

'I'm sorry, Cat. We didn't handle this situation well at all.'

'Neither did I.' Her voice cracked and Ryan's eyes held

hers a moment longer before she looked down. She found it difficult to look at him without tearing up again and she didn't want to cry. She wanted answers. 'I had so many questions, but my mind is blank,' she said.

'Shall I just tell you what *we* know?'

Cat nodded. 'Wait. Is your dad my dad too?' Although Gloria had said he was, that question had been eating away at her. It was clear that Gloria was keeping something from her and she had begun to think it was maybe an extra-marital affair – that would explain why Catherine had had to give her up and why Alan couldn't bring himself to be around her since she'd arrived.

'Yes, he is,' said Ryan.

Cat leaned back into the chair and sighed as relief surged through her body. It wasn't that she was desperate for Alan Knight to be her father. She just didn't want to be the person that tore a family to shreds. It was all too common for happy families to implode when affairs were revealed.

Ryan shifted in his seat. 'But there's something you need to know for all of this to make sense.'

'Oh God. What else?' Her thoughts escaped her lips before she realised.

'You and I were born on the same night, in the same hospital, but to two different mothers. There was a mistake and I ended up with Catherine and you . . .' Ryan's words trailed off. It was as if something had caught in his throat and he couldn't finish what he was saying.

'Catherine Knight is not your mother?' Cat wanted to make sure she understood the implications of what Ryan was saying.

'She wasn't my biological mother.'

Cat struggled to grasp what that meant. 'Are you saying that you and I were switched at birth?'

Ryan nodded and slumped back in his chair as though he had finally unburdened himself.

Cat shook her head. 'That can't happen. That can't be true.'

Ryan leaned forward again. 'It is. This whole thing started thirty years ago when two new mothers just happened to be placed next to each other in the maternity ward.'

'So, you're not . . .' Cat didn't even know what she was trying to say. Her mind was racing with thoughts she was struggling to articulate.

'Dad told me when I was eighteen.'

'That doesn't make any sense.' Cat fumbled in her bag and pulled out her photo album. She flicked to the right page and passed the album to Ryan. 'I have a photo here of your dad and, I think, Rebecca.'

Ryan smiled and nodded. 'That's them. We have the identical photo.'

That shouldn't have been a surprise given that Alan and Rebecca were in the picture, but it was. Blood pounded in Cat's ears as dozens of questions swam through her mind. 'So, Rebecca and your dad have known about this for a long time.'

'Dad has always known. And Rebecca knew long before I did.' Ryan tipped the album up so Cat could see the photo again. 'They decided not to tell me until I was eighteen. I think Dad didn't want me going off the rails or something. Are all of these photos of you? May I take a look?'

'Sure. It's the only thing I have that belonged to my parents.'

'Joe and Jessie, right?'

Cat licked her dry lips and stood up. 'I need some water.'

She left Ryan alone with her photo album and headed to the kitchen. Gloria was pouring boiling water into a china teapot.

'That was good timing, hen. I thought you two could probably do with a cup of tea. Is Ryan still here?'

'Yes. And thank you. A cup of tea would be great.'

'How do you feel?' Gloria put the kettle back and pushed a tray towards Cat.

'Like I'm walking around in a daze.'

'Take your tea. I'll get the doors for you.'

Cat picked up the tray with cups, the teapot, milk and some shortbread biscuits and followed Gloria.

Gloria paused at the door, her hand hovering over the handle. 'It's such a tragic situation, but you can choose to give yourself a happy ending.'

Cat wasn't so sure about that. What was already a complicated situation had just become even muddier.

Ryan didn't look up when Cat returned. He was staring at the last photo in her album. It was a six-year-old Cat laughing hysterically at something. She put the tea tray down on the table in front of the window and sat next to him on the sofa. His breathing was shallow. He blinked hard and turned his face towards the window.

'I'm so sorry, Cat. This should have been my life, not yours. I have photos of every year of my life. Every birthday. Every family holiday. With my dad and three sisters. You should have had that.' A tear slipped down his cheek and Cat took the album from his hands.

Tightness spread across her chest. She *should* have had that, but wishing things had been different wasn't going to change anything. She gripped the album, aware that Ryan had stood to pour the tea. She wanted to tell him that he didn't have to be sorry. That it wasn't his fault. But one question still had to be asked. She just wasn't sure she wanted to know the answer.

'Why did you look for me now?'

Ryan put a cup of tea down in front of her and perched on the edge of the sofa looking directly at her. 'We never stopped looking for you. When Dad found out what had happened, he searched every way he could think of to find you. It was a few years before he succeeded and, by then, you had a family. It was an impossible situation for him. Did he take you away from the only parents you had ever known? What would've happened to me? He agreed with Joe and Jessie that you would stay with them and they agreed to allow him to visit. He thought he was doing the right thing. When your parents stopped returning his calls, he travelled to London to find out what was going on. A neighbour told him about Joe and Jessie's accident. But it was too late to get to you. He had to start his search all over again. The last formal paperwork he saw noted that you had left the local-authority area.'

Cat pressed her lips together to stop her chin from quivering. She clasped her hands and folded her body inwards.

Ryan continued. 'When I was eighteen and found out the truth, I went through all of Dad's paperwork. I even went to the hospital where we were both born. Years earlier, Dad had found a midwife who remembered Mum. Incredibly, she was still working there eighteen years later. She told me everything she could remember, but there wasn't anything that Dad didn't already know. Dad, me, Rebecca – we tried everything we could think of to find you.'

'So, what is it you want from me now?'

Ryan paused until she looked up at him. 'We want to get to know you. We want you to get to know us.'

'Why?'

'Because you're our sister.'

That was all Cat had ever wanted – to find family and know where she came from. She realised at that moment that she hadn't ever considered what she would do if she actually found someone. She had hoped to find one person who could tell her more about her birth mother – someone who knew who her mother was and what had happened. What she hadn't been expecting to find was a whole family that wanted to know her.

'Did Nick know about me?' Cat asked.

Ryan shook his head. 'No. Definitely not. He knows my story but I didn't tell him we'd found you and there's no way he could have figured it out.'

'Gloria did.'

'Gloria has some kind of superhero spy training. I was never able to keep secrets from her. The woman always caught me out.' Cat laughed – she could imagine that. 'Plus, you look like Mum. Nick never met her. He's a good guy. I'm not just saying that because he's my friend.'

'I know.'

'And he gave me a really hard time about not being honest with you when I told him what happened.' She liked the thought of that. She knew Ryan and Nick were close, but she appreciated that he was thinking of her too.

'Dad really wants to speak to you,' continued Ryan. Cat circled her shoulders back and forth, finally easing some of the tension she had been carrying there for days. 'I know I've thrown a lot at you today.' He looked as exhausted as she felt. 'So, take some time and think it through. We're all staying up at Dad's tonight. If you have any questions, come on over. Or even if you just want to hang out and see what we get up to when we're not making chocolate, we'd love to have you.'

Cat stiffened and massaged her temples. She was definitely not ready for a family get-together. 'I'd like to talk to Alan alone at some point,' she said.

'He would like that too. Whenever you want. If you want to do it tonight, the rest of us will make ourselves scarce.'

Cat raised her tea to her lips to avoid committing herself. It was all so much to take in.

'We want you in our lives, Cat, but we'll go at your pace. I know this news is huge. I had a family around me to help deal with the blow and it still took me a year to figure out how I felt about it all.' Ryan's phone rang once then cut off. He moved forward on the sofa to take it out of the back pocket of his jeans. 'If you decide to come tonight, bring Nick if it helps.'

She took a gulp of her tea, hoping to detract from the flush moving up her face, as Ryan stood up and glanced at his phone.

'That's Rebecca.' He held his phone out so Cat could see. 'Your new website is live.'

Ryan lingered for a few seconds as though hoping Cat would stand and follow him out. She couldn't. She stared into her cup and tried to control her breathing.

Gloria spoke the very second Ryan opened the lounge door. 'Is that you away, son?'

Whatever exchange followed between Ryan and Gloria was silent. The front door chimed seconds later and Cat looked up, catching the concern in Gloria's eyes as she came towards Cat.

'How are you doing, hen?' Gloria tidied up the tea tray before prising the cup of cold tea from Cat's hand. 'Can I get you something a little bit stronger? Maybe a brandy?'

Cat shook her head. 'No, thanks. Although maybe later.'

Gloria touched her hand to the side of Cat's face. 'Anytime.'

Cat moved back to the chair that faced out of the window and plucked her laptop from her bag. She switched it on and typed the Thistle Bay Chocolate Company's website address into her browser.

There they were – Cat's words with Nick's gorgeous new photos. She clicked through each of the pages and couldn't help but smile. Despite everything that had happened, she was proud of the work she had pulled together for the website. It looked so much better than what was there before. Cat loved a transformation. It was her favourite part of the job. Taking something that had outlived its purpose and transforming it into something fresh filled her with joy.

Now she just had to do the same with her life.

35

CAT ARRIVED AT ALAN KNIGHT'S HOUSE FOR THE SECOND TIME that day. It was just as picturesque against the early evening sky. Small silver bollards lit the driveway and the house itself had square lights giving off a white glow at even intervals along its façade. She'd dissected her conversation with Ryan as much as she could and knew that her remaining questions could only be answered by one person.

She'd spotted Alan watching from one of the downstairs windows on her approach. His head had then disappeared from view and the front door now opened as she was still walking up the driveway. She suspected Gloria had called him to say Cat was on her way.

With only a nod, Alan led her to a sitting room and poured them both a glass of iced water from a jug on the sideboard. A gallery wall boasted a curated collage of the Knight kids' lives. There were photographs of babies, toothless toddlers, family ski holidays, school dances, graduations. Ryan's family memories spanned decades while hers had smashed to a standstill at the age of six.

Cat sat on the sofa and regarded Alan as he crossed the room towards her with the two glasses. The professional man she'd met in Los Angeles and on her first day in Thistle Bay had vanished. His work attire had been replaced with light-coloured casual trousers and a brown woollen jumper, and he walked with a bit of a stoop.

He sat down on a chair opposite Cat, placing the water glasses on the table between them, and crossed one leg over the other, his hands gripping his knee. 'I'm so happy you came back,' he said. 'Thank you. You must have so many questions and I will answer them truthfully. Everyone is in the kitchen, but they'll give us space to talk. I'm sorry we haven't been honest up to now.'

Cat was about to say it was OK, but she stopped herself. It wasn't OK. They had lied to her and made an already difficult situation worse. She did have a lot of questions and, now, she prompted Alan to start at the very beginning. 'How did Ryan and I end up being switched?'

'Catherine, my wife, was pregnant. After ten years and four babies, we agreed this fourth child would be our last. I loved my daughters. A part of me would have liked a son, too. Catherine knew this. We had talked about it during her pregnancies. When each daughter was born, we loved her instantly and were only ever grateful for a healthy baby.'

Cat didn't like where Alan's story seemed to be going, but she stayed silent and fought to keep her composure.

'At the time,' Alan continued, 'we were living in the Philippines, where I worked. I think I told you that when we met. We wanted the baby to be born in Scotland like the others had been, so when Catherine was a little over eight months pregnant, she flew back to Scotland. The other children were at school in the Philippines so I stayed over there to start with and was going to join her a couple of weeks later. We planned to have the baby, stay on for another couple of weeks in Thistle Bay with friends, then fly back to the Philippines. Catherine arrived in London and, while waiting for her connecting flight to Edinburgh, she went into premature labour.' Cat watched as Alan's eyes glazed over as if he was reliving it. 'Everything I know about what happened next is from what Catherine told me.'

Cat listened as Alan told her the story as he understood it.

At the hospital, Catherine gave birth to a healthy baby girl. Soon after the birth, she overheard the young woman in the next bed confirming she wanted to give her son up for adoption. From the nurses' chatter, she understood the young woman to be a drug addict who felt incapable of looking after the child.

Catherine was in great pain and called out for attention, but when no one came she walked along the hall in search of a midwife to give her more pain relief. She passed an unlocked cupboard and saw packs of baby milk, tiny nappies and a box of blank identity tags. Something compelled her to take one.

Exhausted from a long labour and woozy from drugs, Catherine decided to swap her baby girl for the baby boy that was to be given up for adoption. She wrote the name Catherine on the identity tag and attached it to her daughter's wrist. She stretched and pulled the other one off and also removed the tag from the baby's ankle.

Catherine then lifted the baby boy out of his crib and laid him on her bed. She removed his pale blue blanket, wrapped it around baby Catherine and placed her in the empty plastic crib in the bay next to hers.

She yanked the tag off the wrist of the baby whose first name in the world was 'baby boy unknown'. He had no tag on his ankle. She placed the baby boy in the crib she had taken her daughter from only moments before and stumbled back to her bed.

When Catherine next woke up, a midwife was taking her pulse.

'Good morning,' the midwife said. 'I'm Penny. My shift only started an hour ago so I'll be looking after you all day today. I think the little one is ready for a feed.'

Catherine looked behind the midwife at the baby stirring in the crib. Penny turned and scooped the baby up.

'The little lamb had wriggled out of his identity bracelets, but I've reattached them for you,' she said. With a bright smile, she handed Catherine the baby.

Catherine sat motionless, her hands by her sides, staring at the little face. The baby's dark eyes were wide and still.

'That's not my baby,' said Catherine, a wailing sob escaping her lips.

Alan looked drained. Thirty years of carrying this weight on his shoulders had been lifted to reveal a broken shell of a man.

'Even through the fog of her despair, my Catherine wanted to give you a piece of herself,' said Alan. 'Unable to take you home, she gave you her name. I'm so grateful to Jessie and Joe for not changing it.'

Cat couldn't remember her parents ever telling her where her name came from, although they had always been open about her adoption so they had quite possibly mentioned it. They had called her their little kitty cat and 'Cat' had stuck. Catherine was just the name she used to fill out forms and book flights. It had never occurred to her that it might have been connected to her birth mother.

'We can take a break, if you want to,' Cat said to Alan.

Alan shook his head. 'No. It's better we just get it all out there.' He took a sip of water and shifted in his seat.

'When I arrived, Catherine was pretty out of it on medication to calm her down. The hospital told me that she was struggling to bond with the baby. That's how they phrased it. She begged me to find our real baby, but the hospital assured me that there was no mistake – Ryan was our child and Catherine was suffering from post-natal delusions. I brought her to Thistle Bay as planned and she told me the whole story almost as soon as we arrived. I'm ashamed to say I didn't know whether to believe her or not. She had been through so much and she was struggling with the day-to-day things. It wasn't long before I knew we would have to come home for good.'

'How can that happen? You give birth to a girl and take home a boy.'

'No one would tell me. I found a midwife a few years later who remembered that night. She was a trainee at the time and, even years later, was still cautious about saying too much. I think someone made a mistake, or thought they had made a mistake, and their attempts to correct it prevented the truth from coming out once Catherine realised what she had done.'

'Did you consider getting a paternity test?' Cat asked.

Alan nodded. 'I did, but it wasn't as accurate back then. The first tests could only confirm it was possible we were the biological parents. It was four years before testing was able to confirm that Ryan wasn't biologically ours. By that time, we were his parents and Joe and Jessie were yours.'

Cat opened her mouth to speak, but memories of Joe and Jessie swirled in her mind.

'Your parents were wonderful people. I can recall the anguish on Jessie's face when I tracked her down and told her what had happened. She was terrified that I'd come to take you away. And, honestly, that was my first instinct, but I thought about how I would feel if someone knocked on my door and tried to take Ryan away. Leaving you after each visit was agony.'

'You visited me more than once?'

'I did. You don't remember?' Cat shook her head. 'You were too young, I suppose. Jessie told you to call me Uncle Alan. It seems silly now, but I had hoped you might recognise me when I met you in Los Angeles.' Alan paused as if hoping his words had jogged her memory.

When she kept quiet, he continued. 'Joe was angry that such a situation could have been allowed to happen. I knew the only way forward was to be completely honest with them. I told them what Catherine had done and why. I told them how dreadful I felt at not having initially believed her, not having done more in those first few weeks. They looked at my photographs of the other children. The resemblance between you and Elizabeth as youngsters couldn't be denied and confirmed that I was telling the truth.'

Cat looked to the ceiling and pictured Elizabeth in her mind's eye. Apart from their hair colour, did any of those early similarities remain? Gloria had already told her how much she resembled her mother. Whose looks she'd inherited had been a question that Cat had pondered a lot over the years and now she had the answer.

'Your parents allowed me to meet you,' Alan continued. 'You were such a happy child. You dragged me to your bedroom to see your doll's house. It was a gift from Santa and you beamed with pride when we entered your room. You had decorated it yourself, you said, which meant you'd scribbled on every interior wall with coloured markers.'

Cat wiped a tear from her cheek. 'I didn't know I had a doll's house.'

'I have a picture of it. Would you like to see it?'

Cat stared at him open-mouthed. 'You have a picture of it. How?'

Alan stood up and strode from the room. Cat gawked after him in utter disbelief. She'd had a doll's house that she'd scribbled all over. That was the kind of childhood detail only parents remembered. And he had remembered.

Alan returned with a deep-burgundy box file and placed it on the table in front of Cat. He also handed her a silver photo frame, which she took by the very corners so as not to transfer fingerprints onto the polished metal. It was a duplicate of the image she had in her album – a five-year-old Cat, a teenaged Rebecca, her parents, and Alan. 'We keep that photograph on the wall in the kitchen,' he said.

Alan popped the button on the side of the box file and opened it. Cat recognised Jessie's handwriting on some letters. It was the same scrawl that graced the back of some of the photographs in her album. Alan rummaged inside and produced a photo of a cheerful Cat leaning against a doll's house that was almost the same height as she was. 'You're four in this photo,' said Alan. 'After my first few visits, Jessie sent me the occasional letter with updates and a handful of photos of you.'

Cat flicked through Alan's file skimming the letters and studying the photos. There were no other duplicates, just twenty or so snapshots of the best parts of her childhood that she'd never before seen. Her gaze lingered on an image of a younger Cat in a paddling pool, her sunhat so low on her face that her eyes were hidden. She held an ice cream in her chubby little hand and her grin was wide. Joe was seated on a bench behind her smiling towards the camera, his legs stretched out in front of him.

So many memories that Cat tried to keep buried came rushing back. For too long she had allowed thoughts of her parents to remind her of what she had lost. It dawned on her now that the devastatingly short duration of the life they'd spent together didn't diminish the strength of the love they'd had for each other.

'This is how Rebecca found out,' said Alan. 'She stumbled across the letters and photographs in my office when she was searching for a book on the Highland Clearances for a school project. She was fifteen – old enough to understand, but too young to carry the burden of that knowledge on her own for so many years. It's the reason she is the way she is. She became a mother figure to the other children at a very young age and is fiercely protective of Ryan in particular. We both carried with us a fear that we would lose him just as we had lost you.'

Cat pulled the box file onto her knee and cradled it in her lap. 'You could have chosen any of these other photographs to frame. Why did you choose the one with my parents in it?'

Alan seemed to ponder her question for a moment. 'It felt right. Joe and Jessie were a part of your family and that made them a part of mine. They didn't have to open their home to me. They could have reported Catherine for what she'd done – and who knows how that might have ended. Instead, they chose to put you first and allow you to have a relationship with me, despite how grim that must have been for them in the beginning. Of course, none of us knew of the tragedy to come and how fleeting that relationship would be as a result.'

Cat reached for her water and took a gulp. 'Does Ryan know his birth mother?' she asked, redirecting the conversation while she wrestled with her own traumatic memories of losing her parents.

'No. I found out she died from a drug overdose a year after giving birth. It's a tragic tale on many fronts. But out of the trauma came these two beautiful babies.'

Although she could see it was difficult for Alan to talk about all of this, she struggled to comprehend how he could remain so calm and rational. Was it just because he'd been living with it for so long? And, moreover, Ryan had been nothing but welcoming to her since she had arrived. But then, she supposed he'd also had years to process what had happened.

'When did Ryan find out about all of this?' She wanted to hear what Alan had to say about this detail that she found so hard to understand.

'I told him when he was eighteen. I wanted to tell him before, but I worried it would send him into an unhealthy spiral during his already difficult teenage years.'

The stories she was now hearing were inconceivable, but at least they matched. 'He seems . . .' She struggled for the right phrase – well-adjusted, perhaps, considering he was born to a drug-addicted mother and then snatched as a baby to be raised by a family that wasn't his. All that early trauma must have affected him in some way.

'He's grown into a wonderful young man. Of course, it took him time to find himself. His mother . . . your mother – Catherine – she wasn't around for much of his life either so I expect that actually made it . . .' Alan had a glint of tears in his eyes. For a long time, Cat had lived with the mix of emotions her family situation stirred in her. She'd spent many hours thinking about how her birth mother must have felt giving her up. Had she been relieved? Had she been sad? Would she want to meet Cat one day? Cat had also considered that her birth mother might not be alive. Not once, she realised, had she considered that there might be other members of a family dealing with their own emotional consequences of that decision of her mother's to give away her baby.

'We don't have to talk about this,' said Cat. She had only known Alan for a short time but it was difficult for her to see him like this – his commanding poise diminished by pain.

He shook his head. 'You have a right to know. You have a right to ask any questions you want answers to.'

'I find it strange that I had no family . . .' Cat's eyes darted towards a movement at the door.

Rebecca appeared, dressed in black leggings and an oversized tan-coloured jumper. With bare feet and bare lips, it was a vulnerable-looking side to her that Cat hadn't seen before.

'The website looks good,' Cat blurted out. She didn't know what to say to Rebecca and thought work was safe territory, but she cringed as soon as the words were out of her mouth.

'It looks good because of you. Thank you.' Rebecca looked down at her hands then back up at Cat. 'I'm so sorry for all of this.'

'I thought you didn't like me much,' said Cat.

Rebecca shook her head and joined Cat on the sofa. 'It wasn't that at all. I was frustrated because I knew this was likely to blow up in our faces but I felt powerless to stop it.'

Cat could imagine how that must have been for

Rebecca. She suspected the self-assured Rebecca didn't feel powerless in many situations.

'It's not her fault,' said Alan. 'It was me. When I told Ryan about his origins, the first thing he did was disappear – only for a few hours, but those hours were torture. I had an eighteen-year relationship with him that brought him back. When I thought about telling you in Los Angeles, I dreaded you having the same reaction and being five thousand miles away from us. That's why I brought you here. But I should have told you, and I'm sorry.'

Rebecca raised her hand to stop Alan from speaking further. 'It wasn't just you, Dad. It was all of us.'

Megan cleared her throat to announce her presence in the doorway, flanked by her twin nephews. 'It technically wasn't me. I told her the truth as soon as I saw her.'

'Well, that's true,' said Cat, laughing now.

Liam and Oliver ran into the room and jumped onto the sofa, wedging themselves between Rebecca and Cat. With their dark eyes and even darker hair, there was no mistaking them for Rebecca's children.

'Boys,' said Rebecca. 'Do you remember Cat?' They both nodded. 'Well, Cat is your auntie. Just like Auntie Megan and Auntie Elizabeth. Grandma Catherine had a baby who sadly got separated from the rest of the family. Cat was that baby and we were finally able to find her. That makes Cat my sister. And your auntie,' she clarified again.

The boys eyed her, their little minds no doubt trying to work it out.

'We're having a sleepover with Auntie Megan tonight. Can you come too, Auntie Cat?' asked Oliver.

Or perhaps there was nothing to work out when you were five years old. You just took it for granted that what your mum told you made absolute sense. Just as she must have done when Jessie had introduced Alan as Uncle Alan. 'Em, maybe another time,' she said.

'OK,' said Liam.

Rebecca kissed her boys goodnight and ordered them upstairs with Megan. They jumped up and ran out of the room as quickly as they had entered it, creating a commotion in the hallway as they went. Rebecca rolled her eyes and turned back to Cat. 'I hope that was all right,' she said. 'It's just occurred to me now that you might not want people to know.'

'I just . . . well . . . em.' Cat looked at Alan. 'I thought you might not want people to know.'

Rebecca narrowed her eyes in confusion as though the thought had never occurred to her.

'Why would we not want people to know about you?' asked Alan. 'We've been looking for you for such a long time. You're our family and we certainly don't want to hide that.'

Cat caught an exchange of looks between Alan and Rebecca. 'I mean, it's not just my story,' said Cat. 'How can we tell people without them questioning what happened and so finding out more about Ryan, and maybe Catherine?'

'Sure,' said Alan. 'Some people will gossip. But everyone that matters already knows about Ryan. He didn't hide it. I was going to offer you DNA testing so you could be really sure of what I'm telling you, but Rebecca says you've done that already.'

Cat shook her head. 'I haven't taken a DNA test.'

Alan looked at Rebecca. 'On that website. Isn't that what you need to do to register?'

Rebecca nodded.

'Are you talking about Find My Family?' asked Cat.

'That's the one,' said Alan. 'You give them your DNA, don't you? Then they tell you if you have a match.'

Rebecca took a deep breath. 'You haven't checked your emails then? I'm CocoB13.'

It was dark by the time Cat left Alan Knight's house . . . her dad's house. Would she ever be able to call him that? She walked back to Gloria's on her own. Although Ryan had offered to walk with her, she wanted the space to think things through before she saw anyone else. Rachel had sent her a few texts just checking in that Cat hadn't yet replied to. And she still wanted to see Nick.

When Rebecca had said she was CocoB13, Cat had immediately grabbed her phone and logged in to her Find My Family account. It was true. There it was – an email from Rebecca telling her everything. She'd had almost the full story sitting on her phone for days. She just hadn't read it.

When Cat had received the notification that CocoB13 had replied she'd stopped herself from reading the email so it didn't influence her decision about staying in Thistle Bay. But, she realised now, she had already made her decision. That morning on Blakely Hill, watching the sun rise over Thistle Bay, Cat had never felt more at home. Then, when Megan had blurted out the news, there had been so much going on that Cat had almost forgotten about the email.

She stood now at the end of Main Street, with Gloria's to her left and Nick's to her right. Cat looked up at Nick's flat. A faint glow was coming from the glass doors in his living room that led to the small terrace above the gallery.

She crossed the road. Her hand hovered above the doorbell at the gallery door. She was exhausted. After the day she'd just had, she wasn't sure she could face the rejection if Nick didn't want to see her.

She turned and headed back to Gloria's.

Cat caught Gloria's eye through the lounge window – she was sitting in the chair that Cat had occupied for much of the day. As soon as Cat opened the front door, there was Gloria.

'Oh, come here.' Gloria opened her arms and an emotional Cat fell into them.

36

Nick pinned an image of a solitary seashell on the sand to his wall of photographs. He stood back and appraised his work – fifty prints that captured the essence of Thistle Bay. Everything he loved about this town. It was the side of the town he wanted to share with disillusioned locals – of which there were a few – and with tourists who had yet to discover all that the town had to offer. The project had proved to be a useful distraction after Cat walked out. Even more so now that she was back but hadn't come to see him.

'I think we're done,' Nick said. He peered around the sliding door into the gallery but Skye didn't even bother to open her eyes. She lay stretched out in front of the stove where she had been for the last hour drying herself off after their early-morning run along the beach. Nick left her to sleep and gathered up the five mugs that he'd used then discarded across multiple surfaces. He sighed as he scrubbed the coffee stains from the ceramic. For a sleepy little town, a lot had happened over the last couple of days.

Nick had long known that Ryan was not Alan and Catherine Knight's biological son. Alan had told Ryan when he'd turned eighteen and Ryan had gone straight over to confide in Nick. It was the summer before they went off to universities on opposite sides of the country and perhaps this was the bond that had kept them close. From that day, Nick had always admired how Ryan handled the situation; it would have been so easy for the news to damage the relationship he had with Alan and his sisters.

Nick still remembered how Ryan had trembled the day that Alan told him. Nick's parents were hosting a barbecue at their house and he had invited Ryan, as he often did. Ryan turned up an hour early and Nick had initially thought he was ill – his pale skin was clammy with sweat and his hands were shaking. They'd sat in the dining room as Nick's mum prepared the food and his dad washed the garden furniture before their guests arrived.

'How does a hospital accidentally mix up babies?' Nick couldn't believe the story he'd just heard. 'How do you feel about it?'

'I don't know,' Ryan had said. 'I really can't remember much about my mum. About Catherine, I mean. But I can't help but think her illness was caused by me. The others grew up without their mother because of me.'

'Are you angry with the baby you were switched with?'

'Of course not.'

'Why not?'

'It's hardly her fault. She was just a day old when it happened.'

'Exactly.' Nick had drawn him to the point, but he could see the thoughts still spinning around Ryan's mind – the confusion, the regret, the undeserved guilt. When Ryan sighed, Nick continued questioning him. 'So, the other baby is a girl. Do you know where she is?'

Ryan shook his head.

Nick's mum had peered around the dining-room door at that moment with a mug of tea in her hand and a plate of shortbread biscuits. She put the mug in front of Ryan and smoothed the hair off his face. 'I've put some sugar in your tea, love. It'll be good for the shock. Drink up, then go and see your dad. It sounds like you both have lots to talk about.' Later, Nick had asked his mum if she'd known about Ryan before. She hadn't. It was hard to keep a secret in a small town but it seemed as though that one had remained hidden for almost two decades.

Over the next year, Nick had kept in regular contact with Ryan as he came to terms with his background and, during holidays when they were both home from university, he'd watched Ryan rebuilding his relationship with his dad. Alan had found out that Ryan's birth mother had died from a drug overdose within a year of him being born, and a midwife who remembered the case had told him that she was just a teenager when she'd given birth. There was no one in the delivery room with her and no one had waited outside for her. There was also apparently no record of who his birth father was. That had quashed any desire Ryan might have had to further trace his ancestry. He'd focused instead on trying to find the baby girl he had been mistaken for, but without success. Until now, it seemed.

When Ryan had texted Nick last night to say that Cat had reappeared and they'd told her the full story, Nick had typed out and deleted three messages to her. He plucked his phone from the back pocket of his jeans again and reopened his messages, empathising a bit more now with how hard it must have been for Alan to find the words to tell her the truth sooner.

But Nick locked his phone again, flicked the switch on the kettle and dried a mug. Letting Cat walk away from him that day went against every instinct he had, but he had done it anyway. He thought he knew better than to try to force someone to stay where they didn't want to be. He saw now that he was wrong. A message wouldn't cut it. He had to see her. He fixed himself a coffee while he waited for a more respectable hour and moved to head back into the gallery.

He stopped in the doorway. Skye was on her feet, her tail wagging. Kneeling down beside her was Cat, stroking Skye's ear with one hand and holding a package in the other.

She looked up at him, her face pale and serious. 'Hi.'

'How are you?' he asked.

She stood up and shrugged. 'I'm not sure. I didn't know if you would want to see me.'

'That's all I wanted to do.'

She stepped forward and put the package she was carrying on his desk. He ignored it and walked towards her, put his coffee down and wrapped his arms tightly around her. She melted into his arms and buried her face in his T-shirt.

He was reluctant to let her go and just held her until she took a deep breath.

Cat pulled back and pushed her hair off her face. 'Can you believe all of this?'

'It was a pretty unbelievable story twelve years ago. But this . . .' He struggled to find the words and indicated that they should go and sit by the stove.

Cat took off her coat, unwrapped a green scarf from around her neck and sat down. She leaned forward to warm her hands in the stove's heat.

'They're good people, you know,' said Nick. 'They haven't handled it well, but they would never want to hurt you. Honestly, I think they had just been looking for you for so long that they didn't know what to do once they'd found you.'

'I can relate to that. I freaked out a bit too. And I took it out on you and I shouldn't have.'

Nick shook his head. 'You don't have to deal with this on your own, you know.'

'That's my default position.'

'It's time to change that. You've got a dad, a brother, three sisters. And me,' he added. Ever since the night a jellyfish had got its tentacles on her foot, he couldn't stop scouting the town for her. His eyes zeroed in on Josef's stall whenever he left the gallery, he scanned the tables in Mystic's café umpteen times a day, and he'd even taken to walking Skye up Main Street at lunchtimes hoping to catch a glimpse of Cat in the chocolate shop. He wanted her in his life. He knew she had a lot, probably too much, to sort out first; if he had to settle for being her friend right now, he would do that.

Cat put her head in her hands. 'I don't know how to deal with this.'

With *this* or with *him*? He didn't like to ask. 'Do you want a distraction?' he said. She sat up straighter and bit her lower lip. 'I want to show you something.'

'Are you taking me upstairs again? The last time you did that you plied me with wine and then made me get up at silly o'clock in the morning.'

Nick laughed. 'I'm pretty sure the early morning came before the wine.'

'If you say so.'

'This time I just want to take you through there.' He gestured behind him and stood up. She got to her feet too and followed him into his back room, Skye scampering behind them not wanting to miss the action.

Nick dug his hands into the pockets of his trousers and watched her take in the wall covered in his photographs. She examined each one. He saw her shoulders relax as she moved from picture to picture, touching some of them on her way past.

'What is this?' she asked.

'It's how I see Thistle Bay. It's the photos I'm going to print, frame and sell in the gallery.'

She looked down at her feet then lifted her eyes slightly. 'I'm sorry about what I said and about the flyer. It wasn't my place to tell you how to run your business.'

He shook his head. 'You just verbalised everything I'd been thinking but was too slow to act on.'

She stared back along the wall. 'They're incredible, Nick . . . Do you have space for one more?'

Before he could reply, she headed back into the gallery and returned a few seconds later with the package she'd left on his desk. 'I got you this. An apology, you could say. Although, thinking about it, I ordered it at the same time as the flyer so it's not really an apology, it's the second part of me meddling in your business.'

He took the package from her outstretched hand and peered inside. He wiggled the frame out and recognised the eerie beauty of a cool blue sky with the golden glow of the sun peeking above the horizon. A scattering of clouds reflected in the tranquil sea, together with a strip of sand at the base of the image, brought texture to the photograph. The print had been set within a thick white border surrounded by a sleek black frame, and a typed caption at the bottom read *Sunrise in Thistle Bay*.

Cat crossed her arms over her chest and cleared her throat. 'It's one of my favourites. I emailed it to myself when you weren't looking. My method was sneaky, but my motive was honourable.'

'I love it, Cat. But I won't be selling this one. I've got the perfect spot for it upstairs.'

Seeing some colour return to her cheeks was a relief. He felt a morsel of hope that they would be together and he clung tightly to it.

She raised a hand to fidget with her earring. 'I don't think Josef has seen me yet. Do you want to come over with me? We could say hello and then take a walk along the beach.'

Nick grinned. 'Yeah, I do.'

Skye, who had been sitting just inside the doorway watching them, suddenly burst into life and leaped towards Cat.

'Are you coming too?' Cat asked, reaching down to ruffle the fur of the spaniel. 'Did you hear the word walk?'

Skye spun in a circle and darted back and forth between Nick and Cat. Nick savoured Cat's laughter as it echoed through the gallery, interspersed with the clicking of claws as Skye scurried across the wooden floor. Nick laid the picture on his desk and followed Cat and Skye out onto the street.

37

CAT HAD TO WAIT UNTIL JOSEF HAD SERVED TWO CUSTOMERS before she could get near him, but he gave her a nod to indicate he had seen her. A gust of wind blew in from the North Sea and she pulled her scarf tighter around her neck and dug her hands into her coat pocket. When Josef's customers had gone, he got up from his stool and came out from behind the stall.

'Lovely Cat. You've come home.' He walked over and hugged her. 'And I see you two are still friends.' He released her and raised his eyebrows. 'Or maybe more than that?'

'Maybe,' she said, glancing back at Nick, standing a couple of steps behind her, who smiled, which she hoped was a good sign and meant she hadn't completely ruined things with him.

'Let me get you a Berliner for your breakfast.' Josef hurried back to his food stall and Cat was glad to see no trace of his sprained ankle. 'Jam or custard?' he called over his shoulder.

'Ooh, custard, please.' Cat touched her stomach. Gloria had already fed her up with smoked salmon and scrambled eggs so she really didn't need any more food, but Josef's baking was impossible to resist.

Josef leaned forward from behind his stall. 'Nick?'

'Custard is good for me, too. Thank you.'

Josef passed them each a paper bag and rocked back and forth on his toes as he waited, his eyes sparkling as if in anticipation of the praise about to come his way.

Cat bit into the deliciously doughy treat and nodded as her mouth filled with a sweet vanilla custard that was as satisfying as that first sip of hot coffee in the morning. 'Mmm,' she said as she chewed. 'It's so good. This might be my new favourite.'

'I'll show you how to make them one day. You too, Nick. I know you have a certain fondness for my kitchen. Or was it just for the girl in my kitchen?' Josef's laugh was a rumble in his chest. He squeezed Cat's arm and left them to go and serve another customer.

Cat turned to Nick. 'He's not going to let us forget that one, is he?'

'Doesn't look like it.'

Skye ran on ahead of them to the beach and made straight for the water. They walked along in an easy silence for a minute finishing their doughnuts.

'Things are still pretty tense with the Knights,' Cat said.

Nick nodded. He took her empty paper bag, folded it into a square and stuffed it into the pocket of his jeans. 'It'll take time. It's a cliché, I know, but it's true.'

'I still don't like how they handled the situation. Alan should have told me when he saw me in Los Angeles. Or Rebecca could have replied to my message on Find My Family much sooner and we could have taken it from there. But what's done is done.' Her voice came out sharper than she'd intended.

Nick brushed his fingers against hers as they walked, the small movement making her quiver.

'They invited me over for dinner tonight. I'm not sure what I'll do about it yet. I mean, I suppose I'll go. I'll need to do it at some point, right?' She appreciated him giving her the space to think out loud instead of firing questions at her. 'Regardless of what happens with the Knights,' she continued, 'I meant what I said about wanting to stay here.'

She stopped walking and turned to face him. 'I want to build a life here. I want to be with you and hike up the hill to watch the sunrise and play with Skye on the beach.' She slipped her fingers between his. 'I want to spend Sunday mornings drinking coffee in front of the fire at Mystic's. And I want to practise carving pumpkins so we can beat those kids next year.'

He laughed hard, his grin wide. 'I love you, Cat.'

She closed her eyes, stood on her tiptoes and kissed him. No one had ever got close enough to her to say that. And she had never allowed herself to feel it for anyone. But Nick had got under her skin the first night they met and she couldn't deny her feelings any longer. Nor did she want to. Smiling, she lifted her arm to dab at the tears that had formed on her cheek. 'I love you, too.'

Her phone rang in her pocket and Nick softened his grip on her. 'Do you need to get that?' he asked.

'Actually, I do. I'm expecting a call.' She pulled her phone out and answered it as Nick dropped his arms and stepped back. They stood facing each other on the beach as she took her call.

'Iris, hi. Thank you for coming back to me so quickly. Did you get the paperwork?' Aware that Nick's gaze was on her, Cat, standing still on the sand, listened hard for what she was waiting to hear. A huge grin spread across her face as she tried not to squeal into the phone. 'That is such good news,' she said. 'And your timing couldn't be better. I promise I'll look after it.'

Cat ended the call and looked up into Nick's sea-blue eyes. The energy that had drained from her over the last few days suddenly came flooding back. 'I need your photography skills again,' she said. She felt amused as he eyed her suspiciously, waiting for her to elaborate, and decided to string it out. 'I need some new photos for my website. I've had enough of the Karen's Koffee ones.'

Nick hesitated before speaking again. 'I can do that. Are we replacing them with Mystic Coffee shots?'

She shook her head. 'No. They'll be shots from inside my very own home office. And an additional headshot with me standing in front of that beautiful exterior.' When he tilted his head in confusion, she knew she couldn't keep it in any longer. 'I've just taken a lease for Seashell Cottage.'

A smile crept onto his face, but she didn't let him get a word in as it all came tumbling out of her. 'That was Iris, Mrs Dean's granddaughter. I called her and asked if she would consider allowing me to rent the house until her grandmother is better. It means I have a place to stay and she doesn't need to keep driving over here every other week to check on it.'

A spark of joy lit up inside Cat and she fought the urge to shriek. This was really happening. Nick pressed a kiss on the top of her head and she shuddered as she leaned closer to him.

'I said I'd happily take a month-to-month lease. Apparently her grandmother doesn't want to spend the winter in the house so was happy to give me a six-month lease initially until she's decided what to do long term.' Cat cast her eyes towards the sea and sighed. 'I adore that house.

And it's got the beach, the coffee shop, the airport isn't too far away. The only other thing on my list that I'll need to sort out is the Wi-Fi.'

'Does it have a mattress?'

Cat laughed and shook her head. 'The spare room is empty so I'll need to buy one.'

'It sounds perfect.' Nick grasped her hand and stepped forward to close the gap between them. 'I can't wait to see where life takes us next.'

'Would you be disappointed if it was just cosy nights in with Skye and pretzels at Josef's in the morning?'

He smiled and kissed her. 'That also sounds perfect.'

EPILOGUE

Cat locked up Seashell Cottage and stood back to admire her handiwork. Under Josef's supervision she had pruned the overgrown ivy to clear it from the window, weeded the busy flowerbeds and mowed the grass, which Josef assured her she wouldn't need to do again until spring.

Despite the only piece of furniture Cat owned in the cottage being the comfy king-size bed she'd had delivered two weeks ago, the house already felt like home. Workdays were spent at Mrs Dean's writing desk that had already been ideally positioned in one of the upstairs windows and featured a calming view of the sea. Early evenings often involved a stroll along the beach with Nick and Skye before returning to the cottage to close the curtains, light some candles and enjoy dinner. The good energy Cat had felt on seeing the adorable cottage for the first time had yet to wane.

Thistle Bay Art Gallery had been closed for four days while Cat and Nick reconfigured the display stands, refreshed the paintwork and built a new table against one wall that Nick was intending to offer to local artists. They spent a full day planning together where Nick's newly curated prints of Thistle Bay would go. Nick had meticulously framed all the photographs himself and Cat had sketched out the ideal position in the gallery for each piece and had delivered flyers for the windows of local businesses to advertise the official reopening tomorrow morning.

Last night they had sat on the floor of the gallery and eaten takeaway, washed down with red wine to celebrate the hard part being done. All they had left to do was fix the photographs into position and they were ready for the relaunch. Tonight, though, was a private celebration with friends and family.

Nick had sent Cat home that morning so he could pull together the final displays on his own. He'd told her he wanted to surprise her, too. So Cat, taking Skye with her to keep her out of Nick's way, had spent the day in Seashell Cottage just enjoying the feeling of finally having a place to call home. Before Rebecca had revealed the Knight family's secret, Cat had already stopped allowing the search for her biological family to consume so much of her life. Thistle Bay had been the first town she'd ever moved to where she felt truly present and didn't always have one eye on where she would go to next, and she intended to make the most of every single moment.

Cat now made her way back along the promenade accompanied – or, rather, led – by the little black spaniel tugging on her lead towards her own home. Nick was waiting outside the gallery when they arrived. Cat unclipped Skye's lead and the dog scampered over to Nick, whirling around him in excitement.

Nick crouched down and vigorously rubbed Skye's ears. 'I hope you've missed me just as much,' he said to Cat. He stood, leaned towards her and kissed her, his lips lingering on hers for a few seconds.

Cat shrugged. 'I guess so.'

Nick laughed and held up a green-and-navy-tartan scarf. 'I don't trust you not to peek.'

'This better be worth it,' Cat said as Nick covered her eyes with the woollen scarf and tied it loosely behind her head. She clutched his hand as he led her into the gallery. They stopped just a few steps beyond the doorway and Nick guided her to one side. The door clicked closed and Nick fumbled with the scarf behind her head.

'Ready?' he asked.

'Ready,' she confirmed.

He untied the scarf and peeled it away from her eyes. Cat delighted in the bliss that engulfed her. He had transformed the gallery from a soulless collection of random art with no relation to the town into a vibrant space that showcased the best of what Thistle Bay had to offer.

Cat wandered among the framed photographs, her heart swelling with joy at the pride she saw on Nick's face as he witnessed her reaction. With only his camera, he had taken the ordinary and made it extraordinary. Every image was like an invitation into Nick's private world. The gallery was now a permanent exhibition of unique photographs that seamlessly blended landscapes, people, wildlife and casual objects into a cohesive theme, allowing the consumer to soak up the atmospheric beauty of the town.

Her gaze lingered on a photograph of Main Street. He had taken it from the beach in summer, judging by the array of brightly coloured flowers that crowded the hanging baskets lining the street. He'd captured the town's thoroughfare during one of the rare moments when it was completely empty. Or perhaps he had edited out any stray pedestrians –

she wasn't sure. The line of the street drew her eyes to Blakely Hill in the distance, jutting out above the town. She thought back to their hike up that very hill, when Nick had questioned how many photographs of the same thing he could sell. Thistle Bay was the theme that held all these photographs together, but each one was different.

There were images of landmarks Cat could easily identify and of tranquil sunrises that showed the subtle transition between horizon and sky. Other images captured the tiny details most people would overlook – the rusted chain of a bike that had been stationary for so long it had greenery growing through its gaps; an umbrella pelted by rain and held by a hidden owner; a crab scuttling across wet sand back to the safety of the ocean bed. 'This is beautiful,' she said, touching her hand to a photograph of a stag in an open field. The animal had turned its head at just the right moment for Nick to catch it looking directly into the camera lens with its mouth open ready to give a deep throated roar to perhaps intimidate an unseen rival. Her skin tingled as Nick moved behind her and planted a kiss on her neck.

She paused at the table he had included for local artists – he was still showcasing other artists' work, but now he was only interested in holding pieces that had an association with Thistle Bay. A glass display cabinet held sterling-silver jewellery adorned with sea-glass pendants, as well as photo frames and trinket boxes made from reclaimed driftwood found on the beach across the street.

The front door creaked open behind them and Nick darted across the floor to pull it open wide. Mystic and Josef stood on the other side, their faces glowing with excitement at seeing the changes. Or perhaps their glow was the sheen that came from having spent hours in the kitchen to cater for the party.

'Are you ready for us?' Mystic asked.

'We are indeed.' Nick lifted the trolley Mystic had been dragging behind her into the gallery and wheeled it over to the guest artists' table.

Cat took one of the two bags that Josef was carrying and he brought the other one across to the table himself. 'What do you think of the new gallery?' she asked.

Josef abandoned his bag of food and shuffled between the displays. 'It's absolutely perfect.'

Mystic took it all in and flashed Nick a broad smile. 'It's very you, honey.'

'Is that a good thing?' he asked.

Mystic laughed and pulled Nick towards her for a hug. 'It's a fabulous thing.'

Cat smiled as she watched them. Mystic had unwittingly given Nick the best compliment she could have. He'd never said as much, but she suspected that the previous stock had had less of Nick's influence than he would have liked. She knew, and he did too, that the only way he could truly realise his vision for the gallery was for him to forget about what he thought an art gallery should look like and instead share only the art that sparked joy in him. Mystic was right. Nick's creative flair and his love for the town permeated every photograph he displayed.

They unloaded the trays of food. Cat peeled back the plastic wrapping from a huge fruit platter, sandwiches with a variety of fillings, sausage rolls and a bowl of salad. Josef arranged pretzels and bite-sized biscuits on plates and Cat stashed the now empty bags and Mystic's trolley in the back room. Skye sniffed around the table hoping to snatch some dropped crumbs. Her luck was in as Josef took pity on her and snuck her a sausage roll. Cat cleared her throat behind him and Josef play-acted a jolt of surprise.

'She's a sneaky one, that little dog,' he said.

'I know who the sneaky one is,' said Cat.

'Knock, knock!' came a familiar voice from the doorway. 'I hear there's a party.'

Rachel stepped into the gallery and whooped with delight as soon as she spotted Cat. She ran over and wrapped her arms around her, hoisting Cat an inch off the floor.

'I'm so glad you could make it,' said Cat.

'There's no way I would've have missed it.' Rachel released Cat and said hello to Mystic and Josef, both of whom she'd met before when she had been in town to help Cat move into Seashell Cottage. Nick joined them and Rachel pulled him in for a hug too. Cat loved that her best friend and her boyfriend seemed to like each other.

The other invited guests arrived en masse and soon the gallery was buzzing with chat and laughter. Josef and Rachel had paired up and were sharing some joke or other while Cat took charge of the drinks, weaving among the revellers to top up champagne flutes or deliver the odd orange juice to a non-drinker. She refilled Gloria's glass and lowered the half-empty bottle when Alan Knight covered the top of his glass to show he'd had enough.

'You've done a truly wonderful job here, Cat,' said Alan.

Cat shook her head. 'It was all Nick.'

'That's not what he tells me.'

'Hey, sis,' said Ryan, coming up behind Alan and thrusting his glass towards her. 'Top me up and don't be shy now.'

Things with the Knight family were a work in progress. Cat had spent more time with them over the last few weeks, and the initial awkwardness was fading. They didn't yet feel like family, whatever that was supposed to feel like. The others had bonds that stretched back decades and she wasn't sure that any amount of time would give her the same alliance. But they always made her feel included, pausing regularly to share childhood stories as they bickered and laughed their way through family dinners.

Megan had returned to Majorca, despite Ryan's objections, and Rebecca's hard edge had softened considerably. Cat understood now that Rebecca had taken on a parental role with her siblings and so the sudden appearance of a long-lost sister had left her floundering in uncharted territory. Cat had spent the most time with Elizabeth and they were already close enough to share a bottle of wine at Seashell Cottage on the weekends.

'Where's Nick?' Ryan asked after gulping his champagne. She was closer to Ryan than she was to any of the others, even Elizabeth. Although not biologically related, they shared a history that none of the others did. It was a history neither of them could remember experiencing but it gave them a link that was just theirs. He called her 'sis' a lot, and it seemed as natural as when he shortened Elizabeth's name to Lizzie. He'd even once called her Kitty Cat, a name that he couldn't have known had only ever been used by Joe and Jessie. The affectionate nickname had deepened her fondness for him.

On cue, Nick appeared by Cat's side.

'Congrats, man, the place looks superb,' Ryan said, raising his glass.

'Thanks.' Nick raised one of the two bottles of beer he held and tapped it against Ryan's glass.

'What? No one told me there was beer,' said Ryan.

Nick laughed and handed Ryan the other bottle. 'There isn't. These are from upstairs.'

Ryan took the bottle, tipped his head back and drained

the champagne from his glass, ready to move on to the beer. Cat took the empty glass and Mystic snatched it from her hand.

'You've done enough work tonight, honey. Let me help.' Mystic took the champagne bottle from Cat too and wandered off to pick up refills duty.

Nick slipped his arm around Cat's waist and anchored her to his side. 'I suppose I should make a speech,' he said.

'You should,' she agreed and kissed him on his cheek.

Life had dealt her many shattering blows, but she had begun to piece herself back together. She stood surrounded by friends, some of whom she could call family, in the town that had welcomed her when she hadn't known where else to go. Cat's throat tightened and she swallowed down the emotions stirring inside her. Nick squeezed her tighter and, in that moment, she felt at peace.

AUTHOR'S NOTE TO THE READER

A letter from Claire

DEAR READER,

Thank you so much for reading *Sunrise in Thistle Bay*. If you've read this far, I'm hoping that means you've enjoyed Cat and Nick's story. The idea for this book has been rattling around in my head for years. It was such fun to build the characters and watch their stories unfold.

I'm a sucker for a small town romance with a happy ending and have always wanted to write my own. Now I've done it! I've loved spending time in Thistle Bay and hope you have too.

One of my favourite characters is Josef, the German baker, and I just had to write his backstory. He has a real emotional connection with the town. You can read all about it in New Beginnings – A Thistle Bay Short Story.

I grew up in a seaside town on the East Coast of Scotland. It wasn't quite as idyllic as Thistle Bay, but Scotland is a pretty wonderful country to live in. If you get the chance, come and visit.

If you enjoyed *Sunrise in Thistle Bay*, please consider leaving a review. Hearing from readers is amazing (and slightly nerve-wracking!) but reviews help other readers to take a chance on new authors.

Thank you again for reading.

Claire x

WHAT TO READ NEXT

Looking for more Thistle Bay?

If you're not quite ready to leave Thistle Bay, read *New Beginnings*. It's a short story that reveals more about Josef and how he ended up running a street bakery on the promenade of Thistle Bay.

Look out for the pub quiz at The Smugglers Inn - it's one of my favourite scenes.

ACKNOWLEDGMENTS

I'd like to thank Katharine Walkden for her editorial expertise.

Thank you to the team at MiblArt for my gorgeous cover design.

Thank you to my mum and dad for telling everyone they know, and plenty of people that they don't know, about their author daughter.

To everyone that reads my books. Bestseller status is surely the dream of every author and seeing that little orange flag beside my bestselling book on Amazon was beyond brilliant. Thank you so much for making it happen!

And, as always, to Gavin, Evie and Stuart – for championing my writing and never being afraid to share your opinions – I love you.

ABOUT THE AUTHOR

Claire Anders was born and raised in a seaside town in Scotland. She now lives in Edinburgh with her husband and daughter. When she's not writing, you can usually find her walking her dog in the nearby woods or with a book in one hand and chocolate in the other.

Between Moons was Claire's first historical fiction novel. Claire also writes contemporary feel-good fiction with a touch of romance. All of her books feature strong friendships and supportive communities with a secret or two thrown into the mix.

f facebook.com/claireandersauthor

ALSO BY CLAIRE ANDERS

Historical Fiction

Between Moons - A gripping WWII historical novel

∼

Contemporary Fiction

Sunrise in Thistle Bay

New Beginnings - A Thistle Bay Short Story

Printed in Great Britain
by Amazon

87692458R00161